EDITORIAL REVIEW

Dragoria: The Lost Dragon Realm
Book Five

ROYAL ALLIANCE

"Emelyne, newly revealed as the kingdom's lost princess, must rally the survivors of Paddosha Palace village to rebuild their home and stand against the coterie's growing power, while Samara braves the enemy's hidden caves to free her beloved from an evil orb. In this thrilling fifth installment of the Royal Alliance series, the two heroines fight separate battles that will shape the fate of their kingdom." Meghan P., Line Editor, Red Adept Editing

"Warfare across magical realms has left countless beings in ruin and Paddosha Palace village in ashes. Now, with a crew of rescued dragons and ragtag villagers at their side,

Princess Emelyne and sorceress Samara must draw on mental fortitude and magical training to—hopefully—fend off the coterie anew." Libybet R. G., Proofreader, Red Adept Editing

ROYAL ALLIANCE

PART TWO

DRAGORIA: THE LOST DRAGON REALM
BOOK FIVE

KATRINA COPE

COSY BURROW BOOKS

DRAGORIA: THE LOST DRAGON REALM BOOKS

Part One

Dragon Moon

Dragon Heart

Dragon Breeze

Part Two

Dragon's Royal

Royal Alliance

Royal Resistance

Dusk ~ A beautiful soul and my sorely-missed writing companion.

Blurb:

Hope can rebuild a home—but only courage can defend it.

Emelyne is determined to rise from the ashes. The village lies in ruins, its walls shattered and its people broken, yet she refuses to let despair win. Stone by stone and step by step, she leads the fight to restore what was lost. But survival will demand more than rebuilding—it will demand warriors.

When the dragons return from Dragoria, they bring more than firepower. They bring a gift that could change everything.

Meanwhile, Samara faces her greatest trial yet—rescuing Paxton from the sinister orb's grip. But is he still the man and ally she remembers... or has the darkness claimed him forever?

With their world balanced between ruin and redemption, both heroines must discover whether their strength

lies in magic, dragons, an unyielding fire within, or all
these together.

CHAPTER ONE

Ominous clouds pressed in from every side, the darkness overtaking the sky like a blanket smothering the light of day. The monotonous thrum of the large dragon's wings was a rhythm of hope—hope that this darkness could be pushed away. Emelyne leaned back, her mind almost one with Monut's as the gray dragon dived toward the ground below. Twinkling lights of the village bounced up to meet them, casting their hope onto her.

Monut straightened, giving Emelyne a bird's-eye view of the settlement below. This land was her territory, her kingdom. She needed to reinforce and strengthen it so they might rise against the coterie. Cool air brushed against her face, carrying with it the enthusiasm of the people who had placed their faith in the rough young stranger who was a far cry from their last official princess. She closed her eyes, and images of her past flashed before her. Her life had changed suddenly from that of a simple blacksmith girl in a dwarven village to that of a leader charged with rebuilding a *human* village. She was the lost princess—the lost royal of the kingdom.

The weight was heavy on her shoulders. She didn't have any magic—no special talents other than black-smithing and sword fighting. The only thing that made her special was the bond she had to a dragon, and oh, how that felt good. With a bond like theirs, there was no way she could ever side with the coterie, even if she didn't have to aid and protect the people. A lot of work was needed to return the village to the state in which it had been before the coterie's oppression.

Wind whipped loose strands of long dark hair across her face, drying the dampness left by the storm's heavy humidity. Lightning flashed in the distance, and a slight terror passed over her at the memory of the sorceress's recent visit to the outskirts of Paddosha Palace village. The experience had left scars across the villagers' hearts. So much damage had been caused in a very short time, and the sorceress hadn't even entered the village. She could easily imagine the damage a powerful sorcerer could cause from within. But when her nerves had settled, her optimism set in and reminded her that with the lightning came a storm that would bring much-needed rain to the newly planted fields, providing produce for their future, building their strength bit by bit, so they could rise up.

The large dragon beneath her banked to the left, and her fingers dug under Monut's scales as she tucked her calves under his wings. When he suddenly shifted to the right then weaved up and down, her fingers clung harder to his scales. Her arms wrapped around his neck as she shifted rapidly across his bare back. The adventurous side of her reveled in his different maneuvers, but her heart still thumped in her ears when she nearly slipped off the side.

"Monut! I'm barely hangin' on 'ere!" she screamed against the thunder, too busy trying to hang on to talk to him through their bond. Her dwarven accent—dropping *h*s at the beginning and *g*s at the end of her words—remained prominent after her short time mixing with the humans in the village.

The large dragon peered over his shoulder and nudged her straighter on his back. *It looks like you'll have to get that saddle made. Don't worry! I'll never let you fall.*

"I know. But I'd still rather not risk it." She frowned. "Wouldn't a saddle constrict ya?"

Not if it's tailored for me. Dragons used to wear them in the past, especially the ones bonded to humans during times of war. His wings steadied their beat as he straightened. Peering over his shoulder again, he retracted his lips and showed off his teeth in a wide smile. *I have a feeling you'll enjoy your flights much better when I can spin and dive with you hanging from the saddle. After all, you have the thirst for adventure that comes with intense dragon flying.*

Emelyne found herself imitating his smile. "Ya know, I think ya may be right! That sounds like me kind of flyin'."

Monut widened his flight, taking her farther from the center of her village and past its borders.

Their flight over the closest parts of her kingdom had become a nightly ritual—a way to clear her mind from the worries of the day and the hard work of rebuilding the village, especially after the destruction the sorceress Mist had brought upon them. Her arms ached from the days of blacksmithing and building followed by training the villagers in sword fighting in the afternoons. She wished Thiznabo was still with her. Not only did she miss her friend dearly, but Thiznabo would have been a much better trainer, as she was the more skilled sword fighter of the two. Anger burned in her abdomen, and her desire for revenge grew as she remembered how the handsome coterie sorcerer killed her dwarven friend for simply standing in his way. More fuel for her hatred of the coterie.

There were some fighters in the village with the potential to be quite good. She had hope that they would end up as the village's warriors if need be. As to how they were going to defeat the coterie, she had no idea. They only had one sorceress on their side, as far as she knew, and Samara did not have enough training in magic. There was another potential sorceress still within the coterie, yet she was no use to them outside the village walls. On top of that, Samara had left to rescue her beloved.

A low grumble rumbled from Monut's throat. *My bonded, I can feel the deep sorrow in your heart and thoughts. You must not let these things get to you this way.*

I know, Monut. But so much is restin' on me shoulders, an' at the same time, I still mourn me friend taken from me by the coterie. They have taken so much from me, an' now I have to protect more.

Now that she had settled, she concentrated on speaking through their bond, uninterrupted by the noise of the storm. *We need more people and dragons on our side an' more magic wielders to go against the coterie. I'm honestly worried 'bout these people an' their chances.* Emelyne looked down on the village below, its twinkling lights now slightly in the distance.

I understand your concern, but we don't know what Cyrra and the other dragons are up to or what they have found. There is still much to come together. It is only the early days. You need not fret. Take one day at a time. He circled the outskirts of the village again, following the line of the newly constructed metal fence that served as an external barrier. *Besides, while you weren't looking, I blessed each spike in the fence with dragon fire. All your efforts to protect them with the fence was only the first step—a good first step to protect all of your villagers.*

Thanks, Monut. She stroked the back of his neck in front of her.

You should be very proud of that fence. It should stand strong against these cold-blooded people.

Ya should be proud, too, with ya handiwork in dragon-blessin' each spike. Hopefully, it's enough to keep them out, but just in case, we're also goin' to build a rock wall farther in as a second barrier. She gazed into the distance. *I wonder whether the elven realm, Clialarion, is friendly to us humans or if they have sided with the coterie.*

Monut flapped his enormous wings several times in silence. *I don't know. I'm not aware of anyone who has heard from them in hundreds of years. I guess we won't know until one of ours crosses the borders.*

Hmm. It doesn't help that the realm of the witches, Wraeyanor, blocks our access to Clialarion. And accordin' to Samara, the hidden realm of the dragons, Dragoria, also lies between them. The sorceress Callista put up the boundaries between the kingdoms to make sure the elves an' the humans couldn't collaborate. Samara did say that some members of the coterie are elves, but they could differ from the norm because they've been brainwashed by the coterie.

Boisterous thunder rolled through the air and caused Emelyne to jump, knocking her sword hilt against her boot moments before lightning split the darkness. She sucked in a breath, trying to calm her pounding heart. *That was close. Let's do one last circle. I want to scan the horizon to make sure danger is not approaching. Then I think we should get out of the sky.*

Monut pumped his large wings several times in a monotonous beat. *Already done. I can't see any danger approaching on this night.*

Emelyne took another deep breath and let it out slowly. *As much as I want to take comfort in that, there is somethin' stirrin' in the depths of me belly that feels like a warnin'. Like this is the quiet before the storm, so to speak. I ain't sure if I feel that way 'cause of the recent attack or if I'm actually feelin' somthin' comin'. I ain't sure if the sorceress Mist has managed to make her way back to the coterie base to warn them of me presence at the village, or even to the border to tell the sorcerer managin' it.*

Hmmm. Monut's neck vibrated with the noise. *True. I don't know how much time we will have before they attack again.* He banked hard to the right then jerked in the opposite direction.

What is it? Emelyne squinted, focusing ahead.

The dragon continued straight, something clearly grabbing his attention. *I see something different in the distance. There seems to be fire involved, although I'm not quite sure with all this lightning in the sky.*

What do you mean by somethin' different?

It's hard to explain, but it looks like many little fires. My dragon eyes are good, but they aren't that good. It is quite some distance away.

Perhaps it is a new settlement or a new village bein' erected. As soon as she'd thought the words, the pit of her stomach churned aggressively, causing acid to rise in her throat.

I don't know. It doesn't give off the vibes of a permanent settlement—more of a camp.

That seems rather odd if it's a large group. Emelyne's stomach churned again.

Yes, it does, unless it's a group of soldiers. I would fly higher under the cover of the clouds, but this storm is too strong, and I especially don't want to drag you through it. The last thing we need is for you to be hit by lightning.

Another thunderous roar echoed across the sky, followed quickly by a crack of lightning.

The storm is getting closer. I have to get you to the ground.

Emelyne shook her head, even though Monut couldn't see it. *No. I can't guarantee the settlement will be there tomorrow. It could move somewhere else. For the sake of the village, I think we should go and check it out.*

Monut snorted, and steam shot out the end of his nose. *I am not happy about this, for your safety, but I understand where you are coming from. We don't want our village in danger, and if they are coming for our village, we should know about it.* He flapped his large membranous wings as they headed toward the lights in the distance. The dark clouds blocked out the stars in the sky, and Monut flew lower to try to avoid the storm. The dragon covered the space quickly, bringing them above the camp after only a few minutes. As they approached, the lights turned into several bonfires in the center of a circle of the tents.

Emelyne squinted, assessing the area and looking for any occupants. Her human eyes struggled to make out the images below. *I can't quite see them. Can you?*

They are strange creatures. Not something I have seen before, especially after spending so much time hiding in the Merciless Sanctuary, though I believe these are the creatures described to me by my ancestors as centaurs. A couple of them helped with the rescue of Princess Bianca. The large dragon dipped, bringing Emelyne closer so that she could see.

Emelyne frowned. *They look like horses but with a human torso.* She eyed the bulging muscles on the bare chest of one as he lifted a bow off his shoulder and nocked an arrow from the quiver on his back. In a rapid and fluid motion, he aimed at them and released it.

CHAPTER TWO

The thudding of hooves reverberated through the ground, leading Samara to duck behind a destroyed building. The sun's heat beat against the stone wall of the derelict structure and reflected onto Samara. Beads of sweat trickled down her forehead and cheeks. The trip from Paddosha Palace village, which would have taken her a day on horseback, had taken almost a week on foot. It had been even more tedious needing to take cover behind bushes—or whatever else she could find—to hide from any people or beings who crossed her path. It wasn't worth the risk of running into somebody from the coterie —or somebody who supported the coterie. She and Ulrieg needed to stay out of any unnecessary danger. There was too much at stake for them to be captured now, and she knew that her magic was still not strong enough to compete against one of the more skilled coterie members.

The clopping of the hooves slowed to a steady beat as the being neared. It could have been a horse, except she was within centaur territory, where they guarded the border of the human realm, Slosiaran. She was close to where she and Ulrieg had created a hole for a few people to escape out of Wraeyanor, the realm of the witches. The hooves slowed even more, as though the being was looking for someone.

The branches in the tree above her swayed as an invisible weight landed on its branches. It must have been Ulrieg, for she knew of no other creature that could cause that kind of disturbance within the leaves without being seen.

Ulrieg warned Samara through their bond. *Whatever you do, don't come out. That centaur is stalking something, and I'm pretty sure it must be you.*

Tucking the skirt of her beige dress around her legs, Samara crouched lower, hiding within the foliage of a bush that lined the side of the derelict building, and peered through a few leaves. She had no intention of showing herself, even before Ulrieg gave the warning.

The clopping of the hooves slowly passed her bush, heading toward Wraeyanor. Her eyes caught a glimpse of a male centaur, his bare torso visible underneath a tan leather vest, his arrow nocked and ready to fire.

His long brown hair swished from left to right as he turned his head quickly in search of his target. He must have spotted her at some point on her journey and followed. She wasn't sure how good centaurs' eyes were. If they were better than hers, he could've spotted her miles before she was aware of his presence. She pulled her knees closer to her chest, trying to make herself tiny, and subtly buried herself deeper into the foliage.

He's certainly taking his line of work seriously. Samara

kept her mouth silent as she spoke to Ulrieg through their bond.

Ulrieg mentally huffed. *I guess that's why the centaurs are in charge of manning this side of the border. Besides, it's near impossible to cross the border anywhere other than Callum's opening because of the magical barrier splitting the realms. But they had to make sure by planting these centaurs along the fence line. Just the distraction of the buildings alone is enough to put people off. It's clear that this is an area that isn't peaceful.*

The centaur slowly passed her and stomped his feet, apparently agitated. He traveled in a circle, with the arrow pointing outward and his eyes flicking in all directions, most likely searching for any sign of her or Ulrieg.

After the centaur completed a full circle, he galloped farther, sometimes rechecking areas—probably to make sure he didn't miss any sign of movement. When he reached the border of the realm, he began pacing up and down the invisible barricade.

Samara held her breath. Not far away, her arrow remained stuck in the magical barrier, creating an opening to Wraeyanor, the realm of the witches. If he saw the arrow, it would be the end of their secret hole, and nobody would be able to come through. With her and Ulrieg's help, many people had escaped, including all of her family and those of Blade and Paxton. Only Henriette's and Peadar's families still needed to escape, but the hole was best left in the same spot so Henriette could tell them where to find it.

When the centaur was far enough away, Samara wriggled out of the bushes and instantly felt the sun's rays. She wiped away the sweat gathering on her forehead from the midday heat. It was probably best that she remain hidden until the fall of night.

She carefully searched around the damaged homes that had been abandoned during the war against the Sacred Flame coterie. Spotting one with most of its walls intact, she decided to camp there for the day. After checking the area for the centaur again, she made a dash across several yards of open space. When she reached the entrance, she noticed the door was missing. Having a door to close would have been ideal, but at least this building would conceal her better than those without full walls. She snuck in and investigated the dark interior, illuminated only by a couple of holes in the roof and in some of the walls. The insides were empty other than a table that had lost a leg. The few internal walls had collapsed, leaving only the shell of the building.

After weaving through the rubble, Samara sat in the darkest corner, the one with no windows and no holes in the roof or nearby walls. She was glad for the long sleeves of her dress to ward off the coolness within the musty hut.

I'll stay on the roof and keep watch. Ulrieg's talons scraped lightly on the roof, and a soft sigh passed through their bond. *It's nice to get some sun on my wings.*

Samara smiled, imagining him pressing his stomach against the roof and spreading his wings like a bird sunning himself. *Thanks, Ulrieg. Enjoy that sun. I'm going to stay in here until nightfall. I think it's best that I go to the border in the darkness. Hopefully, there'll be enough moon for me to see tonight.*

If not, I'll guide the way. Dragon eyes are always better in the dark than humans'.

After lifting her backpack from her shoulders, Samara pulled out some little bags of snacks and took a sip of water from a canteen, then she retightened the top and secured it back onto the pack. She unfolded a little cloth containing several nuts and dried fruit. Her tummy rumbled. It had been a while since she had eaten. She ate rapidly, trying to quench her hunger. She needed to build up her strength for the night's journey.

With a little food in her stomach, it wasn't long before her eyes drooped with tiredness. It had been a long trek so far, and she was far from finished. Traveling by foot was too slow, much slower than she'd anticipated. She hadn't realized before heading out how much slower she would be. She would've been back at the coterie building by now if she'd had a horse to ride like last time. On the other hand, she couldn't risk being out in the open, which made walking the safest way to go. Thinking of horses reminded her of the centaur pursuing her. She sat upright, listening for the sound of hooves. Pleased to hear only silence, she slumped against the wall.

Weariness took hold, and she let herself surrender to its pull as she drifted to sleep.

The sound of hooves outside woke her with a start as her ears sprung to life, homing in on the source of the noise.

She blinked, realizing that the inside of the cottage was darker than it had been when she had fallen asleep. *It must be night already.* Even so, a nearby centaur would make it impossible for her to travel safely just yet. She rocked up from her backside and leaned against the wall as she climbed to her feet. She slowly and quietly made her way to the small window. Though he was barely visible in the dim moonlight, she spotted the centaur's frame in the distance, clip-clopping along this small pathway between the trees. She would have to be extremely careful, even in the darkness, as she made her way to the hole she had left in the magical barrier. She leaned farther out the window and watched as the centaur headed in the opposite direction. She watched him until he was no longer visible and the sound of his hooves vanished into the night. Quickly, she tiptoed to the open doorway and pushed out into the darkness, ready to take the final leap into the witches' realm.

"Halt!" A male's voice cut through the quiet night.

Samara paused, the opening she'd created to Wraeyanor only a few paces away. Slowly, she turned around and held up her hands. When she faced the centaur, she locked eyes with him, taking minute side-steps in an attempt to distance herself from the opening. The last thing they needed was for the floating arrow to catch the centaur's eye. If it did, it would be the end of their use of that hole from either side of the barrier.

"I said halt!" The centaur growled. Under the moon-light, his brown horse body glimmered brightly, though his facial features were harsh, his eyes shadowed beneath robust eyebrows. Samara traced the line of his muscle-bound shoulders and taut arms, flexed, fingers clasping the string of a nocked arrow pointing directly at her.

CHAPTER THREE

The arrow whistled past, barely missing Monut's wing. He dodged quickly to the right as the arrow whooshed past Emelyne's ear. Metal sang as she whipped out her sword and swung at the next arrow aimed at them, slicing it in half. The broken arrow had barely fallen from her sword before another arrow was headed their way. Emelyne swung again, cutting the tip from the shaft.

These arrows are too close for comfort. Monut flicked his tail aggressively as his mighty wings took them higher, out of the arrows' reach.

I think it's safe to say the centaurs are enemies of the drag-ons. Emelyne clasped her sword tighter, her eyes peeled for more arrows heading their way. *There would be no mistakin' that you're a dragon from that distance. It's a shame. Ma and Pa taught me about them many years ago. They are excellent fighters, but the coterie must have brainwashed or bullied most of them to gain their loyalty.*

Monut circled the camp, attempting to avoid the storm clouds. *Yes, and I believe many were used to bring down*

Paddosha Palace village. But there might still be some on our side. If there were some willing to help hide Princess Bianca when the palace was destroyed, then there must still be some friendly centaurs out there.

What do ya think they are doin' here? Samara said there were several of them livin' near the border of Wraeyanor, a coterie army in waiting, but this is far from that border line.

I don't know, but I don't believe it's good. We'll have to keep an eye on them. But let's get you out of this storm.

A jolt of lightning split the air only a few feet away just as Emelyne heard the whoosh of arrows sliding past her ear.

Monut darted to the side, but an arrow pierced one of his wings near the bone. He let out a roar as the tip of another lodged underneath one of his softer scales in the pit of his back leg.

Emelyne wrapped her arms tighter around his neck and dug her fingers into his scales as Monut dived to the left.

All right, that's it! It's time to go back. Not only are they still shooting arrows at us, but the lightning also isn't ceasing. It's too dangerous for you to remain here.

Emelyne huffed. *Too much danger for me? You're the one who got hit.*

For me, that was a minor irritant with a slight amount of pain. For you, that could have been fatal. I'm not willing to risk it. The arrow remained embedded underneath Monut's scale as he beat his wings. *For me, it is like getting a splinter under a nail.* The dragon increased his speed as more arrows swished past, then he glided a while before gravity took hold, pulling them downward. Each beat of his wings took them closer to Paddosha Palace village.

Arrows and lightning bolts chased them as thunder roared its intent, seeming angry it hadn't brought them down.

Emelyne's fighting leathers creaked as she clung on tighter to Monut's neck. *Is it just me, or does it seem like the storm is also upset that it hasn't caused us to crash to the ground?*

I'm pretty sure it's all in your head, although it does feel like that. The only way a storm would do that to a dragon and a person on purpose is if it was powered by evil magic. Unless the sorceress who attacked our village is still around and hasn't lost her memory, I think it is all in our imagination.

The lights of Paddosha Palace village beckoned them.

Emelyne peered over Monut's shoulder, glad to see the fires of that little encampment fading into the distance. They were still a fair way from the village, but even so, they couldn't treat the camp's distance from the village lightly, especially after the aggression they had just faced. The centaurs were clearly against the dragons, which meant they were an enemy of Paddosha Palace village. She would have to prepare her people for more confrontations and reinforce the metal fence with an additional one in stone. They would be devastated if, after the hard work they had put into restoring their home, the village was destroyed. The streets had finally begun to show the sparkle of life they had been missing for decades.

Emelyne had no way of knowing whether the group of centaurs was headed toward Paddosha Palace village. Word of dragons in the village had not likely spread. The people had sworn to secrecy, and barely anyone left the safety of the village. If they did and valued their safety, they would keep the secret.

Lightning pierced the darkness, and thunder rattled the sky right as the clouds released a torrent of moisture. Monut angled downward, farther from the threat of Mother Nature and closer toward their home.

The wind and rain whipped against Emelyne's face as Monut landed with a thud in the middle of the open village square. Emelyne kicked her legs to one side and slipped off Monut's back. Her boots hit the hard stone ground, her eyes immediately scanning their surroundings.

Raucous laughter echoed up the street. The attitude of the villagers had certainly changed since her first encounter with the people. They had gone from poverty-stricken and starving, ready to kill anybody who even dared look at their produce, to open and friendly, secure in their safety behind the dragon-blessed bars of their new fence and out of reach of the coterie.

The joy of the streets was in stark contrast to the turmoil that whirled within Emelyne's mind, especially after seeing the camp of centaurs. Although peace had found them, she doubted it would last for long.

The people had faced no direct threat since the sorceress had destroyed the village. Emelyne didn't know if that was because Samara's friend had blinded the sorceress's memory or if the coterie were just giving them a break for a change after hearing about an invisible protector of the village. Perhaps the coterie thought the boundary the sorceress had hit was permanent and would hold them at the village's periphery.

A villager rushed up to her. "Princess Emelyne, this is

for you." The young woman proudly held out a pewter cup of what appeared to be red wine. She was dressed in a beige tunic covered with a pale-blue pinafore, her blond hair wrapped around her head in a braid. "It's from the grapes of our field, our first wine. The vines were there before but have flourished since the farmers arrived."

"Fantastic!" Clasping the cup, Emelyne took a long swig. The combination of bitter and fruity flavors flowed down her throat, dampening the uneasiness in her stomach. "It's delicious. Jus' what I needed." She took another long sip, the warmth radiating through her body, as the young woman watched her response with pleasure.

Emelyne reached over and whacked Monut's leg in a playful gesture. "I'm gonna need a few more of these to dampen the worry I jus' encountered. It's a shame ya can't drink this." The princess snorted, her words slipping back into the strong dwarven accent.

The young woman looked pleased. "If you need some more, I will bring you some. Is all well with you?"

Emelyne took another gulp of wine. She felt its effects taking hold as a relaxing fullness washed over her. Not wanting to alarm the village at this point, she waved a dismissive hand. "It was jus' a rough ride in the storm. In the makin' of ya fields, did ya come across many rocks?"

The young woman frowned. "We did. We pushed them all to the outskirts, closer to the metal fence. Why?"

"That's perfect!" Emelyne downed the last of the wine and handed the cup back to the young woman. "That will make it easier to build the solid stone fence we need inside of the metal one."

The young woman grabbed a canister to fill the cup

again, the red liquid swirling within until it reached the brim.

"Thanks. Ya awfully nice. An' how have I earned this pleasure?" Emelyne wasn't accustomed to being waited on. She was slowly getting used to the idea of being called Princess, but none of it had gone to her head after her humble upbringings as a blacksmith's daughter in the dwarven village. Another habit she'd kept from her upbringing was a healthy appetite to drink.

Lightning struck from above, and Emelyne and the young woman darted under the awning of the nearest building.

Monut moved near them, stretching his wing to the awning to give them more coverage from the storm. The arrows were still visible, sticking out from his wing and the pit of his back leg.

Emelyne handed her cup to the young lady. "Let me get them for ya, Monut. They must hurt."

They are rather bothersome. The large gray dragon positioned his leg so that Emelyne could get to the arrow. She yanked it out, and a small trickle of blood oozed from the wound. She then tugged the arrow from his wing. Monut tilted his wing to have a look, pouring water onto the princess in the process.

Emelyne chuckled at her drenched flying leathers. "Well, if I wasn't wet before, I am now!" She inspected Monut's wounds in the dull sconce light of the street. "Thankfully, neither of these were near major arteries."

Emelyne retrieved her cup from the young woman and finished the rest of the wine in one gulp.

The lady farmer studied the arrows and the wounds they had created. "Where did they come from?"

"Jus' a little mishap. Don't worry ya-self 'bout it." Emelyne held out her cup for a refill.

The young woman gladly poured her another as a couple of the tavern's patrons filed out onto the street to join them.

"Thanks. I think that'll do. I have to get up early tomorrow an' start some more work on buildin' the village's protection. I'm gonna need some helpers to build a rock wall. If ya know of anyone who is free, please send them me way." Emelyne directed her comments to the young woman and the people who had joined them. "It's a matter of urgency. I know ya want to rebuild ya houses first, but protection is the most important thing for this village right now."

"Certain farmers have an offseason. We have done what we can for now, so we'll be able to help," said a man in a loose tunic and brown pants who was standing near the young woman.

"That'll be a great help." She turned to the rest of the people standing around. "For anyone who offers to build the wall, I will make rebuildin' their houses me first priority when we're done." Emelyne downed her wine and handed her cup back to the young woman.

Sensing the group was happy with her offer and would turn up in the morning to help with the wall, Emelyne headed to her damaged palace room, ready for bed.

CHAPTER FOUR

Dragon moon! *Where did this guy come from? I thought we lost him.* Ulrieg spat. *He's supposed to be a centaur, not a stalking cat with silent footsteps.* The branches on a nearby tree bounced suddenly as the dragon rejoined Samara, now invisible since they'd exited the safety of the building.

I don't know. Samara clenched her teeth, annoyed with herself for not seeing the centaur sooner. *Perhaps he's been hiding in the bushes this whole time, waiting for us to emerge.* She shifted a couple more paces away from the arrow sticking out of the ward.

The centaur stomped his foot, his chest muscles flexing under a tan vest that reached just over the top of the brown horsehair at his waist. "I said halt!" His bicep muscles bulged as he pulled the string taut, his fingers curled around the bow string.

Samaria gave a slight chuckle. "I'm sorry. I'm just a little clumsy. I had a bit to drink." She stumbled a few paces farther from the hole.

The centaur stomped his foot again and snorted. Although the snort came from his human half, the sound could easily have come from a horse.

She pretended to ignore him and wobbled a bit more, slurring her words as she reached for her bag. "I just wanted some…" She reached for the leather canteen dangling from the side of her bag and held it out to him.

"Put that away," he demanded.

"Suit yourself," Samara slurred. "But it's good stuff." She hooked it back onto her bag. "I could've used a little more." She stumbled a few more paces away from the hole then turned to him, relaxing her facial muscles to appear blurry-eyed. "I must have gotten myself lost. I have no idea where I am."

"Then you can sleep it off in our camp." Face set in displeasure, the centaur made a couple of quick jabs with the arrow tip still nocked in the bow, indicating she should move away from the barrier. "You must have been drunk for at least half a day if you're still drunk now. It's a good half day's walk from the closest village for any person."

Samara grabbed for her canteen and pretended to take another swig.

"Oi! Put that away!" The centaur growled.

Samara pouted, slowly hooking the canteen back on her bag. "Oh! You're no fun! You males are all the same—all seriousness and no fun. My boyfriend—or should I say ex—was the same. He just broke up with me because I wasn't serious—"

"Enough! I don't want to hear it!" the centaur snapped.

Samara stumbled forward a few paces, tripping over a rock then taking a few steps to correct herself. "All right, all right. No need to be mean." She weaved her way forward, the centaur following close behind.

"Keep going straight ahead." He kept his arrow nocked as his footsteps clip-clopped behind her. He directed her out of the tree cover and into the direct moonlight. "Is that pink in your hair?"

Panic bubbled to the surface, and she froze momentarily.

Ulrieg encouraged her. *Steady Samara. You've been doing good up until now.*

Sucking in a deep breath, Samara twirled like a dog chasing its tail, trying to see the back of her head. "I don't see any pink."

The centaur rolled his eyes. "It looks like pink to me. You must be that traitor the Sacred Flame are looking for. I'll be rewarded greatly for bringing you in."

"Oh, no. You have me mixed up with someone. Do I look like I can do magic?" She chuckled boisterously as she tried to think of a way out of the situation. Nocking her own arrow would be impossible without him catching her in the act. She was at a disadvantage. She wished she'd had some way of learning more magic since leaving the coterie. She had to do something about that.

Leaves above them rustled as Ulrieg landed closer on a nearby sapling. His invisible weight pressed the center of the branch down unnaturally. The centaur spun and pointed his arrow upward, his eyes searching for what had caused the sudden movement. After a few moments, he gave up and pressed forward. He exhaled loudly out of his nose, his gaze jumping between the trees above and Samara before him.

Samara's mind continued to race. She needed to determine a way out of her current predicament, yet no option seemed plausible. *Do you have any ideas of escape, Ulrieg? This is not going the way I had planned, and I can't go to his camp. I imagine it'll be even harder to get out with more centaurs watching me.*

She twisted her hand and pointed it discreetly at a bush, vaguely remembering a spell she used to use. She wriggled her fingers, and the leaves rustled, pulling in her direction. Seeing the results, she cursed herself for not remembering the spell when Mist had been attacking her and the village. It would have made her life easier.

At the rustling sound, the centaur jumped and spun in that direction, accidentally releasing the arrow in the process.

Pain stabbed through Samara as the arrow embedded into her shoulder. She cried out in agony and slumped forward.

Samara, are you all right? Ulrieg's panicked voice echoed within her mind.

Groaning, she straightened and clasped her shoulder before turning toward the centaur. "You shot me." Acting drunk became more of a challenge.

"Maybe that'll sober you up a bit." He grunted. "Keep going!" He shooed her forward with the hand holding his bow and reached for another arrow from the quiver on his back.

Samara stumbled. "Aren't you going to help me get the arrow out and stop the bleeding?"

"Nope. If you come along without causing any trouble, I'll consider it when we get to camp."

Wingless flight. He's a heartless one. Ulrieg mentally

grunted. *I imagine it'd be a different story if he'd been the one hit.*

Staggering from pain, she braced her shoulder with her hand. She had to find a way to get out of this. Gritting her teeth and trying not to focus on the soreness, she twisted her dangling hand and used her magic to pull on the leaves again before he reloaded his arrow.

The centaur seemed very jumpy for someone in control. She noticed he was about to pass close to a bush, and she called to the branches, pulling them toward her. She'd hoped it would block the centaur's way, but he quickly darted to the side as the leaves swayed over his path. He stomped his hooves as he followed behind her and let out a loud, angry breath. "Hurry it up."

She staggered some more, keeping up the appearance of being drunk, but the pain had dampened her enthusiasm for the performance.

Ulrieg suddenly called to her through their bond. *Samara, duck!*

Bracing her injured arm, she fell to the ground as cries of pain sounded from behind her. She gazed back to see the centaur with his chest forward and back arched. His bow discharged, flying into the branches above as he spun on the spot, searching for the cause of his sudden pain. Crimson trickled from deep gashes down his back, glimmering in the moonlight through tears in his vest. Ulrieg had created a brief distraction.

Samara quickly darted to the side and hid in the bushes, taking advantage of this time as Ulrieg attacked him again and again while in his invisible form. The centaur lost his composure. Panic seemed to rise the longer he couldn't spot his attacker.

She clenched her teeth to prevent from calling out in pain as she ran the few hundred feet toward the hole in the barrier, keeping behind the protection of the bushes as much as she could before resting behind a large tree only a couple feet away from the entry. *Ulrieg, are you ready to come through the hole? It should be safe for you to leave him now.*

Another loud cry of pain exploded from the centaur, his hooves clomping erratically on the stones. A few moments passed after Ulrieg's attack ceased, and the centaur calmed briefly before letting out an exasperated groan when he realized he had lost her. "I'll find you." The centaur's scream rippled through the air like a deathly chill. "I'll find you, and I'll find some way to get you to the coterie. You have defied a soldier of the Sacred Flame."

As soon as Samara was through the barrier, she dropped behind a bush. A gush of wind pressed down on her as Ulrieg flew overhead and landed by her side.

Samara huffed, her breath a whisper. *Dragon moon! That was close. I can't afford any more of those.*

Don't you think you should take the arrow out of the barrier? It might be a good idea, just to be sure. Ulrieg's hot breath washed over her arm.

I don't want to do that. If we close the hole, then we won't know where to send people to escape this realm.

There was a sudden whoosh of wings as Ulrieg pushed off the ground. Still in his invisible form, he grabbed the arrow, yanked it free from the barrier, and dropped it by her side. *Have some sense.* He huffed. *It's too dangerous. I get that it'll take energy to remake the hole, but the last thing we need is for it to be discovered. It would alert the coterie that there could be more.* He landed next to her and shoved the arrow closer. *Removing it solved the current problem. Even if he spots us, he'll have to go all the way around to the opening in the border before he can attempt to chase us.*

Samara picked up the arrow and twirled it in her fingers. *I guess you're right.*

You know I am. Ulrieg's voice was full of confidence. *If you're worried about its positioning, we can stay here, behind the safety of the tree, and wait for him to go. Then we can recreate the hole and still tell others to come this way. The centaur will never know it was here.*

Seconds later, the clip-clop of hooves grew louder as the centaur passed them on his path along the invisible barrier that divided the two realms. The moon cast deep shadows over his face, emphasizing his discontent and annoyance.

CHAPTER FIVE

In the early hours of the morning, Monut's thunderous footsteps followed Emelyne as she walked down the pebbled streets of Paddosha Palace village. Several heads turned their way as individuals rushed to their jobs and prepared for the day. Although the people were becoming accustomed to seeing Monut walk through the streets, the princess and her bonded still drew many looks as villagers took in the large dragon's features, disbelief not entirely gone from their faces. Emelyne had been surprised by how easily the people had accepted Monut. But she supposed it also helped that she was the princess. They were willing to accept anything that came with her. Either that or they were willing to accept *any* enemy of the coterie after the mistreatment they had received.

A young girl with blond plaits braided down the sides of her head rushed up to Emelyne, carrying a hunted rabbit over one arm, her blue eyes wide with enthusiasm. Her long blue pinafore flowed to the ground, the material snapping around her calves as she hurried. "Can I give this to your dragon?"

Emelyne smiled, stepped to the side, and gazed up at Monut. "I'm sure he'd love a treat, if ya family can afford it."

"Pa said we can. He caught an extra this morning, and I asked him if I could give it to the big dragon." Excitement tumbled through her words.

The girl's tone rose in pitch as Monut stood tall, making himself seem larger. His big golden eyes gazed down at her over his large snout. He was not used to so much direct attention, especially after having lived in the Merciless Sanctuary for such a long time.

Monut didn't move, and he seemed to be put out a little.

What do ya think, Monut?

Don't you think this rather odd, that a little human wants to bring me food? I can catch my own.

Emelyne cringed. The girl's gesture had apparently disrupted his regal ego.

I know, but this is the little girl's way of interactin' with ya. Besides, it'll look betta, an' ya'll be loved more if ya let a few people feed ya. An' we need to look approachable.

After a few moments, Monut's eyes softened, and he peered down at the girl. He lowered his head to her level, sniffing at the rabbit. He nodded. *It smells fresh and tasty.*

See? She's doin' somethin' nice for ya.

Monut kept his eyes at the girl's level. *You're just a young one, aren't you?* He chose to speak to her directly.

The girl giggled, clearly loving that the dragon spoke to her through her mind. But then her face turned serious. "I'm not that little. I'm ten summers old."

Well, excuse me, young miss. You are still much younger than I.

The girl smiled. "That's okay. A lot of people think I'm too young."

He expelled a nostril full of steam, covering the young girl with it.

She squealed in delight. "That was strange and funny." She giggled. "Can you do that again?"

Monut repeated it a few times, entertaining her. His whole posture had softened, and he even seemed to be enjoying the interaction. After some time, he paused. *What is your name, young miss?*

"I'm Maisie. And you're Monut."

The dragon chuckled, seeming genuinely amused. *Yes, I am.*

She held out the rabbit. "How would you like me to give it to you?"

How about you throw it as far as you can into the air, and I'll jump up and catch it.

The girl squealed with delight. "That sounds like fun. I'll do my best to throw it as high as I can."

Holding the rabbit firmly in one hand, Maisie started to spin, swinging the rabbit around in a circle. Surprisingly, the girl started to build more and more speed, steadily swinging the animal lower on one side and higher on the other. After a few more lopsided spins, she released the rabbit on the elevated side, sending it high into the sky.

The instant it left her hands, Monut sprung into the air, pushing his wings down to lift himself even more. He followed the rabbit a couple stories high, then he snatched it in his large maw and gulped it down whole.

He landed on his talons a few feet from Maisie and gazed down at the girl with soft eyes. *Wow. That was a very big throw for someone your size.*

Smiling, Maisie clasped her hands behind her back and rocked on her toes.

"Who taught ya how to throw like that?" Emelyne placed a hand on Maisie's shoulder. "That was very impressive."

She looked pleased over the compliments. "Pa taught me."

In many ways, the young girl reminded Emelyne of herself when she was younger. She squeezed her shoulder. "He taught ya well."

Nodding, the young girl's attention moved back to Monut. "Can I touch you?"

Monut was standing, making the girl look very small. *Of course.* Monut then sat, lowered his head, and stretched out a talon.

Tentatively, the girl reached out and touched him, stroking his long talon. "I wish I had a dragon friend."

Maybe one day you will. Monut tilted his head to one side, looking slightly fascinated with her small size and large attitude.

Her blue eyes turned serious. "Maybe a lot of us could if we defeat the coterie and the dragons are free."

Maybe a lot of you will if we can do just that.

She walked closer to him, touched his nose, and flinched. "Oh! That's very warm."

Monut chuckled—a deep, throaty laugh. *That would be because of my internal fire. It's always waiting to be used.*

"Oh. Can I see it?" Eyes wide with a mixture of excitement and pleading, she stepped back expectantly.

Monut looked thoughtful, then he lifted his head. *All right. Stand back farther.*

Maisie clapped and stood to the side, giving the dragon space.

Sucking in a deep breath, Monut exhaled a large plume of fire, shooting it directly down the pebbled street, away from the houses.

When the flame receded, the girl embraced Monut's leg, giving it a cuddle. "Thank you. That was spectacular! I hope you enjoyed your snack." She turned quickly and skipped down the cobblestone street.

I think ya got some admirers. Emelyne petted Monut's side. *But I ain't surprised. Ya are a special bein'.*

Monut rose, and they walked down the street until they reached the blacksmithing building. Emelyne rubbed her eyes. It had been a restless night. She'd been worried about the centaur camp not far from their village. The last thing they needed right now was another attack—when they still had so much to rebuild.

Leaving Monut standing guard outside, Emelyne walked in to check on her father and Silut, following the sounds of clanging metal. Today, the little shop buzzed with song as Silut and her father sang together, hammering in time with the rhythm.

Within the tiny building, the two dwarven men worked on extra spikes for the fence and other bits and pieces to help rebuild the village. These days, it wasn't uncommon for Silut to start even before her father. He had been putting in extra work since Emelyne had forgiven him for his betrayal and accepted his family among them.

Emelyne had understood he'd been in a difficult situation—his family was being held hostage by one of the evil Sacred Flame coterie sorceresses. She glanced at her adoptive father. She would do anything to keep him and her mother safe.

Since the truth had come out, Silut had been more talkative, bringing cheer to the blacksmithing shop.

"Good mornin'!" Emelyne called over the noise.

"Good mornin'!" They greeted her in unison, pausing their song.

"Are ya comin' to help us today?" Lozzeak, Emelyne's adoptive father, held his hammer still, his red hair ablaze from the light of the furnace. His leather apron covered his long pants and tunic, and his gloves were pulled up to his elbows.

Emelyne shook her head. "Maybe later. I'm goin' to see how the rock wall is comin' along an' to see if they need a hand. Monut an' I saw a centaur camp last night that wasn't friendly. It's not too far away from here an' is makin' me nervous. I'd like to get the village more secure in case they're plannin' to pay us a visit."

"Can't ya go for a ride on Monut an' see what they are up to today to put ya mind at ease?" Lozzeak asked.

"Nah. There ain't a cloud in the sky. They were already firin' at Monut last night, an' they would certainly have a go at him today."

Lozzeak placed his hammer and steel on the anvil, the orange heated end of the steel cooling to red. "That ain't good. Do ya think they were expectin' him, or do ya think they were surprised at seein' a dragon?" He tugged at his long braided beard.

Emelyne crossed her arms over her chest. "It was too hard to see from the altitude we were flyin' an' in the darkness of the night. But the fact that they were firin' at Monut is a sign they are with the coterie an' don't like dragons."

"I see. Let's hope that's not the case." Lozzeak reached up to place a hand on his daughter's shoulder.

She placed a hand on his. "My life today is a far cry from what it was in our quiet dwarven village. But I guess that's part of bein' the royal of the kingdom."

Lozzeak nodded and squeezed her hand. "Ya ma an' me are always here for ya. Never forget that."

"Thanks, Pa." She gave him a half smile. "Is there anythin' ya need today to help get ya work done?"

He shook his head. "Not so far. What about you? Is there anythin' ya need to help ya get through the day?"

"I could use ya cart to lug around some large stones."

"Take it. Ya know where to find it. We don't need it today." Lozzeak picked up his hammer, ready to resume his work.

"Thanks. I need to get to the fence an' organize the buildin' of the stone wall. Love ya." She kissed him on his forehead, the taste of salty sweat on her lips.

CHAPTER SIX

Shoulder aching from the arrow wound, Samara clenched her jaw to keep from crying out in pain. She remained huddled behind a bush as the centaur paced the area along the invisible barrier. She avoided glancing around the bush to see what he was doing until she was certain the clopping of his hooves sounded from far away. Only then did she risk sticking her head out in time to see his loose dark hair glimmering under the moonlight, his shadow lurking behind him.

When she was certain he wasn't returning, Samara reached for the arrow still sticking out the back of her shoulder. She hissed in pain when her fingers touched the shaft. *I'm not going to be able to do it.*

Do what? Ulrieg's glowing red eyes filled with worry.

Pull the arrow out by myself. Do you think you'll be able to?

Ulrieg frowned, his black scales bunching on his forehead and crowding his horns. *I don't think my talons will close tightly enough, but I should be able to use my teeth.*

All right. That's sounds like a solution. She dug through

her bag. *I'll just find something to use as a gauze to stop the bleeding.* She found a tunic and ripped a strip from the bottom, flinching in pain every time she moved her arm. When she had gathered enough, she folded it to make a thick patch then sat on the ground. She grabbed a stick to clamp her teeth onto so she didn't scream and alert the centaur of their position. *All right. When you're ready.*

Ulrieg circled to her back. Careful not to jab her with any of his horns, he fastened his teeth over the shaft and yanked it out.

Samara breathed heavily through her nose, and the darkness closed in around her as she struggled to remain conscious.

Ulrieg clasped her arm with his talons, digging them slightly into her flesh. *Are you all right? You're not looking too good.*

She took a few more deep breaths, concentrating on the pressure of Ulrieg's talons in her arm. Her world stopped spinning, and she became aware of the warm trail of blood flowing down her back. *Oh. I feel fantastic!*

The dragon smirked and tilted his head. *Do I detect sarcasm? I am rubbing off on you. I guess you should be fine, then.*

In all honesty, if I don't stop this bleeding soon, I'm going to bleed out. She held out the cloth. *Can you put this on the hole and put pressure on it? Hopefully, it'll stop the bleeding.*

Ulrieg held out his talon, and she placed the fabric in the middle of his claw. She flinched as the cloth touched her wound. When she had regained her composure, she attempted a few healing spells, aiming them at the injury, without any luck. Her healing spells never seemed to work on herself. With the amount of blood she felt trickling down her back and arm, she needed to do something fast if the wound didn't clot.

A wolf howled in the distance, breaking the silence of the night.

Now what? Ulrieg asked after some time had passed.

We need to see if the bleeding has stopped.

Ulrieg removed the cloth, and a fresh stream of blood trickled down.

That's not good. Can you add pressure again? She caught a glimpse of concern in his fiery red eyes. *Don't worry. I'll think of something.*

His back straightened as he snarked. *You better! Don't you dare think of leaving me. We have a lot of work to do yet.* His eyes and his shoulders softened. *Surely, I can do something to help.*

She reached for a dagger she'd packed in her bag and held it out to Ulrieg. Yes, you can. *Can you please breathe fire on this and make it hot?*

When she was met with a look of disbelief, she explained. *I need to cauterize the wound. It may be the only way to stop the bleeding.*

Ulrieg took a deep breath and breathed out from the depths of his throat. Fire flew out of his mouth. The dragon had hardly ever breathed fire since he'd bonded with Samara, and the sight was spectacular, filling Samara with awe. There was something special about dragon fire. After a couple of minutes, Ulrieg pulled away the gauze, giving Samara access to place the heated blade against the wound.

Her flesh sizzled, and she gritted her teeth, groaning in pain.

Ulrieg pulled back. *Wow! That looks like it hurts.* The dragon stood tensely as he watched her in silence.

Samara sucked in a quick deep breath. *It's the only way I can stop the bleeding. After this, I'll have to find some herbs and make a poultice to place over it.*

It's going to leave a nasty scar unless we find a miracle worker to heal it.

There's not much I can do about that. Her mind traveled to Paxton, remembering how his healing powers were way beyond anybody else's in the coterie. If only he was free and by her side, this pain would be over in no time. She wished she could ease the pain and suffering he was going through right now. The thought was a sudden jolt to her system. What she was going through right now was nothing compared to him.

The sizzling stopped, and she pulled the dagger away. She picked up her bag and threw it over her other shoulder. *We've got to get going. We must save Paxton as soon as possible. It's been too long that we've left him in there.*

Like I need reminding, Ulrieg scoffed. *I just hope his head is still with us and not corrupted by the evil magic of the orb.*

Me too. We won't know until we manage to get him out. She paused and checked for any signs of the centaur. *First, we should recreate the hole in the barrier, or else we won't be able to send anyone through it. I can't see the centaur anywhere. Can you?*

Not the slightest sound or movement.

Samara lifted her bow from her body and reached for an arrow in the quiver. *Good. Then can you press up against me while I spell this arrow and fire it?* Rough scales pressed up against her leg as Ulrieg's body heat warmed it through the material of her dress. She positioned herself and let the arrow fly, watching with satisfaction when it hovered midair, tip embedded into the barrier. She poked her arm through the hole and smiled. *I love how we discovered this. It's ironic that Callista taught me the initial part of the spell. I'm sure she never thought I'd be able to pierce her barrier spells separating the kingdoms.*

Humph. She got what she deserved. No one should have that much control over the kingdoms.

The beating of drums sounded in the distance. *That sounds like it's coming from Kellam's camp.*

Ulrieg turned to face the source of the sound. *Maybe you should make another hole farther away from the border opening. The last thing we need is to lose this option if one of them finds the hovering arrow. From the sound of those drums, I don't think this is far enough away from their camp.*

That's a good idea. Samara turned and headed in the opposite direction, traveling farther away from the camp. She followed the barrier by dragging her fingers softly along its resistance. Without anyone in sight, Ulrieg remained visible by her side. They traveled several hundred feet until they reached two large trees, their leaves touching the barrier. A gust of wind picked up, and the trees swayed, the leaves hitting the ward.

Here looks good. The two trees should hide the arrow floating in the air.

Ulrieg pressed up against her leg as she grabbed, spelled, nocked, and fired her arrow. It hit, remaining hidden among the leaves. She repeated the process near the second tree, the two holes combining to create a larger passage than that of the first escape route.

Samara huffed her amusement. *I was always disappointed that I never seemed to have a special gift, but I think this is pretty special, especially since this is how we found Dragoria. I just wish I had a gift I could use to fight others—especially the coterie members working against us.*

You'll just have to practice what you can remember and hopefully get Henriette to teach you some more. Her magic has increased greatly since we left the coterie.

Satisfied with her new entry point, Samara turned to head back toward Kellam's camp. She wished they could steer well clear of it, but it would add too much time to their travels. As they retraced their steps along the barrier, they the beating of the drums slowly grew louder. Ulrieg disappeared, using his invisibility as they neared the camp. Even though they stuck to the shadows in the moonlight, it was best to remain cautious. Only the soft crackling of leaves and twigs would give away Ulrieg's location.

Samara's nerves fired like lightning the closer they got, her head spinning to assess any movement. *I should've made the first opening in the barrier farther away from Kellam's camp.*

You didn't know for sure we would be sending people this way when we traveled here with Henriette and Pixie. Besides, I think it's very unlikely that anyone in the camp will find it. If they do, now you have an additional hole farther up. It'll be harder for Kellam, the ogres, or his snub-nosed monkey to find it.

Samara's forehead creased as she maneuvered under a low-hanging branch. *I guess you're right.* A flickering caught her eye, and she turned to see a bonfire glowing in the distance. It's red embers fired into the air before turning to black ash. Several enormous green figures banged on drums hanging from their necks, dancing with only loincloths covering their bodies. Not far from the joyous ogres, the watchtower loomed menacingly.

A puff of breeze brushed over Samara a moment before the branches on a tall tree swayed with invisible weight. *The ogres look rather cheerful, like they are having a party. Perhaps the evil sorcerer is away.*

Samara tilted her head, listing to the cheerful grunts joining the beating of the drums. *Huh! It does sound too cheerful, doesn't it? Nothing like it was when Callista and Kellam were here on our first visit. I couldn't image Kellam allowing them to make so much noise.*

I don't blame them if they are. That sorcerer would never treat them nicely. I imagine he'd be breathing down their necks all the time, happy to belittle them.

Samara nodded. *I saw enough of how he treated people when I was in the coterie. He especially hated humans and halflings, even though they were coterie members—people he was supposed to respect.*

Loud footsteps nearby, followed by the crack of a large branch, sent Samara dropping to the ground.

CHAPTER SEVEN

E melyne pulled as many workers as she could to start on the stone wall. She even pulled individuals from weapons training for the day, as they needed the security of another barrier in case of an attack. This had become glaringly obvious after seeing the centaur's camp last night.

If centaurs gathered outside their dragon-blessed steel fence, their arrows could easily go above or through the bars, hitting anybody within reach. She wanted to repair the buildings of Paddosha Palace village quickly not only to provide everyone with secure homes but also to restore the village back to its former glory. Unfortunately, they had to concentrate on security first, or there wouldn't be a village at all.

This security became more vital each day. News of changes happening at Paddosha Palace village would travel fast. Inevitably, someone would let it slip to the outsiders that the princess or dragons were there, that they were rebuilding, or that the village was getting back on its feet. The word could spread as a message of hope, but it could also reach the wrong ears, alerting the coterie of their progress.

Despite the poundings they'd received from the coterie over the last decades, the village had changed rapidly since Emelyne and her family had joined them. Not only had they started to rebuild, but the morale of the villagers had also improved greatly. People walked around with smiles on their faces even though resources were still sparse. They were learning to improve their lives with farming and pulling together as a community.

The visit from the from the sorceress of the Sacred Flame coterie had scared them immensely. Emelyne's exposure to members of the coterie had been sparse, and the power that they held was beyond her imagination. She had heard they were a source to contend with, but never in her life had she imagined something like the attack the villagers had endured. She never thought they would have had to defend themselves against lightning. The thought was scary.

The dragons had been gone for a while, so she hoped they would come across more beings to join their side. Samara and Ulrieg seemed confident that they had found Dragoria. She hoped they were right. They could certainly use the help against the coterie. From their description of the hidden and secure border, they had likely found the hidden realm. She hoped they would find many more dragons there and that those dragons would come to their defense. But even with extra dragons on their side, she didn't know how they were going to stand against the whole coterie.

The people had much more to learn. They faced a long struggle to defend this village, let alone the whole realm.

Emelyne had Monut drag the cart full of stones to the wall they were erecting. For a time, she oversaw the process. She marveled at how the stonemason would cut the stones to fit, with the flat side showing to the outside of the wall. Muscles bulged on the arms of every person helping to lift the larger stones.

She joined in the effort. Peering over her shoulder, she spotted more people coming to help. Many came from the farmlands, and most of the villagers joined in, especially the men. The farmers had taken the day off to help build the wall. Emelyne's father also headed toward the rock wall to join the others. Many of the farmers had even brought their own carts full of stones. The farm horses drew the carts towards the wall as the workers progressed.

Maisie approached Emelyne, her long blond braids hanging down her back. "Once I heard you needed help, I told my father to grab all the rocks they had and to bring them. And he rounded up all the other farmers. Now he has brought the rocks and the labor to build the wall quickly." She rocked on her toes and clasped her hands behind her back, looking pleased with herself.

Emelyne was astounded that a young girl had been so proactive. "That was very clever of ya."

The girl raced to Monut and hugged his leg, and the dragon seemed perplexed by the girl's open affection.

She looked up at him with her big blue eyes. "I'm so sorry. I don't have any more rabbits. That's all we had to spare."

Monut lowered his snout to her level and looked her

in the eyes. *That's okay. I'm very grateful for what you gave me, but I'm perfectly capable of catching my own. It was nice that you thought of me.*

Maisie pulled her attention away from Monut, releasing his leg, and studied the crowds building the rock wall. "They all seem so dreary."

Emelyne squatted to her level. "It's hard work buildin' rock walls, an' we need it built quickly to protect us as soon as possible."

Maisie's eyes filled with intensity. "But everyone could still be happy while doing it. Papa always tells me that work is easier to do when you sing. And it's such a beautiful day. The sun is out, and Papa says the sky is as blue as my eyes. Even the fluffy white clouds look happy to be part of this day."

Emelyne leaned on one leg, amused by the girl's instructions. "And what do ya suggest they sing?"

"They could sing something that has a good beat, like 'Hey ho, here we go, the rock wall we must build. The faster we do it, the stronger we'll grow, getting that rock wall built.'"

She repeated the lines a few more times before she caught her father's attention, then he smiled and joined in her song. His baritone filled the air alongside her sweet soprano.

That's actually kind of catchy. Monut tapped his talons in time with their beat.

Before long, another person joined in. Their voice was rough as they carried and hoisted the rocks, but it didn't affect the flow of the song. Then more joined in. Even the stonemason sang as he chipped away. When the rocks were secure, the workers filled the gaps with lime mortar, setting the stones in place. Once the mortar had hardened, they would lean ladders against the wall and pass more stones up to make the wall taller. More workers joined in the song until all their voices blended as one, creating the sense of a relaxing, joyous day despite the labor.

Emelyne was glad to see the song lift the workers' spirits. "That was a fantastic idea. Good thinking. Your dad must be a very intelligent man."

The little girl nodded, skipping along the wall as the men sang and loaded the rocks, her sweet, high-pitched voice joining in. Emelyne couldn't help but join in as well.

It looks like you have it all under control here. I'm going to go dragon-fire the rest of this steel fence. Monut stopped his talon tapping. *I want to make sure it's as strong as possible.*

Emelyne nodded. "That's a good idea. I'll stay and help build the rock wall."

They parted ways as Emelyne continued to sing. Her alto voice blended with the tenors and bases as she worked alongside Hamon, Samara's elven father, and Marcel, Paxton's human father. Pride filled her as the wall came together quickly with help from so many villagers. They had changed greatly since she had come along as an unknown. She'd first been accused of stealing food, and now she was accepted and respected.

When it came time for lunch, the group walked back to the village square, where the ladies from the bakery had brought several loaves of bread and all sorts of treats for them to eat. The food was offered free of charge, another way for the villagers to pitch in.

"Perhaps when they're all done with the wall, they could rebuild the palace quicker." Hamon took a large bite of his bread filled with shredded possum. "Then you might have an actual room to sleep in instead of a makeshift chamber with a partial roof."

Emelyne shook her head. "As delightful as that sounds, me current sleeping arrangement works quite well. I ain't gonna have villagers go without so I get some fancy palace." She shook her head. "Nah! It's more important that the village is rebuilt. A palace is jus' an additional plus. We'll look at that when the village is completely restored. Me an' me parents have enough with a roof over our heads. There were at least two rooms salvageable in the palace."

"It's not good for the princess to be sleeping rough." The farmer took another bite of his roll.

"Well, there ain't a lot of princesses who grew up in a dwarven village. I'm fine with what I've got. Simple is fine. The palace is more an emblem of the strength of the village."

"Hail to the giving Princess!" a farmer with a burly blond beard yelled. "And that's why we love her—because she puts us first. It's not all about her and her image. She puts what is important first, not vanity."

The workers eating around her raised their cups in cheer.

"That's why all the farms are taking off and growing abundantly, because of all the help she's focused onto them," Hamon called.

Emelyne felt her cheeks warm. She was not used to such attention. Even though she was technically the princess now, she quite liked being just one of the normal people.

"That's exactly right," said Marcel, who was next to

Hamon. "This has been the most welcoming village that I have come to and lived in for a very long time. Our mixed marriage isn't even looked at twice, and my half-blood child is never ridiculed."

"You should be very proud of what you've done here. And I'm sure that because of your humbleness, you'll raise a lot of support for each task you need to do," one of the women said.

CHAPTER EIGHT

Samara remained behind a bush, squatting. She pulled her dark cloak hood over her head and kept her eyes peeled on her surroundings to determine where the loud footsteps had come from.

Suddenly, the branches of a tree swung apart, and an ogre peered through the opening. His enormous eyes were alert as he scanned the area. He snorted, and traces of snot shot out of his large nose, which looked to have been beaten almost flat. His gaze landed on the bush behind which Samara was hiding.

She held her breath, determined not to make any noise to pique his curiosity. It seemed like forever before he released the branches and backed away, annoyance on his face. She let her breath out quietly. *That was close.*

No kidding! Ulrieg remained in his invisible form. *I think it's time we move away from their camp and give it a wide berth.* The branches above Samara bounced as his weight lifted. *He's headed away—far enough for us not to be seen. Let's get out of here.*

Following Ulrieg's advice, Samara redirected her path to steer clear of the camp. Whether Kellam was there or not, at least one of the ogres was clearly taking his duty seriously. Once she could no longer see the bonfire and the sound of the drums had faded, she heard Ulrieg land and begin walking by her side. His body heat and the slight swish of air from his movement reached up to her waist on one side. Her mind traveled to Monut's size, and she was glad that Ulrieg wasn't a dragon to ride—especially since she didn't enjoy heights. Still, his personality made up for his small size.

She reached out and brushed her hand gently over his invisible cheek, managing to avoid his many horns. *Let's hope this trip will be over soon and that we are able to get Paxton out of the orb.*

I completely agree with you, but you do realize that this could be our last mission ever? Samara felt a sadness in Ulrieg's voice.

Oh. I realize what you're saying. But Ulrieg, let's not think like that. We have to be positive.

Pfft! Always miss positive. Always thinking on the bright side gets rather tiresome. Ulrieg snorted. *It's disgusting!*

She sighed. *I know it's not in your nature, but it's a way of dealing with everything we are going through.* She picked up her pace and heard Ulrieg scrambling to keep close for a few hundred feet until he launched into the air, loose twigs scattering from the force of his wings.

Although they had left the beating of the drums far behind, Ulrieg found it much easier to fly than to walk. They traveled through the rest of the night, only resting in the early hours of the morning. They then continued through the next day and night, avoiding villages until the light broke through the darkness. Samara could feel exhaustion growing in her bones, but she didn't stop until they had reached the village near the forest surrounding the coterie building.

The hood of her cape had fallen, so she pulled it back up until the rim reached her forehead. Most of the pink had grown out of her hair, but just in case the rays of the sun heightened the color, she wanted to make sure it was covered—especially since they were so close to the coterie hiding spot and there were most likely more spies among the villagers.

She was tempted to call on the people she had sought refuge with before meeting up with Forgrac to run from the coterie. But she wasn't sure how things had panned out for them over the last few months. Things could have taken a turn for the worse if the coterie had suspected the villagers harbored their escapees.

The banging of a blacksmith's hammer reverberated through the village the moment she set foot on the main street. The sound was strangely comforting after she'd spent so much time with Emelyne and the residents of Paddosha Palace village.

Samara made sure her stride remained confident so as not to appear she was hiding. Acting self-assured was the best way to avoid unwanted attention. With her chin down, her eyes darted all around to take in every movement. She was determined to spot and avoid anyone likely to question her.

The wind picked up, threatening to blow her hood from her head and whipping the lower part of her cloak around her legs. Trees swayed from side to side, and loose leaves scattered down the dirt road. A stick struck her legs, thankfully through her thick cloak and dress. The change in weather caused people to seek shelter when they could.

Wanting to get off the street as quickly as possible, she headed to the local inn to seek a bed for the night. She cracked the door open, gripping it tightly so it wouldn't be caught in a gust and slam open. She felt Ulrieg crawl past her as he slid into the building. It was only midmorning, but the tavern was well alight with joy and the cheer of drunken chatter, the people too preoccupied to notice her joining them.

Despite the ruckus, she was glad to be out of the strong winds. A storm was likely coming, and she would rather wait it out before heading toward the coterie. The visit was going to be difficult enough without the weather working against her as well.

The aroma of warm stew wafted on the air, dampening the smell of stale ale. Her stomach rumbled. She hadn't had a proper meal since she'd left Paddosha Palace village. Nerves firing on edge, she walked toward the bar. She stayed alert as she studied every patron, watching their joyous celebrations and listening to their drunken slander.

Her body swayed as Ulrieg climbed her waist and perched on her shoulder, steering clear of the injured side. She did her best to counteract the weight, wincing from the ache caused by the slight movement. She groaned.

Am I hurting you? Concern marred his voice.

A little, but that's okay. It's better than having your talons scraping on the floor. Although I don't think they'd be heard over this ruckus.

I'll climb down, then.

Her body shifted again, and she stiffened, standing near a wall until he had reached the floor. She hoped her strange movements wouldn't be noticed by anyone in the tavern. With Ulrieg beside her once more, she locked eyes with a man at a table near the bar. Curiosity filled his eyes, sending her into a panic.

I think we might have trouble. Samara was unsure whether she recognized the man.

Which one?

The one in the far corner, near the bar. He's sitting by himself with a tankard in front of him.

I'll fix that.

A gust of air brushed against her. He must have pushed off the ground, heading toward the man. The ceiling was tall enough for a smallish dragon to fly over the top of the patrons without hitting any of them.

Trying not to be too obvious, she set her eyes on the man watching her from the corner. A few moments later, his hood was pushed off with a gust that also brushed back his hair. Within moments, his face distorted with displeasure as though he had smelled something rank, and sweat built on his skin. He turned his face in the opposite direction, facing the wall.

Ulrieg's chuckling echoed through their bond.

What did you do?

I flatulated in his face. He roared with laughter.

The age-old boy joke. The corner of her mouth twitched. *How incredibly childish and brilliant of you.*

And rather effective?

It seems that way.

While the man was distracted, she quickly approached

the bar and grabbed the barkeep's attention. "Do you have a room?"

The barkeep slung his tea towel over his shoulder and grunted, "That'll be two silvers."

Samara dug through her bag, retrieved a couple of coins from the money pouch, and placed them on the counter. The barkeep snatched them up before retrieving a key and nodding in the direction of the stairs. "It's up the stairs, first door on the right."

Samara grabbed the key and glanced toward the corner to see if the man was still turned away.

Ulrieg urged her forward. *Don't waste time. You're taking too long. Go now. He's not watching.*

Samara headed up the stairs and felt the push of air from Ulrieg's wings as he passed over her. When she reached the top, she unlocked the first door on the right. She opened it to find a modest room consisting of a bed and a window. The space was barely bigger than the bed, but the window was perfect for Ulrieg to get out during the night and hunt.

Weary after such a long trip, she decided to sleep until the patron downstairs had disappeared. She had not slept properly, if at all, since leaving Paddosha Palace village. She locked the door and opened the window. *I'll leave this open so you can go hunting, but I need to sleep.*

Ulrieg made himself visible now that they were behind closed doors, the sight of his red eyes and scaly black body a comfort to Samara.

You sleep. I'll hang around for a bit to make sure that guy doesn't come up this way. I can hunt later if we're still here. You need your beauty sleep. You're getting big bags under your eyes.

Lovely. Thanks for that, Ulrieg. Too tired to change her

clothes, Samara kicked off her shoes and lay on the bed. Before long, sleep found her, sending strange images her way. She thrashed on top of the covers as centaurs, ogres, and wrapping vines protruding from the orb weeded their way into her dreams. The nightmare grew increasingly realistic until she was awoken by loud banging on the door.

Sitting bolt upright, she searched the room, squinting against the light that still pierced through the window. Her mind foggy, she wondered how long she had been asleep. It didn't feel like long enough.

The knocking sounded again, and she blinked, trying to clear her vision. *Ulrieg. Are you here?* She saw no evidence of him in the room, and he had no reason to be invisible with just the two of them in the room.

She pushed herself up, threw her legs over the side of the bed, and tiptoed barefoot across the floor. She rotated her shoulder, groaning from the ache. The dagger heated by Ulrieg's flame had stopped the bleeding and warded off any infection, but the wound still needed time to heal. Another round of banging startled her as she reached the back of the door. The sound was urgent and menacing.

She grabbed the handle, turned it slowly, and opened the door a crack, making sure she jammed her foot behind it to block any forced entry.

When she looked up, she came face-to-face with the man who had been watching her from the table downstairs.

CHAPTER NINE

Muscles weary from the long day's work, Emelyne walked through the sconce-lit streets of Paddosha Palace village. Her heart was soaring. Everyone had come together, and thanks to Maisie's advice of a song, their work had been done with cheer and enthusiasm. The sun had set, and the majority of the villagers had finished their work and were lining the streets, waiting for their turn at a food stall. With the villagers' approval, Emelyne had pooled their resources, and the main meals were cooked in bulk and supplied to all.

With Forgrac in charge, several men and women had worked to supply everyone with food for the day. The whole village had come together to eat and drink in the streets of Paddosha Palace village for what had become a festive occasion. The wine and ale were spread around, and everyone seemed happy and joyous.

Emelyne was tired, but her spirits were high. The villagers had welcomed the foreigners, dwarves and elves included. She wished Thiznabo was still alive to see this. She would've loved this community.

The princess had finished eating her meal and intermingling with the villagers, and though she was eager to sleep, she had to do her nightly scout of the area with Monut. She also needed to keep an eye on where the centaurs had gone since the previous night.

With her riding leathers on and her long hair tied into two braids that finished in one at the base of her neck, the princess walked through the village toward the gate and quickly searched the sky for her dragon friend. *Monut, are ya ready?* She hadn't seen him for a while, but that was not uncommon. He liked to spend time in nature out of the village square, most likely missing his dragon friends or hunting. Before long, she heard his reply.

Yes, my bonded. I shall meet you outside the village.

Emelyne reached the front entrance of the village, where few people went at that time of night, and found Monut, his gray scales reflecting the surrounding torchlight. He had on his new saddle made by Marcel, the leather strong and sturdy.

The dragon lowered to his haunches and spread out a wing to help her up onto his back. Emelyne hooked her legs over his wings and fastened the saddle strap around her waist. Her hand ran over the black leather and the fine details added by Marcel and his wife, Jastira. The couple had even added pouches and places to secure her weapons. *They 'ave done an exquisite job on this saddle.*

Monut rose to his feet. *Good. Let's test it out properly tonight.* He pushed into the air, and a couple of leaves swirled below him as he flapped his enormous membranous wings.

Gripping the saddle, Emelyne leaned forward, reveling in the cool breeze pushing back the few loose strands of her long brunet hair from her face. She had loved flying and the adrenaline that came with it from her first flight on Monut's back. Dragon flying was something she'd never expected to do, but not for a second would she want to give it up. The heights and the freedom were almost addictive.

Monut rose high into the sky. *Are you ready for some new maneuvers?*

Emelyne chuckled. *I'm always ready.*

All right, hang on!

Monut tucked his wings into his sides and dived. Then he tilted and briefly flipped upside down, fueling her adrenaline rush. Unfinished, the large dragon flew back into the clouds and dived again, the village lights springing up to meet her before he quickly spread his wings and banked to the right.

Emelyne searched the village below and the surrounding areas while enjoying the rush, the strap around her waist jerking and pulling as it kept her from falling during his antics.

Monut chuckled. *This is so much freedom. I haven't been able to fly like this for so long.*

Couldn't you do this in the Merciless Sanctuary? Emelyne smiled at the joy she could feel across their bond.

Occasionally, we could do this, but we always had to be cautious because we didn't know who would see us. We couldn't risk being caught. There were so many of us too. But now, having so many people know that I exist and loving it, I have a certain amount of freedom. I can fly above them and not fear any repercussions.

She could hear the smile in his voice.

They circled wider to take in more of the surroundings below, each circle taking them farther from the village. Monut rose higher, taking shelter in the clouds when available, even though it was dark, as his gray scales glimmered slightly in the moonlight.

The immediate area looked normal, with no signs of new camps, so Monut circled farther out from the village, keeping to the clouds. They only dropped below cloud cover to give Emelyne a better view or to let Monut search the horizon, as he could see farther in the darkness.

Emelyne, isn't that the camp that we saw last night?

He lowered, and she spotted the centaurs, their faces illuminated by the fires they circled.

I believe it is. Emelyne squinted. *That's quite a lot closer than yesterday, isn't it?*

Yes, much closer. They may be coming to Paddosha Palace village after all.

Something whistled passed Emelyne's ear, and she ducked to the side. The distinct sound signaled that an arrow had passed narrowly by her.

Emelyne glowered over the side of Monut's body at the camp below. *That was close. It clearly is the village from yesterday, and they're still angry 'bout seein' a dragon.* A couple more arrows whooshed past her and lodged into Monut's wing.

Monut growled. *How long until I can breathe fire on them?*

That may be an option later, but right now, ya need to get away from the arrows. I'd hate for them to catch ya in the eye or somewhere where ya vulnerable.

I'm more worried about you. You don't have any armor on. At least my scales are tough, though the arrow sticking out of my wing does hurt with each stroke.

I think we've confirmed that it is the same camp as yesterday. Either that or there's another camp of centaurs that don't like dragons.

I'll go a little farther out to make sure it is the same and not a second one. Monut circled higher, heading toward the spot where they saw the village last night. *I can't see any sign of a camp up ahead. I believe that was the same camp.*

Let's pass over them one more time. We should count how many tents there are, or if there aren't tents, we should count the centaurs.

Monut stayed high until they were nearly at the camp. Then he dived low, swiftly flying several yards above them.

Emelyne did a quick count of the centaurs that were lying around or parked around the campfires. *I count thirty.*

That's not that many.

Except I believe they're trained warriors, whereas our villagers are just farmers and everyday folk. Some of them have hardly even picked up a weapon.

I would say they're not too far from the village. Unfortunately, we'll have to prepare for war. If they're heading our way, they could be upon us by tomorrow.

CHAPTER TEN

Samara wedged her foot harder against the back of the door. The man's features were dark, his eyes hidden within the deep shadow cast by the hood of his cloak.

Gulping, Samara tried to swallow the large lump in her throat. "Can I help you?" She gripped the brass handle, her body ready to react when the man attacked.

The man's shoulders seemed a cave, sending mixed messages to Samara. "It's more like, can I help you?" He glanced from side to side, seeming suspicious or wary. "There are coterie spies everywhere around here. You have a lot of nerve coming back to this village."

Samara wasn't sure what to make of him—whether he was trying to warn or threaten her. She decided to play naive, as it seemed to work at other times. "I don't know what you mean. I'm just passing through."

Shifting closer, he pressed against the door.

Samara's foot remained firm.

"I know you're an ex-coterie member. And because of that, you have brought a lot of danger to yourself and everyone in this village. You shouldn't be here." His warm breath bore the strong stench of ale.

Samara attempted to hold her face steady so as not to give away any emotions, yet her mind was whirling. She didn't know what to do next. He was still sending her mixed messages.

He exhaled loudly, almost snorting, pushing more secondhand ale her way as he shifted closer.

She pulled back, her nose scrunched in disgust. "Look, I don't know what you expect me to do. I'm literally just passing through. I won't be here for long. I'm not meaning to put anybody in danger. I was just after a room for the night."

"Well, I recommend you don't stay here. I am certain that coterie members or people who are on their side have already seen and recognized you. The coterie are too close for you to pretend like you aren't an ex-member who defied them. If people hadn't seen you before, maybe it would be safer for you."

"And how am I to trust you?" She kept her distance, struggling to keep her foot lodged behind the door every time he pushed closer.

"I'm a friend of Forgrac. He would always drop in. I used to help him get all his supplies for the coterie." He tried peering past her into the room. "You should grab your things and get out of here."

Samara sighed loudly through her nose. "I don't know where else to go. I was seriously hoping for a bed for the night while I wait out the bad weather."

"I'm warning you, all it'll take is one member from the coterie to enter this village, and the information will be passed on to them from one of the villagers. I suggest—if you would like to stay alive and free—that you leave immediately. Sleep is not worth the risk, even if the bed is comfortable." He glanced over his shoulder, down the stairs toward the tavern. "If you come now, I can show you another way out of this inn so that nobody will see you."

"Wait here." Shoulders slumped, Samara grabbed her bag, gathered her things, and placed them inside it.

The man entered the room and closed the door behind him.

She spun to look at him, his hooked nose looking larger in the light. "What are you doing?"

"Don't worry. I'm simply making sure that nobody else comes into the room while you're packing." His eyes traveled past her uneasy stance, studying the rest of her room. "Where's your dragon?"

Samara looked down, pretending to be extra busy packing her things. "What makes you think I've got a dragon? Do you see one anywhere?" She waved her hand around the room. "If you don't see one, then there isn't one."

Amusement passed over the man's face. "Forgrac told me all about him. And he told me that he can be invisible. So he could be here somewhere." He reached out as if feeling for something. Coming up empty-handed, he turned to face her. "That's how much Forgrac trusted me."

Samara placed her hands on her hips. "He's got a bit of a big mouth, hasn't he? He's still not here. So you can feel the air all you like for something invisible. You won't find him."

The man placed his hands by his side, giving up on his fruitless search. His hood fell from his head, revealing cropped brown hair. He looked to be only about thirty summers and seemed quite bony, the flesh of his cheeks sucking in and shadowed even without the hood. "He only told me because he trusted me. I helped him out many times when he was stuck in the coterie too. That place is not a good place."

"You've got that right." She quickly packed a few more things into her bag and threw the sack onto her shoulder, groaning as it hit her wound on its way over. The spot was still tender, but at least the bleeding had stopped and the area showed no signs of infection.

When she finished packing, he led her out of the room and in the opposite direction from the tavern to the back side of the building. She wondered if there were more openings than just the front door. But no matter which way she took, it sounded like she was in danger. He brought her to a window overlooking part of the roof then climbed out. Reluctantly, Samara climbed out after him. She tried not to peer at the ground as she followed him to lower roofs of adjacent buildings until they could climb down a ladder.

Once they were on solid ground, he led her down thin alleyways lined with all kinds of items like potted plants and seats placed on the stone stairs. Samara had never been down the tiny streets of the village of Nightscar. The village's name seemed appropriate. She hadn't spent much time there, even though the coterie building was nearby. Coterie members were not usually allowed to go out or travel to the villages. They mostly stayed around the coterie building and continued their studies unless sent out by Callista. She had only visited briefly to seek refuge with some of Forgrac's friends after she'd escaped.

The man led her down several more narrow, dingy streets. They weaved their way through more chairs and plants until, finally, they came to the edge of the village that met the forest.

Samara's stomach rumbled.

"Here. I brought you some stew to eat." The man handed her a pie bigger than her hand from under his cloak, wrapped in a bit of cloth. "I had the barkeep make a pie case for it when I saw you didn't have anything to eat before you went to your room." He chuckled. "He wasn't too pleased about it either."

Shocked by the kind gesture, she took it from him. The pastry was slightly warm, still intact even though he had been carrying it. "Thank you. I am starving—especially for a warm meal."

The man nodded. "I didn't give it to you earlier because we had to get moving." He indicated to the forest with his head. "Find a hiding place in there and eat your fill."

Despite being hungry, she was glad she'd caught some sleep instead of taking the time to eat. She would need clarity when she arrived at the plain where the coterie building sat. The sun was high in the sky, telling her she had only slept for part of the day.

The breeze whipped through the canopy, sending leaves into a loud song and snowing many to the ground. She assessed the sky. Several puffy white clouds floated freely, with no ominous signs of a storm. Relief flooded her.

Noticing her assessing the weather, the man said, "The winds are probably bringing the cold for the start of autumn. There shouldn't be a storm today. I would've taken you to my home, but you have been seen by too many people, and they may search all of the village homes tonight looking for you. If a coterie member comes, it's too risky for my family." He ran his hand through his long brunet hair. "You should be able to find some sort of cave or something in the forest to take shelter and sleep, if it does storm." He nudged her toward the forest. "You need to go now. You shouldn't have come back like this." He glanced over his shoulder at a loud noise from the village. "It's too dangerous. So I'll leave you here."

Without another word, he turned and left, his cape billowing behind him.

Samara stood dumbfound for a moment at the edge of the forest before ducking behind a tree and taking a bite of her pie. It was lukewarm but still delicious. The rich flavors of the rabbit and vegetables, boiled in their own juices, melted in her mouth. It seemed like such a long time since she'd had a proper meal.

Still eating her pie, she called out through her bond. *Ulrieg?* After taking several more bites, she called again, her eyes peeled for any danger that might come from the village or forest.

Samara, where are you? I had a peek in the room, and you weren't in there.

I'm at the edge of the forest. I've been told to get out of the village because it's too dangerous.

Nice. His sarcasm was clear. *Just what you need. This is going to be one rough trip. I can tell. I'll fly around now and see if I can spot you.*

Silence accompanied the wind until a tree branch above her bounced with an invisible weight, showering several leaves on her. She brushed them off her pie and took another bite.

I'm here. I guess we've gotta get going.

Monut reassured Emelyne that he would continue his surveillance of the area.

Wake me if there is anythin' close or if they move our way. If they don't, wake me before first light, an' we shall go for another flight to survey the area.

Leaving Monut with the responsibility, she headed to her makeshift bed of straw in the mostly-intact room on the ground floor of the destroyed palace. Rest wasn't easy. She worried about the village and what would happen the next day. There was no use telling the villagers about the centaurs at this stage. But in the morning, she would have to break the news if they moved any closer.

Just before dawn, Monut's voice echoed through Emelyne's mind. *Are you awake?*

She stirred, scattering a bit of straw from under the sheets. She rubbed her eyes. *Gettin' there. I'll be out in it a little bit.*

After stretching and grabbing a bite of bread she had kept in the corner, she dressed quickly, throwing on her boots and riding leathers. She ran a hand through her disheveled hair and weaved it into a rough braid. Still groggy, she made her way out of the palace and down the steps into the village square.

Monut waited for her there, tilting his head to take a good look at her. *You look rather cheerful this morning.*

Emelyne grumbled at Monut's sarcasm. *Yeah, I didn't get much sleep last night. I'm too worked up and worried 'bout the village.*

There wasn't any movement during the night as far as I could tell. Going for a flight this morning is a good idea so that we can see if they're packing up or doing something.

Emelyne wiped her eyes and hooked a loose strand of her brunet hair behind her ear before climbing onto Monut's back with the help of his wing. She secured herself with the strap and grabbed on to the saddle.

"I'm ready," she said.

Monut leaped into the sky and took them high into the cool air.

Normally, I would be bringin' Pa and Silut their breakfast first thing in the mornin'. But they'll have to wait.

Monut hummed. *I'm sure they'll survive if it's a bit late. Or they could down their tools and get their own.*

I know. I jus' like doin' that for Pa, an' it's a way that I can see him every day. I don't get to see me parents much anymore.

I'm certain your parents understand. Besides, they knew that this could happen when they were raising you.

Emelyne chuckled. *Yeah. Imagine keepin' a secret like that from ya daughter.* Her heart warmed when she thought about how much her adoptive parents had done for her.

When they rose above the trees, the sun peeked over the horizon, stretching its glowing fingers into the sky.

Monut briefly circled the village, checking the boundaries, before spreading his flight toward the camp they'd seen last night.

Let's hope they aren't headin' our way. Emelyne breathed in the early-morning air, relishing its crispness. *Thirty experienced and armed centaurs would be hard for the learnin' villagers to contend with. It would be their first battle, properly standin' up for themselves against the coterie.*

I understand your concern. Monut beat his wings in harmonious rhythm. *There is a slight benefit.*

Oh? What is that? Emelyne pushed a strand of hair away from her mouth.

The centaurs don't have a magic wielder in their midst.

Emelyne tilted her head. *True. It'll be easier than dealin' with lightnin' and whatever other gifts the coterie magic wielders may have.*

With a few more beats of his wings, Monut had them over the camp, flying out of an arrow's reach. *We're here.*

Emelyne squinted, trying to see what was going on below, but the land was still covered in darkness. *I don't see nothin'. I have to rely on ya vision.*

The large dragon circled, flapping his majestic wings just enough to maintain a steady altitude. *They seem to be packing up. It looks to me like they are donning their bows and quivers and setting off.*

Which way are they goin'?

He circled the camp a few more times. *They are heading toward the village.*

Emelyne's heart sank. *We're gonna have to prepare the village for them. It's better to be safe than sorry. We've seen enough.*

Monut turned and headed back to the village.

Emelyne fell into silence as she contemplated what to do. *I wish Thiznabo was still with us. She woulda had better battle knowledge.* Emelyne knew she needed to be strong instead. She still longed for the day she could avenge her friend.

I believe in you. I have learned how you pull from your strength to make wise decisions. Just look at how you won over the villagers' hearts. That in itself is a huge achievement.

They flew in silence as the sun's rays spread over the earth, illuminating it with a dull light that grew brighter by the minute. Carried by the huge wings of the dragon, they returned to the village quickly. Monut landed in the main square, and Emelyne disembarked in the dimly lit courtyard. Serving of the communal breakfast was under-way, with most foods meant to be grabbed and eaten on the way.

Emelyne climbed the steps of the palace to her room, where she retrieved her sword and bow and arrows. Her riding-leather pants swished with each rapid step. Her room was basic, with stone walls, one opaque window, and a sheet-covered straw bed. The walls were mostly erect, as was the roof, leaving only a small hole on one side. She had been told it was the room Samara had stayed in when she visited the village with Callista. There had been a second straw bed, but Emelyne had combined the straw to make hers softer. Only two rooms were still mostly intact after destruction of the palace, and her parents' room was much the same. It provided just enough shelter to keep them out of the harshness of the weather. The rooms were enough for now. Admittedly, it would be nice to have a safer and more pristine building to live in, but the villagers came first—otherwise, there wouldn't be a kingdom at all.

Sword clacking by her side and arrows rattling in the quiver, she ran down the stairs. She grabbed some pastries from her mother in the bakery for breakfast then headed to the blacksmith shop. It was clear that Silut and her father had been hard at work for a couple of hours already.

Lozzeak off-loaded his hammer and set aside the piece he had been working on. "Mornin', love." He smiled, pulling off his gloves and wiping the sweat off his forehead with his long sleeve. "Ah. Are them pastries for us?"

Emelyne handed a couple to her adoptive father and a couple to Silut, then she placed the rest on a bare bench. "Of course. Well, at least most of them. I grabbed ya what I could. We're all up so early, the bakers ain't even got much baked yet." She grabbed one more for herself, leaving an even number of pastries for the two men.

Taking a bite of a berry-filled pastry, Lozzeak groaned. "Hmm. Did ya ma make this?"

Emelyne shrugged. "I didn't ask, but she was in the baker's section this mornin'."

"She has learned a lot of new things since she joined the bakery. I ain't complainin'." He smiled, white sugar clinging to his red beard.

"Ma has always been a good cook." Emelyne finished her pastry, dusting her fingers on her pants.

"Not goin' to argue with ya there." He rubbed his protruding belly. "The proof's right here. Jus' sayin' that she's learnin' new stuff. I like it."

Silut put down his equipment and took a large mouthful

of pastry. "I have to agree with ya. Even though me muscles are growin', me wife is complainin' 'bout me ever-growin' belly." He chuckled. "I think it's 'cause ya keepin' me well fed." Silut tapped his barely-there belly affectionately.

Emelyne smiled. "As soon as ya can, I need ya to do somethin'."

Lozzeak grabbed his second pastry and looked up at her. "Anythin'. What do ya need?"

"I need ya to grab ya horse an' cart an' fill the cart with all the weapons we have. Then bring 'em to the front of the village, where all the wall builders will be waitin'."

The dwarven men frowned. "What's goin' on?" Lozzeak stopped chewing.

"I jus' want to be cautious. Not trying to alarm ya. There's a camp of centaurs that seems to be headin' this way."

Silut's face paled, and he discarded his pastry. "Do they 'ave any members of the coterie with 'em?"

"Not that we can see. From what Monut said, it seems to be only centaurs."

"I ain't seen a centaur before, but I hear they're fantastic archers. I ain't had much weapons trainin' yet." The young father pushed the hair out of his eyes.

"Hopefully, it won't come to that." She nodded to the pastry he'd abandoned on the bench. "But try an' eat up. I know it's hard, but ya goin' to need ya strength. Whether it's for manual labor or runnin' weapons to the more-trained fighters. Ya help is goin' to be needed."

CHAPTER TWELVE

Samara crouched among the pine trees at the edge of the empty plain where she knew the invisible coterie building was hidden. It was strange to look across the space and not see the building she knew was there. The last time she had been here, she was still a part of the Sacred Flame coterie, which allowed her to see the secret building where they trained magic apprentices. She no longer held the status of Sacred Flame coterie member. Although she would never wish to return to the oppressive group that tortured dragons and dragon elves for fun, it would have been helpful at the moment to see where the building was and which parts to avoid as she made her way to the opening of the underground.

The spell on the building had been designed so that nonmembers could not see the building's outline or windows. The space before her appeared to be only an empty plain lined by pine trees. She wouldn't know if someone had spotted her from a window.

Since her escape from the coterie several months

prior, so much had happened. Yet she knew that deep within the ground, the evil orange orb was spinning, pulsating, wrapping its sinister tendrils around Paxton's body.

Ulrieg was somewhere in the trees above her in his invisible form, grabbing a better view of the plain. The wild winds from earlier had settled, creating the perfect afternoon to be out on a walk. Brilliant hues of red, orange, yellow, and blue stretched across the westward sky as the sun began its descent. Darkness swept in from the east, settling over the forest.

Have you seen Henriette yet? Samara spoke through their bond to keep their noise to a minimum.

No, I haven't. There hasn't been a sign of the mischievous sorceress or her ferret anywhere. The branches above her moved slightly, as if Ulrieg was adjusting his position. *Though I could have sworn that I saw Mystique's head appear suddenly out of nowhere, probably peeking out of the main building door. The image was fleeting, though, so I could be wrong.*

Surprisingly, there has been very little action today on this plain. Samara shifted her legs to stretch them, the muscles complaining from the cramped position she'd had them in. *I remember apprentices coming and going regularly to practice in the woods.*

The walk through the forest from the village of Nightscar had taken them a while, bringing them to the edge of the clearing by late afternoon. Since then, they had spent their time scouting the area, waiting to observe the comings and goings of the coterie residents, but they'd had little success in spotting anyone.

I don't think Henriette has come back yet after she helped save Paddosha Palace from Mist. Ulrieg remained in the tree above. *That should mean Mist isn't back either. Hopefully, Henriette managed to successfully wipe Mist's memory.*

Hopefully. Samara tugged at her brunet hair, no longer a brilliant pink from the coterie requests. She had let the color grow out and hadn't replaced it. Only a smidgen of pink remained. The thought of Paxton still underneath the coterie—in a building she could no longer see—was gnawing at her stomach, churning her insides into a sludge of deep worry. If Henriette still hadn't returned to the coterie, Samara wasn't sure how she was going to enter the invisible building. Maybe they'd have some luck and either Devi or Peadar would exit the building on their own. But even if they did, they couldn't make her invisible, and she would most likely be seen trying to cross the plain.

She should probably wait for Henriette to return, but at the same time, with every minute that Paxton stayed in the orb, it could either be corrupting him or ending his life. She had already waited too long. She wished she had some way of contacting Henriette, Devi, or Peadar. She would probably need their help, and they would have no idea that she was there.

Samara groaned her frustration. *Where is Henriette?* Her eyes traveled over the plain and landed on the bush that she suspected concealed the hole into the underground. At least the trees weren't invisible. *I still haven't seen her. It wouldn't be a problem if I didn't need her help to get underground. Being invisible would be very helpful right now.*

Unfortunately, I can't do anything about that. Ulrieg sounded just as frustrated.

I know. I can't either, which is why it's so frustrating. But I really don't think I can wait. Every minute I sit here is a waste of time. I'm thinking about Paxton, trapped in that evil orb, and what it must be doing to him. Now that I'm this close, I want to get in there and do something about it.

Ulrieg's loud sigh traveled through their bond. *That's going to be a very risky move if we try and do something now, without the help of anybody else.*

I haven't got a clue when Henriette is going to be coming back, so I can't wait. She could be ages yet. And when she does come back, Mist will probably be with her, which will make it hard to do anything.

They continued to watch the plain with no sign of sorcerers coming or going from the invisible coterie building. Darkness crept farther into the sky, shrouding them with its protection, yet Samara remained within the cover of the pine trees.

Hide! Somebody's coming. Ulrieg's urgent whisper traveled through their bond.

Samara sat upright. *From which direction?*

From behind us. I can hear footsteps and giggling. It's still quite some distance, but they're heading this way.

Samara crouched down farther, trying to stay under the cover of some of the lower-lying bushes. She peered behind her, trying to spot the people Ulrieg had heard. *Do you know who it is?*

I'm not quite sure, but I think it's a male and a female—judging by the voices I'm hearing.

Samara's heart thumped against her chest as she anticipated who could be heading toward the coterie. If there were two and they were on the coterie side, she would be outnumbered. A nice-sized bush stood near her, and she darted toward it, planting herself in the middle of its leaves, in the center of its cover.

After only a few minutes, she could hear the crunching of twigs and leaves as the footsteps approached. A rabbit hopped by, heading toward the plain. A moment later, she spotted a fox about fifty yards away, then she heard the chatter of a man and woman, and her insides twisted into knots. She would recognize those voices anywhere.

Being careful not to pique the fox's interest, she peered through the branches, trying to spot the two people approaching. Brilliant blue hair came into view through the brush, topping a handsome face—one recently set with an evil edge. Or perhaps she had been blinded to it. Looking at him now, she didn't know how she had been attracted to him before, especially when she wasn't one to fall for outward charm. After hearing what he'd done to Emelyne's friend, her insides twisted in disgust. Although after what she had experienced in her final days at the coterie, she shouldn't have been surprised.

A high-pitched peal of laughter echoed through the forest as Luna tossed back her head of golden hair, her beautiful face radiantly happy. Samara knew that happiness had something to do with Kaine's charm, plus Luna seemed to have embraced the evilness of the coterie. She wasn't using her singsong voice. She didn't have to control Kaine by any means other than making sure he doted on her beauty. And she made sure she flaunted that with her very low-cut neckline amplifying her voluptuous cleavage.

Samara found these two to be an interesting combination. Both magical beings knew how to twist people into voluntarily giving information without even realizing it.

They both had very manipulative ways of controlling people that, at times, could *seem* friendly.

Luna linked her arm through Kaine's as they walked side by side. Her carefree attitude so close to the coterie was one to be envied. Samara wondered if Luna had also been persecuting villages like Kaine had persecuted Emelyne's home of Bhalwahrum. She shivered at the terror a couple of coterie magic wielders could do.

Their footsteps passed close to Samara. She held her breath, doing her best not to rustle the leaves hiding her, glad neither Ginger nor Coco—their familiars—had spotted her or caught her scent. She listened to part of their conversation and realized Kaine was boasting about killing a dwarf in one of the villages. Heat rushed to her cheeks as anger boiled within her. It sounded like he was talking about Emelyne's friend. How horrifying to be boasting about killing people—beings who had done nothing to him other than delay his entrance to a building. Even though it had been the blacksmith building where the princess, Emelyne, had been hiding, Kaine didn't know that.

Loathing filled Samara as they passed. He had probably been to many villages and killed the residents simply because he could. The thought that she had kissed him in the past made bile rise in her throat.

He had become so much like Vexx, the sorcerer who guarded the elven realm of Clialarion. Her memory flashed to her time in the coterie when the apprentices had first been visited by the sorcerers guarding the borders of Wraeyanor. She had thought they were the evil ones, only to learn that, in the end, Callista wasn't any better. The head sorceress just hid it beneath her unemotional face and neutral reactions. But deep down, she was devious, with an evil heart. As much as Samara loathed seeing these two, at least Kaine, Luna, and their familiars were not out terrorizing the villagers at this present moment.

Luna and Kaine entered the plain, eventually going up the invisible stairs and disappearing into the invisible building. Ginger and Coco disappeared with them.

Samara released the pressure in her lungs, realizing she had been holding her breath. It was strange watching them ascend into the air then disappear.

That was close. Ulrieg lowered closer to Samara, his movement made obvious by tree branches swaying under his weight.

Yes, it was, but they didn't appear to be looking for anyone hiding in the bushes. At least I've got that going for me. They must feel extremely comfortable in this area.

Or their power has grown so much since you were here that they are unafraid of people like you.

Way to be encouraging. I honestly must get back to practicing all these spells and learning from Henriette. My education in the world of magic is far from sufficient to go against the coterie. It makes me kind of wish I could have stayed longer to learn how to do more things with my magic.

Impatient, Samara took in the darkening sky. Soon, the night would envelop them. *I'm going to make my way around to the other side. I can't wait any longer. If Henriette isn't here, I'm just going to have to try without her.*

I would've thought that those two magic wielders would have put you off trying without any help. I thought you were smarter than to rush in brashly.

Samara scratched her arm, noticing the pain still radiating through her shoulder with every movement. *It would've been ideal if we had help, but it's almost dark now, and I think it's the best time to go. You can see in the dark and be my eyes when I cannot see properly.*

Don't forget, I'm not the only one, Ulrieg cautioned her. *There are others with familiars who can see in the dark here.*

I know. You'll have to just keep an eye out for them. Twigs cracked, and the leaves rustled under her feet as she worked her way around the edge of the clearing, heading closer to the bush that concealed the hole into the underground.

I hope the underground is not invisible as well after I enter this hole. It'll be difficult to find our way around it if we can't see anything.

Samara stopped under the shelter of the trees at the edge of the clearing, not far from where she expected the back entrance of the underground to be. She shifted forward to step out into the clearing.

Stop! Ulrieg's voice rang through her mind.

She froze, her eyes shooting up to study the darkened plain before her, trying to find the reason for his alert. Squinting, she could just make out a slinky black figure slowly descending the invisible stairs. Mystique. The jaguar's eyes would have easily seen her in the darkness. Her heart thundered within her chest, and she retreated into the shadows.

CHAPTER THIRTEEN

The darkness of the night had set in, making it nearly impossible to see the black jaguar prowling the plain that housed the coterie building. Clouds had hidden the light of the new moon, making it difficult for Samara to see at all.

Ulrieg, what's going on?

The vexatious cat looks to be on the lookout for something, or perhaps us. Oh, wait. Mystique just sniffed the air. Surely she can't smell me from there—can she?

I don't know. It would depend on whether we are downwind. Samara listened for the rustling of leaves and focused on the breeze brushing softly against her face to assess whether their scent would carry to the jaguar. *The wind from earlier today seems to be completely gone. Everything is still. So I don't know how well the cat would be able to smell us from here.*

Ulrieg grumbled. *I don't like this. I'm fine up here, but you have no way of escaping the cat if she spots you.*

What's she doing now?

She's prowling the plain. She is definitely on alert.

Maybe she does that every night as part of her security measures. Samara hoped she was right.

I didn't use to see her do it before. Ulrieg disagreed.

I mean, maybe that's a new protocol since we left. She crossed her fingers and continued peering into the plain from her hiding spot despite not being able to see the jaguar.

I'm not placing my confidence in that. That cat was a pain in the butt from the start.

What do you expect from an evil sorceress's familiar? It's not like she's going to be the opposite of her bonded.

Yeah, well, I'm different from you. I have no patience for stupidity, whereas you're always too nice.

You've got me on that one. Samara's leg was turning numb, and she was itching to move, but she didn't dare in case it created too much noise.

Dragon moon! She's coming this way.

Ulrieg's words sent shivers down her spine. She could shoot the cat with one of her spelled arrows, but then Callista would know she was here. Surely the head sorceress would come looking for Mystique if she didn't return for the night. Samara wasn't sure. Still, it might have been worth the risk. Slowly, being careful not to knock anything, she retrieved an arrow form her quiver then cast a spell over it with a wave of her hand, whispering, "Petra." It was a spell that would put Mystique into a state of temporary paralysis. She wouldn't come out of it until someone removed the arrow. *Is she still coming my way?*

Yes. She's several feet away. It's hard to tell if she knows you're there or just happened to walk this way.

Samara nocked her arrow, slowly drawing the string back to keep the movement silent. If Mystique was stalking her, Samara would be prepared to act quickly.

Ulrieg warned her the cat was close. *Four feet.*

Samara cringed. This wasn't how she expected her first visit back to the coterie to go. She thought she might still be able to see the coterie building because she'd once been a coterie member. But she didn't know why she was surprised. The coterie had zero tolerance for outsiders, especially ones that sided with their original enemy. Of course they would cut her off instantly, blinding her to their sacred building.

Two feet.

She could see the cat now. Mystique's head was angled to investigate the forest, not at Samara's hiding spot. The jaguar stopped, her nose lifting as she sucked in the air. Samara panicked. Surely the cat would smell her now. She fired, the arrow hitting the cat in the leg. Mystique instantly fell to the ground, petrified, eyes open. At times like this, Samara wished she didn't have to hurt animals. She had to remind herself that these were the familiars of evil magic wielders. In the past, she didn't like using magic on Ginger either, even though the fox deserved it for all the trouble she had brought.

Ha! Excellent! You got her. No cat deserved that as much as she did. Ulrieg's voice was full of pride.

Well, I don't feel great about it. Samara climbed out of her hiding spot. *I don't think she spotted me. I just wasn't willing to risk it.*

Don't feel bad. The cat wouldn't have hesitated to harm you or turn you in to Callista.

Samara checked the plain and the surrounding edges again for any sign of coterie members before grabbing Mystique's back paws and attempted to drag her into the forest. Only moving the cat a couple of feet, Samara dropped the legs. *I can't move her. She's heavier than she looks. Ulrieg, can you help me, please?*

Are you serious? I thought you were stronger than that. Wingless flight! You must be growing weak after not training every day.

Hmph. Then why don't you come down here and have a go? I'd like to see how you do.

The leaves rustled above as Ulrieg flew to the ground, still in his invisible form. *Sure. I'll show you how it's done.*

Samara stood back to give him room to work, watching as the jaguar's legs seemingly lifted of their own accord and were tugged toward the depths of the forest. The cat hardly shifted. *So, how is it going?* Samara crossed her arms over her chest and leaned to the side.

The cat's legs were tugged again, with barely any movement. Ulrieg groaned. *All right. All right. You're right. The cat is heavier than she looks.*

Ha! See? Enjoying one of the rare times Ulrieg admitted he was wrong, Samara hunkered down to help him. Ulrieg grabbed one leg while Samara grabbed the other. Together they managed to drag Mystique farther into the forest then left her behind a bush. Samara brushed her hands together to dust them off. *There. This way, if anyone comes out to look for her, they won't find her immediately.*

She gazed out over the plain, still unable to see clearly. *Ulrieg, has anyone else come out while we were distracted?*

Not for now.

Let's not waste any time. Keeping low, Samara set out over the plain, heading toward the area she thought the hole to the underground might be. She didn't know why she crouched—other than the position felt stealthy. The moon remained hidden from the sky, leaving the area dark and limiting her sight. Perhaps this would work in her favor, as any resident of the building glancing out into the night shouldn't be able to spot her either. She glided across the middle of the plain. *You know, I've always wondered something.*

What's that? Ulrieg's footsteps sounded softly on the trampled wildflowers by Samara's side.

If outsiders can't see the building, does that mean they can't feel the building either?

I don't know. I was on your shoulders when I first entered the coterie, and because of that, I could see the building as well. After that, I was invited by you, and because of our bond, I was classed as one of the coterie's familiars and could see the building.

I guess we'll find out soon. I think the outside of some of the building was around here. Although she was walking slowly, her face hit a solid flat surface, her cheek slapping against the cold stone. *Ouch!* She pulled back. *I wasn't even going fast, but that packed a punch.* She felt along the invisible wall and studied her surroundings, trying to work out which part of the building she had run into. *It's nearly impossible to know what part of the building this is. I think it's too risky to stay on the plain.* She gazed back at the forest where they had left the petrified Mystique. *We should go back to the forest and work our way around, out of sight of anyone looking out a window of the coterie building. I don't know why I didn't do that in the first place.*

Ulrieg grumbled. *You go back, and I'll fly to the trees nearest and keep an eye out. I'm not going to run into the building up there.*

All right. Samara hurried back to the shelter of the forest and quickly made her way around the edge of the plain, keeping an eye on her surroundings in case any of the coterie members or their familiars were strolling in the darkness. She was certain, though, that only the familiars with night vision would be able to see well without the light of the moon.

After a several minutes, she'd made it around the edge and spotted the shrub that hid the back entrance of the underground. She hoped that once she went into the hole, the underground wouldn't be invisible to her as well. That would make it difficult to get around. Although there was only one corridor, the stairs were often slippery from exposure to the rain, and they didn't have a railing.

Is the coast still clear?

I haven't seen any familiars or members of the coterie. Just to be sure, I'll stay up here until you're in the safety of the hole.

Thanks. Samara crouched and scurried across the plain again. It was still a fair distance, but much closer than from the other side of the plain. She quickly reached the bush and ducked behind its foliage before shoving it away from the hole. Sitting on her backside, she carefully hung her legs over the side and felt for the first step. Grabbing on to the edge of the hole, she slowly felt her way down the steps with her feet. Relief washed over her with each step downward. Only her torso remained above the ground.

Hurry up. Jet has just come out of the building.

Ulrieg's warning sent shivers through her body, and she quickly took several more steps into the hole. She didn't want to be caught by Zofia's bear familiar. The weapons master was one of the last instructors she needed to run into.

CHAPTER FOURTEEN

Appreciation ran through Emelyne's body as she approached the stone fence. The villagers had started without her, already having laid several feet more of the stone wall, now double the height of a human. Monut joined her, following close behind like an overprotective bodyguard.

Once Emelyne called for the workers' attention and told them of her plan, the clopping of the horses' hooves and rattling of the loaded carriage drew near. Lozzeak and Silut handed out the weapons, and Emelyne directed the archers to set up perches behind the slits they had made in the rock wall. Although the wall blocked the entrance of the village with the help of a looming wooden gate, much of the village was still only protected by the metal fence constructed by the blacksmiths and blessed with dragon fire from Monut. If the centaurs arrived, this would be the first battle to test the boundary.

Lookouts were placed on the towers, and tension mounted as they waited. The day dragged as the sun climbed higher into the sky. A cool breeze bushed against their faces as autumn settled in. The birds whistling in the distant trees provided a stark contrast to the apprehension hanging over the village.

A trumpet sounded a warning, sending a strange dread into the depths of Emelyne's stomach. It was truly going to happen. There would be no running and hiding for her anymore. This is what she had been brought up and trained for, even though she hadn't known it at the time. The work ethic instilled in her by her parents, plus the fighting expertise learned from her friend, Thiznabo, had prepared her for this moment. She gripped the sword hanging by her side tightly. The thought of avenging her friend fueled a strength inside her like nothing else.

She motioned to the strongest villager, Finlay MacKie, a brawny, blond curly-haired farmer who had developed a passion for the sword when training.

Finlay called, "Archers, get ready. Be prepared to spread out, and please take shelter behind anything you can find. Swordsmen, brace yourselves in case they somehow get through the metal fence. But remember, centaurs are excellent archers, so use cover."

Male and female archers spread out, some of them physically shaking.

I hate that I have to do this to them, Emelyne confided in her bonded.

Monut nudged her with his snout. *I know. But I'm sure they understand that if they want independence from the coterie, then they're going to have to stand up to the coterie's allies.*

Emelyne placed a hand on his cheek. *Maybe I should reassure them of that.* She took a deep breath and projected her voice. "I know this ain't the ideal situation, an' I wish I didn't need ya to do this, but if we want to keep the coterie out of our lives, we need to take a stand."

"Too right!" called Hamon, Samara's elven father.

The villagers cheered him on, even the ones who were physically shaking.

A female archer spoke up. "We have experienced the destruction and oppression of the coterie's rule. It has brought us nothing but grief and poverty. Under your instruction, our village has thrived. It is clear what we must do."

Again, the villagers cheered and chatted excitedly amongst themselves.

Finlay raised a hand to still the ruckus. "Then let's prepare to protect our village. May luck be with you all!"

With a last hurrah, the villagers readied themselves for confrontation with the centaurs. Although still high, the tension among them had eased.

With the advantage of a horse's speed, the centaurs were upon them soon after the alarm and gathered near the gate.

A male centaur with a leather vest open at the front and long flowing brunet hair appeared to be their leader. "I demand that you open these gates and let us in, under the order of Callista, the senior sorceress of the Sacred Flame coterie! We are here to collect her crystal. If you don't provide it, there shall be a severe punishment."

Emelyne, standing atop a guard post near the wooden gate of the stone wall, called, "Ha! That ain't gonna happen. For one, we don't know where the crystal is. But even if we did, we ain't gonna give it to ya. And two, this village no longer bends to the will of Callista or her minions."

"Then you leave us no choice but to attack." The male centaur raised his hand and called, "Centaurs, attack!" He quickly grabbed an arrow from his quiver and shot it at Emelyne.

Finlay yelled, "Villagers, defend!" He waved his hand dramatically in the air, his blond hair whipping with the movement.

Emelyne ducked an arrow, and Monut roared as he leapt into the sky. The centaurs scattered, their hooves clopping rapidly around the metal barrier gate, their eyes darting between the rising dragon and the archers poised at the arrow slits in the stone wall and surrounding areas. The fifty archers traced the centaurs' progression with the tips of their arrows while trying to stay covered. The villagers with swords helped wherever they could, standing by in case the centaurs broke through their fence.

Seeing Monut rise above them, half of the centaurs fired their arrows at the large dragon. He swerved, but not before several arrows found their mark in his wings and one in his tail.

Emelyne cringed. *Monut! Don't you dare get yourself killed.*

I'm fine. Although I'd be lying if I said it didn't hurt. They just got lucky.

The dragon growled and spewed fire on top of the centaurs. Several darted to the side, the fire narrowly missing them. A couple were caught in the blaze, and screams of pain mixed with the whistling of arrows being fired from both sides. The village archers hiding behind the arrow slits fired at the scattering centaurs but missed. Their aim had likely been affected by the stress of a real battle. The centaurs fired back, narrowly missing the arrow peepholes, as the village archers on the edges of the stone wall fired at the centaurs running loose around the barred fence. Many of the arrows either hit the bars or flew off course.

Emelyne cursed. *Shattered anvil! The villagers need so much more practice. They haven't done enough to function when under pressure.*

At least you have the first fence constructed. The centaurs can't seem to get through it. Just look at the one trying to slice it with a sword.

Emelyne squinted, searching the surroundings to find the one to which Monut was referring. She spotted him on the farthest edge of her line of sight. He was closer to the farmlands, his blond hair pulled into a low ponytail and his toned arms swinging wildly at the metal.

Maybe centaurs aren't that bright. Like he has a chance of the sword chopping through steel. Despite the situation, there was humor in the dragon's voice.

Emelyne couldn't help but laugh. *Maybe.* Grabbing her sword from its scabbard, she headed toward the centaur. She would fight this one—if she could get to him without being hit by an arrow. The princess swerved as an arrow flew past. A villager fired an arrow at the chopping centaur. The arrow hit his torso, and a cry of pain cut through the air. The centaur stopped swinging and looked down at the shaft sticking out of him before collapsing to the ground.

Emelyne cheered. *Finally, a villager's arrow made its mark.*

Monut banked hard to the left, leaving the lonely centaur on his own.

Emelyne watched him in her peripheral vision as he tried to remove the arrow. *Aren't we gonna stop him?*

There's no use attacking that centaur. He's going to do himself enough harm by pulling out that arrow.

She chuckled. *I think ya right. If the centaur has been around for a while, he should know that pullin' out that arrow would make him bleed to death, especially if it hit a main artery.*

They clearly don't know much. Monut sounded amused.

An arrow whistled past her again, sweeping through the spot where she'd stood not seconds before. *Whew! That was close.*

Monut roared and dived toward the archer who had nearly brought her down. Several centaurs fired at the dragon, some arrows hitting his wings and some bouncing off his tough scales. He opened his large maw and scooped up the centaur. He shook him as he took flight and released him midshake, tossing the centaur's lifeless body several yards away.

The villagers also fired. A couple hit their marks in less significant places, like the equine leg or the human arm, and one struck the human heart. The human part of the centaur looked to suffer, yet the equine body still galloped with ease. Emelyne slid her sword into its sheath, pulled out her bow, then fired an arrow aimed for the horse's heart. The centaur fell, legs twitching as the nerves gave their final protest. She silently thanked Thiznabo for her lessons in keeping calm while under attack. She pulled another arrow and shot a centaur not far from the one that had fallen. She then narrowly dodged an arrow aimed at her from another direction.

A terrifying roar filled the air as Monut dived over the centaur game enough to shoot at his bonded, a plume of fire blazing from the dragon's mouth. The centaur let out a bloodcurdling scream.

Emelyne clenched her jaw. This was war. It was definitely not her favorite pastime. Only thoughts of keeping her village and her family safe spurred her on.

CHAPTER FIFTEEN

I'm in. Samara quietly caught her breath after the initial shock of Ulrieg spotting the weapons master's familiar.

Good. Wait at the bottom of the stairs. I'll be with you shortly. I'll keep an eye on Jet to see that he doesn't catch our scent or find Mystique straight away.

Samara followed Ulrieg's instruction. She might have been out of sight, but if the bear familiar smelled her presence and followed her into the hole, their mission would be finished before it properly began. She found an unlit torch and set it alight. "Ignito." Her eyes slowly adjusted to the dim light of the sconce burning on the wall near the top of the stairs. Relief flooded her when she could make out the corridor and locked doors to the rooms on the left where she and Ulrieg had discovered his deceased cousin, Byzarid. The underground didn't seem to be under the same invisible spell as the rest of the coterie building. Perhaps Callista had been overconfident when she created the invisibility spell and thought her enemies would never know about the underground back entrance. In any case, the oversight worked in Samara's favor.

For what seemed like hours, she waited for Ulrieg to join her. She wondered how they were going to open the door leading to the underground torture rooms. They didn't have the special key needed to unlock it—a key held only by the coterie's instructors and senior magic wielders. Ulrieg used to steal it off the instructors.

Ulrieg was taking too long, causing her to grow impatient. She knew her familiar wouldn't leave her waiting unless he had good reason. Maybe Jet was giving him the runaround. She grabbed the sconce and started to make her way down the corridor toward the ominous door. So much terror had taken place in the large cave behind it and the subsequent little caves. Many dragons and dragon elves had been tortured there and fed to the glowing orange orb—the evil one Paxton's magic was currently feeding. A chill passed through her body. She hoped she wasn't too late, that Paxton was still alive and hadn't turned evil during his time stuck in the orb's sphere. Her impatience had her pulling at the handle and attempting to unlock the door with spells, even though she had tried these before they'd found the special key.

After pulling on the handle many times over and casting several spells, she gave up... until she remembered she'd entered the rooms off the side of the corridor by shooting an arrow into the door, creating a hole large enough for her to crawl through. She grabbed an arrow from her quiver, spelled it, and nocked it in her bow, aiming at the door. She released a breath as she released the arrow, which punctured the door with a *thunk*. The door remained closed, without a hole she could climb through. Her last chance relied on her familiar touching her. They had gotten through the barrier sealing off Dragoria, so surely they could pierce this small door with their powers combined. She would have to wait for Ulrieg, whatever he was doing. She paced the corridor. Surely he should have joined her by now. She hoped he was all right. *Ulrieg, what's taking you so long?*

I'm almost there. Just trying to sort out some things.

Samara moaned at his cryptic nature. Sometimes, he could be frustrating. *I'm getting impatient!*

I understand, but you don't want to risk getting caught, so you'd better wait.

Great words of wisdom. Her reply dripped with sarcasm. *I have to wait for you anyway. I don't have the special key, and my spelled arrow didn't create a hole in the door. The door must be protected by the same kind of ward as the barriers between the borders. I need your dragon power to make a proper spell. Hopefully, it'll open.*

Gotcha! I shouldn't be too long now.

Samara barely resisted the urge to tap her foot as she waited. It was probably best she made as little noise as possible in case someone was on the other side of the door. Although now that she thought about it, the arrow landing in the door hadn't been very quiet. She grabbed the arrow from the door and placed it back into her quiver. With her bow laced over her body, she backed away then hid in a dark corner, listening for any noise from behind the door. Maybe it was a good thing that Ulrieg was taking his time. She had no idea if anyone was inside the cave guarding the orb. The last thing they needed was to break through the door and find the underground full of the senior coterie members.

Dread caused her skin to crawl. The ogres at the border were having a party. Perhaps Kellam was visiting the coterie building.

I've changed my mind. Take your time. We may need to be here for a while.

Something moved near her, and she retreated farther into the dark corner, glad she'd left the sconce near the door.

I'm here anyway. Ulrieg's glowing red eyes appeared next to her, causing her to jump. *Why do we need to wait?*

She held a hand over her heart, trying to still it. *We have no way of knowing if anyone is in the cave. It could be full of senior coterie members, including Kellam.*

Do you forget that I have better hearing than you? He scratched behind one of the horns on his head with his back talon.

Can you hear into the cave? I can't hear anything.

There's only one way to find out. Ulrieg waddled down the corridor, and Samara scrambled to catch up with him, doing her best to minimize the scuffling of her shoes.

What was taking you so long? Was someone else outside?

Zion emerged into the meadow.

Devi's wolf familiar? Was Devi with him?

No. But I had him keep an eye on Mystique to make sure no one finds her before we are finished. Ulrieg pressed the side of his head against the door.

Can you hear anything?

I might—if you learn to be quiet.

Samara gulped. *Sorry. Being on edge is making it hard for me to think straight.*

Ulrieg leveled his red eyes at her. She nodded then remained still and quiet. Time seemed to tick by slowly as she waited for his findings.

After a while, Ulrieg pulled away and shook his head. *I don't think it's safe for us to enter the cave yet. There are noises inside that could be members of the coterie. We should wait here. Even better, I'll wait outside so I can keep an eye on the plain and the entrance to this area. That way, you won't be caught by surprise if members of the coterie or their familiars decide to enter here.*

Disappointment washed through Samara. She was keen to get this mission over and done with. Being in this dark underground brought back all kinds of bad memories. She hoped they didn't have to wait long. Ulrieg left, leaving her feeling even more alone and on edge. Doubt raced through her mind, but she didn't want to leave Paxton inside the orb any longer.

Hours seemed to pass, and the chill of the underground set into Samara's bones, the sound of water dripping down the stairs numbing her insides. Worse still, she had no idea how to remove Paxton from the orb. She hoped there was something she could do, or this was all for nothing.

Right! It should be all right to go in now. Ulrieg's red eyes glowed in front of her, startling her again.

Samara slapped a hand over her mouth to stifle a scream. *I wish you would give me some warning once you're next to me. I'm already on edge, and you're just making it worse.*

Ulrieg smirked, showing off his vast array of teeth. *Sorry. I thought you'd be used to me by now.*

Well, yes. But I'm not exactly feeling safe here, so your sudden appearances are startling me. Samara pushed herself up to stand. *What makes you think it's all right to go through? Did you sneak down the corridor to have another listen?*

No. When I spoke to Zion, I asked him to get Devi to clear the underground of the coterie members. That was a while ago.

How is she going to do that without making people suspicious?

Ulrieg shrugged. *I don't know. She would be the best judge of what to do.*

Have they found Mystique?

No. Not yet. But Zion can't stand guard over her forever. Jet would notice, and other coterie members would get suspicious. That's another reason we're hurrying up the process. Someone is going to notice she is missing soon, and we need to try to get away before that happens.

Quickly, they made their way to down the corridor. Ulrieg scurried to the door and placed his ear against it. *I'll just have a quick listen to see if I can hear anything just in case Devi wasn't successful.*

Samara held her breath until he pulled away. *Are we good to enter?*

I think so. It seems quiet in there.

She stepped back several paces, unhooked her bow from around her shoulders, grabbed an arrow out of her quiver, and spelled it. *Can you press up against my leg? Let's see if your connection works to pierce the barrier like it did for the one separating Wraeyanor from Slosiaran. If that doesn't work, I'll need you to breathe your dragon fire on the tip like you did for the ward around Dragoria.*

Without hesitation, Ulrieg pressed against her leg, touching as much skin as possible. Samara nocked her arrow and raised her bow to point it at the door, ignoring the pain radiating through her injured shoulder. The string twanged as she released it, and the arrow sank into the door.

CHAPTER SIXTEEN

Glowing orange light illuminated their faces, instantly letting Samara know that the arrow had succeeded in creating a hole in the door to the underground cave. Ulrieg turned invisible, and Samara squinted, trying to adjust to the sudden light after having hidden in the dark for so long. The flame of the sconce was weak in comparison to the brightness of the orb. A dull pulse vibrated through the air, sending shockwaves through Samara's nerves.

Quiet scratches told Samara Ulrieg was climbing though the hole, and she readied herself to follow, observing the space she could see for any signs of coterie members. The cave appeared to be free of any undesirable companions. She weaved her way through the hole—leg first, body next, then carefully pulling her other leg through. The arrows in her quiver rattled during her final move, and she gritted her teeth, waiting to see whether the noise had brought any unwanted attention. Nothing seemed to shift, and she straightened softly before stepping toward the glowing orb, remaining alert.

Memories of Callista facing the orb—back arched, arms spread wide as she accepted the power that leached from it directly into her body—rushed through Samara. The energy had clearly boosted the head sorceress's strength. The sorcerer who had created the orb must have been pure evil and overflowing with power. Samara considered Callista a powerful adversary. She couldn't imagine the power and strength a sorcerer must have had to go against the dragons, dragon elves, and all the kingdoms combined.

She studied the glowing orb. She had expected to see Paxton imprisoned within the middle but couldn't see anything but the bright orange glow. For a moment, her heart skipped a beat. Perhaps Vexx had been lying when the sorcerer had told her he'd fed Paxton into the orb. Maybe he'd only said that so she would think all was lost and that she would never see him again. After all, she hadn't *seen* Paxton shoved into the orb.

Edging closer, Samara felt evilness radiating from the orb. When she was only a foot away, she noticed something that made her heart sink. The silhouette of a man floated in the center of the orange glow. The form was difficult to make it out, but the more she studied the dark shape, the more she was convinced it was a man inside.

Pacing around the sphere, Samara wrung her hands, wondering what she should do. If she put her hands into the orb, she feared it would drag her into its center, and she had no idea how to get herself out if that happened. She knew Ulrieg couldn't pull her out since the orb was hungry for dragons in addition to wielders of magic. She closed her eyes, focusing hard as she attempted the pulling spell, the one she used to make an object fly into her hands. When she opened her eyes, she could have sworn the orb had moved slightly toward her. That was not going to do. The last thing she needed was for the orb to roll on top of her. It would undoubtedly swallow her up, and she would be stuck.

She was deep in concentration when Ulrieg's voice interrupted her thoughts. *Hmph. They are still torturing dragons.*

She blinked, slowly registering what he had said. *What makes you say that?*

There are pieces of dragons in these little caves, and they look fairly new.

Nausea wrapped its tendrils around her middle. The contents of her stomach rose into her throat at the horrible memories of dismembered dragon pieces being dragged across the cave and fed to the orb, unashamed trails of blood marking their paths. She wondered how many more dragons they had captured since she and Ulrieg had left the coterie. The thought made her feel responsible for all the dragon deaths.

I know what you're thinking. There was nothing you could do. Any dragons that died after we left would have been impossible to rescue. We couldn't have saved them all, and if we'd stayed, neither of us was likely to survive. Nor could we have done what we have in the other kingdoms. Be proud of what you have achieved. Don't forget Paddosha Palace village. There are many people there who could have been killed by a coterie member or starved to death, but because we found the princess, their lives are looking up. And remember the dragons we saved from the Merciless Sanctuary and led to Dragoria. We've done a lot since we left.

I know, but it's still difficult to see other dragons dying because we aren't here to help. I hate the way the coterie treats others.

Ulrieg's talons clacked on the stone floor as he walked out of the small room. He stood by her in front of the orb, making himself visible. *Any idea what you're going to do?*

Samara shook her head. *I don't know what the orb's going to do if I touch it, let alone stick my hand in to grab Paxton. It may try to devour me, too, or it may shoot out parts of itself like it did to Callista, though she wanted to receive the evil power the orb released. I don't want any piece of it inside me.* She reached an arm forward as if to touch it but stopped midway. She was trying to get a reading on how the orb would react before interacting with it. Just the look of it twisted her stomach into knots. *Would you think any less of me if I told you I'm scared?*

Ulrieg chortled through their bond. *Absolutely not! I've never liked this orb, even before I knew it was fed parts of dragons and now one sorcerer I respect.* He shook his head. *This is just so wrong. What kind of sadist came up with the idea to harbor the evil power from a past sorcerer in an orb? Even worse, to feed other magical beings to it?*

The bright orange light illuminated their faces as Samara paced around the orb, pondering how to get Paxton out. Every time she placed her hand near it, the orb seemed to respond to her gesture. Sections of it lifted, reaching for her. Each time, she shied away before it was able to touch her.

She chewed her bottom lip. The longer she took, the more she worried she wouldn't be able to do it. Yet she didn't have the luxury of time. A coterie member could walk in at any moment. She had to think quickly. As she reached toward the orb again, it creeped toward her. It would be terrible if the orb managed to grab her and drag her into it with Paxton. Then they would both be stuck, feeding it with their magic. She shivered.

It's not looking good. Ulrieg reached a talon toward the orb, quickly jerking it away when the orb lurched toward him. He scurried back, making sure he kept a greater distance. *Perhaps we should have a look through the small caves to see if the coterie has any utensils or gadgets that might be useful to snag and drag Paxton out without us having to place parts of us within its reach?*

Great idea! Relief washed over Samara. *I don't know why I didn't think of that.*

They headed to the caves sectioned off from the large one and searched through the tools used for torture. The thought of torture was bad enough, but the sight of the tools also brought to mind the times she had witnessed the suffering the coterie had inflicted on so many drag-ons. They'd even killed a guardian dragon, leaving her bonded dragon elf clumsy and unable to use her magic.

Looking over various scalpels, long metal nails, and other items, her gaze stopped on a pair of long forceps. Apprehensively, Samara picked them up and squeezed the ends together. The silver stems were approximately a foot in length, with toothed ends. Wild were the ideas of how a contraption like this could be used. Reactively, she threw them down, the metal clattering against the stone floor.

Samara! Are you all right? Ulrieg's voice traveled through their bond as his talons scurried along the hard floor.

Her cheeks heated. She had made too much noise dropping the forceps like that. Swooping, she picked them up. *Yes, sorry. This place fills me with horror.*

That's an understatement. Have you found anything useful?

After a quick scan of the rest of the room, Samara returned to the main cave, holding up her find. *Possibly. I might be able to reach Paxton with these long forceps without having to put my hand inside the orb.*

Oh. They look nasty. Ulrieg tilted his head. *But we can give it a try.*

Together, they approached the side of the orb where Paxton was slightly closer to the edge, their steps slow and unsure. Samara grabbed the forceps by the fold, keeping her hand as far away from the tips as possible. Hand shaking, she held them out, aiming for a loose piece of Paxton's clothing to grab on to.

The metal touched the edge of the orb. *So far, so good.* Sweat beaded on Samara's forehead. The orb hadn't reached for the forceps like it had her hand. *Maybe it can't sense metal objects like it seems to sense flesh.* She moved the forceps farther into the orb.

The orb pulsed like usual but didn't seem to notice the invasion. Courage grew deep from Samara's bones, and she plunged the forceps farther. Paxton was just out of reach. Holding her breath, she braced, ready to delve in farther.

Something shifted. The orb's pulsating increased, shooting panic through her. She froze. Out of the corner of her eye, she saw movement.

Ulrieg dashed toward her. *Look out!*

Suddenly, a large stream of orange light jumped out of the orb and looped around her.

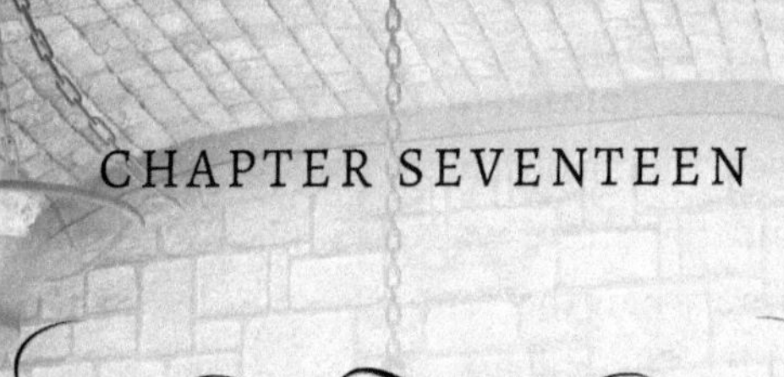

CHAPTER SEVENTEEN

A spine-chilling scream filled the air. Having dismounted Monut, Emelyne spun to see a village archer fall from her spot in an arrow slit. The young woman's red hair blew across her face as she fell backward to the ground. A nearby swordsman raced to her side, and Emelyne took in the carnage on both fronts as another archer took her place in the arrow slit. The woman appeared to be the first casualty from the village, yet the centaurs were a few down, thanks to Monut and a couple of lucky shots from the villagers.

The large dragon swooped toward the centaur who had felled the woman, releasing a plume of fire over him before he could gallop away. The smell of burning flesh was sickening. Emelyne scrunched her nose, not smitten with her first proper battle. She appreciated neither the smell nor the execution of the centaur's death. It would've been a very unpleasant way to go. Digging deep, she braced herself, hardening her response. This is what had to be done to protect the village against the coterie and its followers.

The centaurs continued to fire at any villagers they spotted. Even the swordsmen and swordswomen taking cover behind the stone wall entrance weren't safe from the firing line when the centaurs rounded to the section not yet built. The village archers fired back, but the centaurs had taken to galloping while firing, an art they were trained in. The villagers had yet to be taught to fire at a moving target. There simply hadn't been enough time.

A strange movement in the periphery of Emelyne's vision caught her attention, and she turned to see Hamon, Samara's father, waving his hands as though trying to concoct magic. The elf shot out his hands toward a centaur.

Emelyne shifted to get a better view of the centaur but couldn't see whether it had affected him. However, near them was a new hole in the ground, about the size of a carriage wheel. She frowned. Either he was a bad shot, or his magic wasn't good. She ditched any hopes that something might come of his magic. For a moment, she'd thought strong magic must run in the family, but after seeing Hamon's attempt, she wasn't going to rely on it. Not having met a magic wielder before Samara, she wasn't familiar with how magic was acquired.

Returning her focus to the battle, she nocked another arrow and fired it at a female centaur in the center of the group. Her arrow landed directly in her human torso just as another landed in her equine torso. Before long, she fell to the ground, unable to get up.

Finlay cheered with enthusiasm for their small win, instilling more confidence in the village's fighters.

Coming from behind, Monut flew low again, shooting his plume of dragon fire. The centaurs scattered but were not quick enough to move out of the way. They let out a few cries of pain as their flesh burned in places. Several arrows were fired at Monut, and the dragon flipped and swerved, knocking many of the arrows to the side before flying out of reach.

The centaurs were slowly diminishing in number, yet they fought on. A man's cry rang out as the villager collapsed, a centaur's arrow lodged in his heart. Several more were injured as another centaur attacked with fury. The centaurs' patience seemed to be wearing thin. Monut dived, fire spewing from his large mouth, setting the wildflowers alight along with more centaur flesh. Emelyne shot at a centaur screaming in pain from the dragon-fire burns, killing him on the spot as her arrow went through his head. If it wasn't for Monut, the villagers probably wouldn't have fared this well.

The villagers fired at the galloping centaurs, a lucky hit felling another as it pierced through the horse's abdomen. Suddenly, the centaurs retreated, galloping even faster and firing into the air as Monut descended upon them. Monut flipped to the side, twisting to expose his tougher scales as they shot arrows his way.

The dragon showered them with fire, his laughter traveling through his bond with Emelyne as the centaurs parted to escape his attack. *This is kind of fun. I much prefer this life where I don't have to hide. But I could do with fewer arrows stuck in my wings. They kind of hurt.*

Killing is fun? Emelyne chewed her bottom lip.

No, but defending you and the villagers is, as is the freedom to dive and twist in the daylight.

That's a more acceptable reason. Emelyne watched as he climbed high into the sky again. *The only problem is that if they return to report to Callista, she will know you are here and will come in force.*

Then I'll just have to make sure that they don't return. Monut flipped then dived, this time scorching several of the centaurs. *Maybe I should have done this before they arrived—when they were still at their camp.*

But then we wouldn't have known if they were coming to attack. They could have just been firing at you because you were scary and something they hadn't seen in their lifetime. Emelyne squinted through the arrow slit, trying to work out the centaurs' plan, but they seemed too busy dodging Monut's attacks. They continued their retreat, apparently having decided their numbers weren't enough to take down the village rebels and a large fiery dragon. Emelyne smiled. It must have been a blow to the lead centaur's ego. He'd certainly seemed sure of himself when he arrived. At that stage, they probably hadn't yet seen Monut.

Emelyne remained fixed to the spot where she stood, her eyes on Monut as he chased down the retreating centaurs. As they moved farther away, it became difficult to make out what was happening. Soon she spotted the large dragon returning to the village, his flight path straight. *What happened?*

You don't need to worry about them anymore. He sounded pleased with himself. *I have seen to that.*

Emelyne cringed at the thought of burned centaurs lying abandoned along the countryside, food for the vultures. She turned to face the villagers still in their places, their faces wan after experiencing their first battle. "I'm pleased to announce that it is over. Monut has chased them away an' dealt with the remaining centaurs. Ya all fought well. Ya should be proud."

"But we missed most of the time," one of the men yelled from an arrow slit.

"Never mind what was," Finlay said, trying to be encouraging.

Emelyne nodded. "Ya must remember that ya haven't had much practice. It all takes time. After we have rested an' had some lunch, we will continue buildin' the wall an' take turns in practicin'. This village has been in Callista's sights for far too long, and it needs to fight back." She gazed over their weary faces. "Now, go get somethin' to eat and rest for a while. I'll stay with Monut and keep watch."

The villagers migrated slowly to the center of the village, their mannerisms weary, sad yet slightly lifted. Emelyne couldn't help but admire the resilience of the villagers after all they had been through. They had gone from scared and cowering in front of the coterie to ready to battle and defend what was left of their village in only a short time.

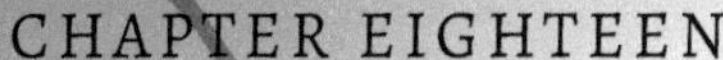

CHAPTER EIGHTEEN

S amara flinched and dropped the forceps, the clatter not registering over her panic. She jerked her arms in toward her torso and wanted to lurch back, but she wasn't able. Surprisingly, the orange stream wasn't touching her but circled close, trapping her near the orb. Her breaths were rapid as terror clouded her thoughts, making it impossible for her to think. She didn't want the orb's energy to feed into her, nor did she want to feed it.

She caught sight of Ulrieg's glowing red eyes, wide with trepidation. She knew he wouldn't be able to help her out of this. If he tried, it would likely devour him too. Her fate was up to her. Bending at the knees, she attempted to go under the swirls only to find they followed her—moving down as her body lowered. The loops tightened, and Samara straightened, sweat now trickling down her face and soaking her back. Her bow remained hooked over her shoulder, her quiver on her back. There was nothing she could do to combat being swallowed into the large evil orb.

Ulrieg disappeared, leaving Samara feeling completely alone yet glad he was getting away from the danger. The last thing she wanted was for him to be caught up in this too.

Unable to think of a way to escape, she closed her eyes and started to accept her inevitable fate and possible death. It wasn't how she had planned on passing. She had hoped to help Dragoria and the kingdoms to rise against the coterie, to do much more than what she had achieved. Maybe, if Ulrieg escaped from the coterie, he would continue their work.

The pulsating intensified, making her head throb with its intensity. It wouldn't be long now before it would snatch her up and engulf her in its evil embrace. At least she would be with Paxton—sort of. Their fates would be the same but would strengthen the orb's power, which in turn would empower Callista and her plot against the kingdoms. Vibrations shook Samara's entire body, and she could feel the orb's power tasting her like a snake's tongue sensing its prey.

Any second now, she would be consumed.

Suddenly, the atmosphere around her changed. She squeezed her eyes shut even tighter. *This must be it.* Her heart thundered within her chest. A mighty gust of air shot from her feet past her head, with another two shooting toward the orb on either side of her. Her hair whipped back violently before draping casually over her shoulders. Samara frowned. It felt like she was still standing, and a coolness touched the parts of her facing away from the orb. If anything, her surroundings felt less charged. She didn't know what to expect inside the orb, but this definitely wasn't it.

Drumming up courage, she cracked open her eyes, daring to witness what was happening. Her eyes widened. No longer was the orb's power whisking around her. Her view to the cave was unobstructed. Swiveling, she caught sight of movement and focused on it. Devi's thin frame paced purposefully into the room, arms extended, palms exposed as she weaved them to control her magic. The instructor's long brown dress, pinched at the waist, flowed around her legs, and her spiked salmon-colored hair was tinted by the orb's orange glow. Her elven ears twitched slightly as she frowned in concentration.

Backing away from the orb, Samara turned to find it still pulsating and reaching for her with its tendrils. She peddled back quicker as Devi pushed her hands forward, the orb shrinking back from the force. Standing in what she hoped was well out of the orb's reach, Samara watched Devi work. The defense arts instructor knew her magic. Beads of sweat gathered on Devi's forehead and temples from the strain of controlling the orb's powerful magic. Samara wished she could help, but she didn't know what to do.

Once Samara had backed away as far as possible, she scanned the room for Ulrieg, unable to find him. *Ulrieg, are you all right? Where are you?*

Yes, I'm fine.

Did you know Devi is here?

Yes, I asked Zion earlier to bring her here, and I left briefly to make sure she was coming. You needed help quickly, and I didn't know how else to assist you.

Thank you. I think you saved me. Samara rubbed the goose bumps on her arm.

Of course I went for help. There's no way I'd let you to be sucked into that orb permanently.

Oh, thank you. But I'm also glad that you didn't stick around. I would have hated for you to be lost in there too. It's bad enough that Paxton has been in there for several months.

Devi continued to fight the orb, sending it back into itself. Her normally relaxed posture was tense with concentration.

Samara asked, "Is there anything I can do to help, Devi?"

Devi shook her head, and a couple of beads of sweat dripped from her face as she continued to battle the orb's power. "I think I've nearly got it, but stay out of the way just in case." Hands still palms-out, she waved her arms back and forth. "Those tendrils are the way the orb pulls you in. You are lucky I arrived when I did."

The battle of wills continued. And if the stories were anything to go by, the orb had a very strong will. Somehow, though, it was contained.

Another major pulse seemed to come from the orb, and Devi pushed back harder. The power snapped back into the orb, restoring the full sphere. Still, Devi remained on guard, her palms still facing out as if waiting for the orb to fight back again.

After several minutes, the orb seemed to have settled, remaining in a neat sphere and not reaching toward Samara or Devi.

Ulrieg, clearly on edge, tiptoed around from the other side of the orb toward Samara and Devi. *Jeesh! That thing's certainly got some spirit, hasn't it? Not something I'd want to contend with.*

"Yes," Devi said. "This orb was once the magic of a very

powerful magician. A magician more powerful than Callista has ever been. Yet the dragons, dragon elves, and guardian dragons managed to bind it into the orb, containing and weakening it somehow. It's because of Callista that it has regained strength, as she has fed it magical food. It gets stronger each time they feed it. It leeches all the victim's power then feeds Callista with its evil magic. She continues the cycle by feeding it with more dragons and magic wielders."

"Do you know how to get someone out of the orb?" Samara asked, hoping the senior coterie member would have an idea.

"If I knew, I would have gotten him out by now. But it's too dangerous a feat for one person. I know that much. To be honest, I've never known of anyone or anything to be extracted from the orb—other than the power Callista leeches from it." Devi leaned on one leg. "I have been down here many times pondering how to get Paxton out without being caught or dragged into the orb myself."

"Well, as you can see, I tried to do it by myself and did not get very far." Samara shivered at the thought of what could have happened.

Devi nodded. Her eyes and face wore a worried look. "I honestly don't know what Paxton is going to be like when he comes out. That orb holds so much evil, and he would have to be a very strong person to come out and not be changed—if he's still alive."

Samara's stomach twisted into knots, sending its contents up her throat. Her main fear was that he would emerge either dead already or evil. "Wouldn't you think his body would have been devoured if he had passed?"

"That is one good point. If Paxton had passed, I couldn't imagine him being in one piece. Though, like I said, I haven't seen anybody come out alive, and I certainly haven't seen any magic wielders pulled out, so I don't know. It would make more sense that if he had passed away, the orb would also consume his body, breaking it down into usable energy. I haven't come down here with Henriette or Peadar either. It has been too risky. All the apprentices are being watched closely. After what you and Paxton did, this has become a very dangerous place, not that it was ever safe," Devi said. "Have you tried the retrieving spell?"

Samara nodded. "I tried it a little. It didn't seem to work. Although, I think it dragged the orb a little my way. If it works, it would be a good spell to use, but I don't trust it enough to know whether I'd just get Paxton or move the whole orb."

"I understand what you're saying. Paxton may be classed as a person or a thing now, so it is hard to know whether the spell will work. But even if he's passed away, we should try to retrieve his body so the orb can no longer feed off him."

Way to kill the mood! Ulrieg groaned.

"I only say this so you're prepared, just in case. Let's see if the spell works now. If it does and any of the orb comes with it, I will control it," Devi said.

Samara nodded and pulled her thoughts together, readying herself to cast the spell.

CHAPTER NINETEEN

It took several minutes for Samara to gather her thoughts. *Ulrieg, can you please press up against me? Your touch has always made me stronger, and I might need the extra strength to pull Paxton from this orb.*

Ulrieg's talons clicked on the floor as he made his way over and pressed against Samara's leg.

Beside her, Devi braced herself. She moved her feet for a more stable stance, ready for action.

Samara closed her eyes, feeling Ulrieg's pressure against her leg and, with it, the gathering of strength. She wasn't sure whether it was his presence or his touch that made her feel better. Or perhaps he was transferring more magic to her. Whatever it was, she was grateful for his presence and his companionship. She focused, narrowing all her thoughts and gathering them together, purposefully thinking of the spell that she needed.

Other than the quick attempt earlier, she had never performed it on a human before. Normally, it wouldn't work because it was meant for things, not living beings.

But if Devi though it was worth a better try, she was willing to give anything a go. Once her thoughts were in order, she held out her hands, ignoring the niggling pain in her shoulder. She opened her eyes and focused on the silhouette of Paxton within the orb, calling to him with her magic. Parts of the orb started to break away and fly toward her, but Devi instantly created a barrier and pushed them back, controlling the orb with her magic and protecting Samara and Ulrieg at the same time.

Samara tried again, but each time, she only moved parts of the orb. The silhouette of Paxton remained unmoved. She tried again with the same results—pieces of the orb reached hungrily for her, determined to devour her.

After the third time without the desired reaction, she stopped, shaking her head, her shoulders slumped. "He's just not moving. I hope that means Paxton is alive and himself."

Devi looked as disappointed as Samara felt. "I honestly hoped that would work, but you can see why I wasn't able to try by myself. The orb is not keen to be rid of him or let him go. It's willing to take on anyone who tries to take its meal."

Ulrieg stopped pressing against Samara's leg and returned to the small caves. He darted from one to the other.

Samara turned to Devi. "Do you have any other suggestions? I honestly don't think I can leave until I know Paxton is safe."

"And you're going to have to act quickly, because I doubt this room will be left unoccupied by the coterie for long." Devi glanced at the door connecting to the inside of the coterie building as if expecting someone to walk through it any minute.

Samara's frustration grew. Devi was right, but it would tear her apart to leave Paxton behind this time. Not only that, but the coterie would see things had been moved, know that someone had been down here, and probably make it harder for her to get back in to try another time. She paced, her thoughts whirring as she tried to think of a solution.

Ulrieg reentered the main cave, dragging a long, thick rope with his mouth. *What do you think about this? Could we use this rope to pull through the orb and perhaps drag him out?*

"It's worth a try," Devi said. "The rope is long enough to go all the way through to the other side and still let us stand far enough from the orb. It'll give us the space we need to fight back."

Samara pressed her lips together. "Perhaps Ulrieg can hold one side of the rope while I circle around to the other, cutting through the orb."

Devi frowned. "Having you so far apart will make it impossible to defend you both."

Do you think putting something in front of me would help protect me from the orb? Ulrieg brought the rope to Samara. *Like, perhaps put one of the gurneys in front and use it as a protective barrier against the orb shooting things or trying to devour me. I'm worried about it shooting out both ways at the same time.*

"That's a good idea, Ulrieg." Devi rubbed her delicate chin between her thumb and forefinger. "That way, I can remain closer to Samara to help protect her." She headed toward one of the little rooms. "Samara, can you help me?"

They found a gurney, carried it out together, then leaned it on its side. Passing one end of the rope to Ulrieg, Samara took the other. Devi, standing guard, followed Samara as the young sorceress slowly circled the orb while holding the rope at the orb's mid-height, aiming to wrap it around the waistline of Paxton's silhouette. At first, the orb put up resistance, but Devi spelled the rope, allowing it to slowly cut through.

Devi and Samara gradually circled the orb, dragging the rope through the center. Several bursts of orange shot from each side toward Samara and Ulrieg. Ulrieg remained protected by the gurney as he firmly held the rope in his mouth, using his talons to steady it over the edge in front of him.

Eventually, they cut through the orb and snagged Paxton around the waist, slowly pulling him closer as Samara continued circling. Devi stayed close to Samara, ready to push back at any power coming from the sphere. Paxton's body neared the edge of the orb, his back facing out.

Parts of Paxton were pulled out of the orb, still clothed in the garments he'd been wearing the day they were captured—the same day Samara had escaped. With the majority of Paxton's body free, they continued to pull carefully, lowering him softly to the floor. Samara used the rope to drag him away as Devi worked to push the evil magic back into its sphere. The orb reached its tendrils for Paxton as though angry and desperate to recover its meal. Orange blasts fired rapidly at Samara and Ulrieg as well, apparently trying to bring them down and devour them too.

Even though Paxton was free, Samara continued to

drag him, shortening the rope as she pulled it until he was most of the way across the floor, away from the orb. Hunkering down and bracing her legs against the floor, she pulled him toward her, arm length by arm length. The more she watched him, the more she panicked. He seemed lifeless and limp. Her heart ached with the hope he was still alive, yet she didn't like the way he looked. He appeared completely unconscious—either that or he had passed away so recently that rigor mortis hadn't set in. With each drag of Paxton's unmoving body, her worries doubled. Perhaps they'd been too late in rescuing him. The signs weren't looking good. Maybe the orb had just killed him, knowing what they were doing. Dread set in as she took in his lifeless features.

CHAPTER TWENTY

Over the next few days, the villagers took turns practicing fighting and weaponry then switched to their essential duties of running the village, feeding the people, and building the stone wall. The wall was coming along quickly, and soon they would finish rebuilding their homes. The sky was murky and overcast, with dull-gray clouds lining the sky. A crisp autumn breeze whipped through the town, piercing Emelyne's long-sleeved tunic and pants and cooling the workers. At least they could build under chilly conditions. The summer heat would've made the manual labor unbearable. Instead, the cooler temperature made it easier to work quickly. They had already reached the section of wall that would give the farmlands extra protection.

With Monut by her side, Emelyne stood at the far edge of a farmer's field of peas and green beans. The pea plants thrived in cooler climates, while the beans were on their last harvest. They had been a perfect choice to quickly boost food production. She picked a long green bean and took a bite. The bean crunched between her teeth as she observed the work before her. It was a shame to block the outside view of the area, but the wall was necessary. The palace was elevated for a view over the wall yet far enough from the border to escape any attacks by arrow.

She tilted her head. *Monut, do you know if it snows here in the winter?*

The scales on Monut's forehead bunched together. *I don't know. But you should find out.*

Hmm. If it does, it will make me semidamaged room an' the rest of the palace rather unpleasant an' cold.

Let's hope that they get to rebuilding it before then, or you might need to sleep with me to keep warm.

Emelyne gazed up at him, and he tentatively stretched out his wing, still healing from the multiple arrow shots he'd received during the small battle. *Ha! I've heard ya sleepin'. As much as I love ya company, ya snorin' is worse than me pa's. I'd probably sleep better freezin' to death.*

Monut raised a scaly eyebrow. *Really? It's like that, is it?*

Only tellin' the truth.

Monut shoved her with his wing, knocking her several feet to the side. *We'll see who's laughing when the snow comes.*

Emelyne regained her balance and backhanded his leg playfully. *I'm jus' kiddin'. But not 'bout the snorin'. Sometimes, it is really bad.*

Haha. Monut exposed his impressive array of teeth. *In any case, we can't let you catch your death in the cold.*

Emelyne started toward the group building the stone wall, ready to help. She dusted her hands on her trousers and headed to the pile of stones set aside by the farmer when he'd plowed the fields.

Whatcha doing, Princess? Emelyne spun, looking for the

familiar voice she hadn't heard in a while. She spotted the brown dragon with beige stripes standing not far away.

"Cyrra!" Emelyne exclaimed and ran to give the dragon a hug. "You're back!"

The dragon wrapped her brown wings around her. As her head was buried within the dragon's wings, several more *thuds* surrounded them.

She stepped back to find the familiar faces of several more dragons who had once lived in the Merciless Sanctuary. "When did you get back?"

Literally just now. It was a perfect day to fly, with all these clouds to hide between. I spotted Monut from up above. It was such an amazing trip. You just won't believe. Cyrra sprang from talon to talon.

Emelyne had forgotten how much she missed the excitable dragon and found her attitude catching. "I can't wait to hear all about it. Was it definitely Dragoria? An' did ya find any other dragons?"

Oh, yes. And yes. Cyrra continued hopping enthusiastically.

Several more *thuds* brought dragons Emelyne hadn't seen before. She counted ten large dragons the size of Monut and eleven smaller ones of different shapes and colors. She was conscious of the humans halting their work to stare at the thunder of dragons.

These dragons wanted to come see the humans of Paddosha Palace village. So we brought them back with us. Cyrra spread her wings, indicating the newly arrived dragons. *There are many more in Dragoria, including the tiny little dragons called guardian dragons. They wanted to stay in Dragoria for now. They said their main connection is with elves, so it is safer for them to stay where they are protected.* The dragon chattered on excitedly. *Oh, it was like dragon heaven. There aren't any humans or elves, although they know the history of how they became separated and how they used to work alongside the humans and elves to fight against the evil magic wielders. You can thank the guardian dragons for keeping them informed.*

She sucked in a long breath then continued, *These dragons were curious to see what it is like in the other realms. Plus, they know there are dragons in the kingdoms who need help. So here we are.* She chuckled.

Emelyne gently placed a hand on Cyrra's snout, attempting to calm the dragon's excitable heart. "It sounds like ya had a lovely time. Ya back quicker than I thought."

Well, a realm isn't as hard to cross when you can fly freely. There were no threats to dragons, so that's what we did. Oh, it was so lovely. She threw back her head in delight.

The princess stroked her snout softly. "I'm so glad for you. But you'll have to keep close to the village grounds here. So far, we have kept Monut's presence a secret to avoid any unwanted visits from the coterie. They visit enough, even though they don't know 'bout me or ya dragons yet. We had a close call just the other day."

What about Ulrieg? Is he keeping out of sight as well?

"Yes. He's always invisible when he leaves the village," Emelyne reassured her. "He hasn't been here for a little while anyway."

Oh, that's weird. The dragon's eyes took in the workers building the wall. *Is Samara still here? I have something I need to give her.* She tugged at a bag looped over her neck.

"Both she and Ulrieg are currently away. They've gone to see if they can rescue Samara's beloved, who was trapped in an evil orb. It is risky, an' I wanted her to stay and help, but I could see it was tearin' her up not knowing if he is alive."

Cyrra gasped. *I hope she's all right and makes it back.*

"Me too." Emelyne turned to see the workers still staring. She called them over with a motion of her hand. "Come over an' meet these other dragons. They have jus' come from Dragoria. They won't harm ya." She turned to Cyrra and asked quietly out the side of her mouth, "Will they?"

Oh, no. They are here to be of help.

Confusion washed over the people's faces, yet it didn't stop them from getting a closer look at the different types of dragons attentively sitting just outside of the field. The dragons and the people studied each other, the dragons sniffing the humans and the humans feeling the texture of the dragons' tough scales.

Emelyne marveled at the interaction, holding hope for their future.

A young woman, whom the princess knew as Anayah, was slightly older than Emelyne. She cried out in surprise as a large female dragon touched her with her nose. Anayah's hand jerked back in alarm yet returned quickly to the dragon's snout, her eyes wide with wonder. "I don't know what just happened, but I suddenly feel extremely connected to this dragon."

Emelyne smiled, pride and amusement washing through her. "Congratulations! You have just bonded with your dragon."

Monut roared, proud and loud, causing several of the humans to jump. *We are going to have more dragon riders.*

This is good for the future of Paddosha Palace village and Slosiaran.

Cyrra started jumping excitedly again from talon to talon. She chuckled. *Oh yeah. That's right. I forgot. The guardian dragons said that many humans from Paddosha Palace village once bonded with the large dragons, making many of the villagers dragon riders.*

CHAPTER TWENTY-ONE

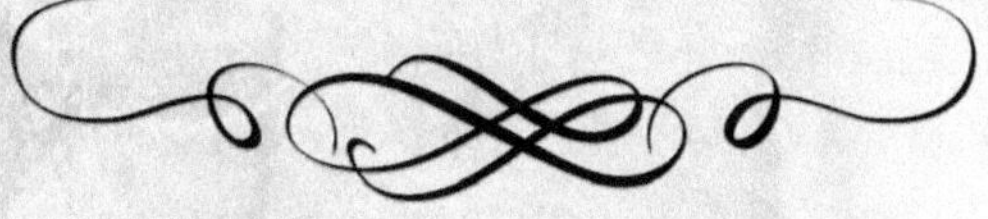

Heart thumping, Samara dragged Paxton behind the gurney by his legs to hide with Ulrieg from the orb's shots of power.

Slightly to the side, Devi stood with her hands raised, ready for any of the orb's shots that might bypass the gurney table's protection.

Shoulders slumped, Samara gazed over Paxton's still form as he lay on his back. His dark hair, with only the slightest remnants of green from his coterie coloring, was pulled roughly into a ponytail. His face rested, expressionless, and his skin was wan. His thin and muscular body lay motionless in every way, as though dead. She hadn't known what to expect. Whether he would be covered in some sort of goop. Instead, he was bone-dry, as though the power of the orb floated on the particles of air, constantly swirling, all the light blending to make it seem like one giant sphere.

She reached for his carotid artery, searching for a heartbeat, and pressed her ear up to his mouth, listening for any breaths. She couldn't hear any. Focusing solely on searching for his heartbeat, she shifted her fingers to find a better spot on his neck. A very soft *thump* resonated from under her fingertips. A small amount of relief washed over her body. He was alive, but he wasn't in good condition.

Devi shifted to shelter behind the gurney with them, seeming semiconfident the orb had settled. "How is he?"

"His heart is barely beating, and I can't see or feel any breaths." Samara placed her hand on his chest, feeling for a rise or fall. "It doesn't look good."

"I imagine the orb stuns its victims. That way, they can't fight against it with their magic when trapped inside." She felt his forehead. "Perhaps that is what happened, and maybe, if we can get him out of this, he'll be fine."

"How am I going to get him out of here if he can't move? Ulrieg's not big enough to carry him, and I can't carry his weight far enough to get us out of here." Panic rose from her toes, causing her to fidget.

"I'll see what I can do." Devi gave her a reassuring smile before she leaned over him, rubbed her palms together, then gently placed them against Paxton's temple and his heart.

Seeing Paxton like this was heart-wrenching for Samara, his soft and caring brown eyes sealed shut and the spark of his warm personality gone. She longed to see his vitality shine through again. She missed him—missed his help, his heart, and his good intentions. She hoped the orb had not changed him.

Samara's thoughts were interrupted when Ulrieg piped up. *Somebody's coming. I can hear footsteps outside.*

Devi sat straight, her eyes wide, and Samara followed suit. "Quick, let's get him out of here." Ulrieg and Samara lifted him from under his shoulders, and Devi grabbed his feet. Then, as quickly as they could, they carried him across the room and maneuvered him out of the underground cave through the hole Samara had made with her arrow.

Once they were in the corridor leading to the back entrance, Samara yanked out the arrow, closing the hole behind them. "We didn't have time to clean up the room and make it look like we weren't there."

"I don't think it's going to matter, because whoever's coming in there is going to notice Paxton isn't in the orb anymore. So moving things back isn't going to make much difference." Devi stretched her back after carrying Paxton's weight.

"What are we going to do? They know about this entrance, too, and they could come through this way as well." Samara felt her panic rising.

Devi went to the door and waved her hands over it, spelling it with an extra lock. "That may keep them out for a little longer, but we're not going to be able to stay here if they come looking for us." She looked at Ulrieg. "Can you call to Zion and get him to help us while I concentrate on Paxton?"

Of course. Ulrieg closed his eyes for a short while.

Devi wiped her hands on her skirt. "We should move a little farther from here."

Samara and Devi carried Paxton's body farther toward the stairs, trying to get away from the door as much as possible, and Ulrieg scurried after them to help. Devi leaned over Paxton again to instill more healing magic into him.

Soon, Samara heard footsteps above. In a panic, she looked up to find Zion's large wolf form coming down the stairs.

Relief flooded Devi's face. "Zion says we're free to go out around the building, but we need to hurry and get straight to the bushes."

"We're going to need help to carry Paxton as quickly as possible." Samara straightened her back. "He's not big, but he's still too big for us to carry that far quickly. I can't see the building anymore. Can you keep an eye out for anyone watching from the windows, Devi?"

"Of course." Devi readied herself to lift her end of Paxton. "I'd forgotten about that. I haven't been out of the coterie in so long that I just automatically assumed ex-coterie members can see the building."

"All that I see is the meadow and a few trees," Samara said, indicating for Ulrieg to grab Paxton's shoulder.

Yep. That's it. We only found this area because the hole isn't part of the coterie building and mustn't be included in the invisibility spell. Ulrieg grunted as he helped pull Paxton up the stairs.

The bush swayed wildly as they pulled Paxton out of the hole into the darkness of the night. Fumbling, they dragged him across the plain. As soon as they reached a safer spot, Devi would be able to work on him. When they reached the bushes that were hopefully out of sight from anyone entering the grounds, they stopped. Devi set to work on Paxton again, trying to heal him and bring him back to consciousness.

"If I don't bring him back to consciousness soon, I'm

going to have to leave you and work on him again later." Devi pressed her hands against Paxton's temples.

Why is that? Ulrieg seemed worried.

"Because they're going to notice I'm gone. If they suspect me of anything, that would put Henriette and Peadar in danger as well, plus anybody else who has been talking to me more lately." She closed her eyes for a moment and tossed her head back, her hands remaining on Paxton's temples. "We can't risk that kind of problem."

"Is Henriette back from her trip?" Samara asked.

Devi glanced questioningly at Samara. "No, she's not. Although she's been gone for quite some time. I didn't know you knew she was gone."

"I ran into her a couple of weeks ago at Paddosha Palace village. She helped protect our village from Mist, though she was invisible while doing it, so Mist doesn't know. I don't know what's happened since she left. She said she was going to wipe Mist's memory so she wouldn't remember anything about her failed attack on the village. I'm hoping Henriette is okay."

"It sounds like she's already in deep trouble. That's not good." A worried look passed over Devi's face. "I'm afraid our days at the coterie are numbered. We will have to leave shortly. It's getting too dangerous to be around here. They're not fools. They knew about you a long time before they approached you, but they were trying to catch Ulrieg."

"I know." Samara nodded. "Callista admitted as much on my last day here."

After working on Paxton for a while, Devi froze.

"What is it?" Worry washed over Samara. "Is he okay?"

"Zion has informed me that they know that I'm missing. Because I distracted them from the underground, they now suspect me of helping you. Even though I was very careful to cover my tracks when I came down, we can't go back." Devi said. "If we do, we will be in major danger. I'm so worried about Henriette and Peadar. I hope they haven't connected the dots between us, as I've been personally giving them defense lessons outside of class." The sorceress turned back to Paxton. "Callista was always wondering how you got away so easily. She knows that you had help. Even though Paxton was caught, other things happened that didn't seem to come from you and Ulrieg."

"I'm so sorry," Samara said. "You can always come with us, and hopefully Peadar and Henriette will be okay."

"I think I'm going to have to. Perhaps we can get messages to Peadar and Henriette."

I can go find Peadar now if you like. I can let him know.

"That would be a good idea, Ulrieg." Devi suddenly froze again. "We must move now. Zion said people are heading this way with Mystique. They found her under a spell earlier. They've released her, and she is now sniffing us down with Jet, followed by Zofia and Callista. We have to go."

CHAPTER TWENTY-TWO

"We have to think of some way to get out of here." Samara bit her bottom lip as she peered at Devi, barely able to see her eyes through the darkness.

"You're right," Devi said. "They're going to follow us, and Mystique and Jet are quick, with an excellent sense of smell. They'll probably track us down before we get a few yards." She sucked in a large breath. "I'll see what I can do." She stepped out from the protection of the bushes and into the dull moonlight, palms outstretched, shooting magic at Mystique as the cat prowled toward them.

A wince sounded a hundred yards away, and Devi turned to find Zion being attacked by Jet, the sun bear, pinning the wolf down, teeth barred on both.

Mystique pounced on Devi while she was distracted, the distance between them devoured in a split second. After knocking her down from the side, the jaguar rolled her to her back and used her front paws to pin the instructor to the ground.

Devi thrashed, struggling to get the cat off her.

Mystique's teeth grazed her arm, and crimson slashes—almost black in the moonlight—streaked Devi's skin.

Quickly, Samara grabbed an arrow from her quiver, muttered a quick spell, and shot it at Mystique, petrifying her again.

Groaning, Devi shoved at the jaguar's dead weight, finally pushing Mystique to the side. As her blood trailed to the ground, she said a healing spell. With a swipe of her hand over the injury, she was on her feet again, cheered on by the snarls of Jet and Zion. Her wounds were no longer bleeding but remained unhealed. Devi seemed able to ignore the pain and direct her attention to the fighting familiars. The sounds were terrifying, and Devi likely felt every blow Zion received.

The defense arts instructor ran toward the animals, and Samara joined her. Several gashes marked Zion's light-copper coat, and blood glimmered dimly in the moonlight on a few angry bite marks in Jet's hide. Zion had put up a strong fight but was now pinned to the ground.

Forcing out her hands, palms crossed and forward, Devi shoved a magical force toward Jet, knocking him off Zion. The wolf scrambled off the ground and crouched on all fours, stalking Jet with barred teeth and blocking the bear's path to Devi.

In the distance, something caught Samara's eye. She turned to spot Callista's dimly lit form coming from—what seemed to be—out of nowhere. In reality, she must have been exiting the building. Callista fired magic at Samara, knocking her down and sending her backward. She scrambled to her feet and hid behind some bushes.

Devi and Zion stood their ground. The sorceress kept

her hands flexed and ready, and the wolf circled in front of Jet, blocking his path to his bonded. Jet slowly backed away, teeth barred yet not quite relenting.

Samara spelled and nocked an arrow, finding a peephole through the bushes to aim it at Callista. She took in a deep breath and released it, firing it at the head sorceress. The arrow aimed true until the sorceress waved her arm, knocking it from the sky to the ground several feet away.

Callista moved closer, followed by Zofia and Kellam and the snub-nosed monkey, all heading straight toward them.

Ulrieg. We've got to go. There are too many of them out here. They're attacking us. Where are you?

I'm coming. I've just found Peadar. I'll warn him about what's happening, and then I'm on my way. I had to call out to him because there was no way of finding him inside a building I can't see.

Samara squatted lower behind the bush, spelled another arrow, and aimed it at Callista.

Suddenly, Kellam lurched forward—a reaction Samara had seen a few times before when invisible Ulrieg had attacked someone from behind. The snub-nosed monkey squawked his disapproval, climbing his sorcerer's back to his shoulders, ready to defend him from behind.

The dragon's attack barely slowed the senior coterie members. Determination marked their every movement as the three continued toward Samara, Devi, Paxton, and their familiars.

Paxton still lay unmoving on the ground—a deadweight that was sure to slow them down. Samara hoped he would wake soon, although even if he did, she didn't know what condition he would be in. He could be just as much of a burden awake, maybe even more so. They needed to do something fast, but what, Samara didn't know. They were too outnumbered to stay and fight.

Devi continued her battle against Jet. Eventually, she pushed back with magic so forceful that the sun bear was thrown against a tree, knocking him unconscious. She instantly turned her attention to the three instructors coming from the coterie building.

While Kellam and his monkey were busy with Ulrieg's attacks and Devi concentrated on Callista, Samara spelled more arrows, shooting one at Zofia. The weapons master whipped out her sword and sliced the arrow in the blink of an eye. The two pieces fell to the ground like discarded sticks. Samara nocked more arrows, firing them at the weapons master in quick succession as Devi continued her attack on Callista from the side.

With a rapid movement of her lips and a quick swipe of her hand, Callista installed a ward in front of her, unprepared from Ulrieg's attack from behind. She screamed in frustration and pain, aiming her palm backward to shoot some magic, trying to find Ulrieg. She had wised up to his attacks since the last time, and she attempted to petrify him. However, Ulrieg had also learned from the past and managed to dodge her attacks.

Samara shifted her focus to Kellam, aiming a spelled arrow at his heart. He shifted at the last second, and the arrow landed in his shoulder. The sorcerer fell to the ground, his face distorted in pain and terror as he faced his worst nightmares.

Callista continued toward them, creating a barrier in front of her every few feet to block their attacks while shooting magic into the air in defense against Ulrieg's assault.

Shifting to the edge of the trees, Devi hunkered down behind a thick bush, Zion by her side. Once she'd gathered her strength, she thrust her palm to the ground and spread her arms wide.

Unsure what the defense arts instructor was doing, Samara continued shooting arrows to provide a distraction. She launched another arrow at Callista, only to have it bounce back once it hit the edge of the forest.

"Your arrow isn't going to get through. Quick, come this way." Devi beckoned Samara closer. "Let's grab Paxton and go. I have raised a border as far as it can reach, along the edges of the forest. They have been trapped within the plain—for now. Jet and Mystique are on our side of the barrier but currently out of action. We need to go quickly before they wake up and before Callista can cut her way through the barrier I have installed."

They scooped up Paxton, Samara at his head and Devi at his feet, then carried him off into the forest as quickly as they could go, pausing regularly for Devi to install more barriers behind them.

"You can never be too sure with someone like Callista, or even Kellam or Zofia. It's best to have as many barriers as possible. If nothing else, it'll slow them down." Devi spread her arms out wide, showing the barrier where to go.

They continued, Devi's power growing weaker with each barrier she created. "I don't know how many more I can do." Devi's shoulders slumped, and she looked tired and weak.

"Do you think you can teach me?" Samara couldn't stand seeing the instructor's strength depleted that way.

"Possibly, but you might need Ulrieg to stand by your side to give you more power while you do it."

That I can do. Ulrieg was by Samara's side, visible and pressing up against her before she could call him.

Looking pale, Devi went through the instructions for how to make the barrier. The first time, Samara's barrier was neither large nor strong, and Devi could get through it easily using her magic. Samara practiced over and over until she'd created a stronger one that was more difficult for Devi to break. The longer Samara practiced, the more she noticed her energy draining. Sensing her weakness, Ulrieg pressed harder against her leg. His touch would give her more energy but nothing that could be maintained over a long period.

They left the pine forest and traveled through the hardwoods, farther away from the danger. Still, they dared not stop, even when the sun started to spread its light through the darkness.

The leeches of doom are still coming. Ulrieg updated them several times during the night. *Although they seem to be slowing down.*

Eventually, as the sun peeked over the horizon, they found a cave that led deep into the mountainside. With a couple of wards placed around the entrance, it would be a perfect place to recover while staying out of sight. Here they could hide, sleep, and work on Paxton. Together, they set up a few barriers and headed into the dank darkness. The dark stone walls and ceiling loomed around them as they trekked farther into the mountain, the light of the entrance growing smaller with each step.

CHAPTER TWENTY-THREE

Emelyne gazed at Cyrra in disbelief and asked Monut, *Wouldn't ya think that would be important news to remember? I mean, it's good news that many of the villagers of Paddosha Palace were once dragon riders. I jus' thought it would've been one of the first things she would tell us.*

The large gray dragon looked knowingly at Emelyne. *Yes, it is, my bonded. Don't forget that although Cyrra always means well and is a wonderful companion, she's not really the brightest dragon. Probably not the best messenger the wise guardian dragons could have used. She may remember much important information a long time after she should have let us know.*

"Cyrra, what 'bout the smaller dragons?" Emelyne asked.

The brown-and-beige-striped dragon stood near Monut, reaching only half his height. *What about us?*

"Do the smaller dragons bond with humans?" Emelyne asked.

Dramatically, Cyrra shook her head. *Oh, no. The*

guardian dragons said we are normally just companions. Although, apparently we helped heaps in the war between the evil sorceress and the peace-loving realms and dragons. That's another reason why the sorceress Callista hid our realm and cut us off from the rest of the realms.

Cyrra left to join the smaller dragons, the elation of finding more of her kind never seeming to dull.

Emelyne and Monut watched carefully as the dragons and humans continued to interact, looking for more pairings, but none came. It hadn't occurred to Emelyne that the dragons would bond, but it had seemed natural when it happened. Change seemed to be blowing in on the wind. These freshly planted seeds would bloom with the strength to rise against the coterie and protect their village.

Once the dragons and humans had spent time getting to know each other, Cyrra investigated the stone wall. *What are you doing here, anyway?*

Monut nudged a loose stone onto the center of the wall. *They are building an additional fence around the village to protect it. The steel fence is dragon blessed by me and should be strong enough to withstand great pressure.*

Emelyne leaned up against Monut's side, crossing one leg over the other. "But the bars leave us open to attack from arrows an' other weapons that can be thrown." She sucked in a breath. "As we recently experienced. They won't be able to penetrate the stone wall. We've got no idea what the magic wielders from the coterie will throw at us. The two fences won't protect us from the lightnin' a sorceress struck us with not so long ago."

Cyrra's jaw dropped. *They can create lightning?*

At least one of them can. Samara and her friend managed to stop her. Monut sat, keeping Emelyne's weight supported. *Then we had centaurs attack us, looking for a crystal. They fired arrows through the bars.*

Hmm. Cyrra tussled her wings. *We can't have that! What can the dragons do to help?*

At first, Emelyne was surprised, then she thought of something that would help quicken their pace. "If ya can lift stones, ya can help find more rocks an' place them one on top of another on the wall. The humans can straighten them so they line up."

Cyrra gazed at the other dragons, and a silent communication seemed to pass among them before she turned back to Emelyne. *Done! They're ready to start now.*

"Great!" Emelyne clapped her hands excitedly, and the humans set to work.

Several of the dragons started with the pile of stones already near the fence. One by one, they took a rock between their talons and flew it to the stonemason for him to cut it to size. They then flew the cut stone to the top of the section currently being built. Before long, a large section of the wall had been added.

The remaining dragons searched on either side of the fence for more stones. Soon all groups were working together like clockwork in a sequence that moved the work along quickly. The wall was extending twenty times faster than it had before. Their newfound ease and efficiency was unbelievable.

Monut and Emelyne joined in, and before they knew it, they had reached the part of the small forest where the dragons had initially landed on the day Emelyne joined the village. Creation of a safe area for the dragons was important. The smaller ones especially needed shelter and protection from outsiders. As hard as they'd tried to keep it a secret, news of dragons in the village would probably spread soon—if it hadn't already. People couldn't help but gossip, especially about something so unusual.

Several days passed, and the stone wall was finished. Not only that, but the dragons were introduced in the main square, and the remaining nine large dragons bonded with humans from the village. The bonded dragons roared in triumph, as though they had finally been chosen for what they were born to do.

Emelyne smirked, happy to see their army growing in ways she had never thought of not so long ago. "It looks like dragon ridin' lessons are in order, on top of weapons trainin'."

Monut nudged her with his snout. *It should come naturally to them like it did with you.*

Overhearing the conversation, Cyrra joined in. *Oh yeah. The guardian dragons said that the dragon riders used to also be very experienced with war darts.* She said " war dart" slowly, as though the word was strange on her tongue and she was questioning whether she'd gotten it right. *They said they are fantastic weapons to use from a dragon's back.*

Emelyne gazed blankly at Cyrra before turning to Monut. *Then we definitely need dragon-back weapons training. Even I will need to learn how to throw them correctly.*

Cyrra nodded enthusiastically. *That's right! And you'll also all need saddles. Do you know anyone who can make them? The guardian dragons said that they will also need lots of pockets and attachments that can hold different types of weapons.*

Emelyne's mind spun as she tried to think of someone who might be gifted in making items with leather. "Do you know of anyone, Monut, especially someone who could spare the time?"

He nudged her slightly. *The parents of Samara's beloved are good with making things with leather. They used to make a lot of things with sheep's leather and are now tending the sheep farms here. They did an excellent job on our saddle.*

A gruff voice sounded behind Emelyne, speaking in a dwarven accent. "Travelin' bunions! I hope I don't have to supply food for all them dragons too."

She turned to find Samara's dwarven friend, Forgrac. He and Samara had joined to find Emelyne, disguising themselves in a traveling theater show. The little man rocked on his toes, his thumbs tucked into the belt of his pants, showing off his small belly. His bushy dark-brown beard was brushed and cut straight at the bottom, giving his face a square shape.

"No, I wouldn't do that to ya. Ya have enough people to look after in the village. You've been doin' a wonderful job supplyin' the villagers with lunch and supper."

His hazel eyes looked sincerely over his large, hooked nose. "I don't do it on me own."

Emelyne smiled. "I know. But you oversee all your helpers. And the food is delicious."

Monut reassured him. *As for the dragons, they prefer their food raw and freshly caught. They are usually happy to catch their own.*

"Good," Forgrac grumbled and rubbed the back of his head through his short chocolate-colored hair. "Me heart was fluttering when I saw that many big mouths to feed. I used to supply Ulrieg with some off-cuts at the coterie after I met him. But that was a novelty." He looked at

Monut. "I hope there's enough wildlife out there to keep them fed."

I believe there is. I have seen plenty of wild animals on my nightly flights.

"It's hard to believe that the large dragons have already bonded with people of the village. It's like they were born for each other." He wiped his hands on his apron. "Good things are comin', I tell ya. Good things are comin'. I have waited such a long time for this."

Emelyne leaned on one leg. "We have a lot of work to do yet before the village is even close to how it used to be before Callista's rein."

"Ain't that for sure! I'm jus' glad that I get to see it in me lifetime. There's hope for me children's future yet." He threaded a white apron over his head. "Well, I've gotta get back to work. This crowd ain't gonna feed itself." He tied his apron behind his back as he walked away to the main base of his communal kitchen.

CHAPTER TWENTY-FOUR

After carrying Paxton for so long, they laid him down gently on the stone-and-dirt floor of the cave to catch their breath. Exhausted, Samara collapsed, and Devi sat on a rock not far away from her, igniting a small flame on her palm to give them a slither of light to see by. Samara's stomach rumbled loudly, the sound reverberating softly through the cave.

Way to drop a hint! Ulrieg quipped. *All right, all right. I'm going to go hunting.* He stretched his front legs forward, raised his hips, then shook, loosening his muscles. *What do you think, Zion?*

Samara couldn't hear Zion's answer, but the wolf headed toward the door of the cave, walking with a slight limp from the injuries Devi hadn't finished healing. Gashes could still be seen in his side, but after executing so many wards and trying to heal Paxton, the sorceress had run out of energy.

Devi called after him. "Be careful."

Zion looked over his shoulder on the way out, the

communication and love between the wolf and Devi evident in their eyes.

Samara knew Ulrieg would be careful. They had spent a lot of time out of the coterie now and knew what to watch for. But Samara wasn't sure what Devi and Zion had endured over the last several months within the coterie. She pulled her eyes from the defense arts instructor and studied Paxton. A faint rise and fall of his chest was the only indication he was still alive. His face was so pale, even in the darkness of the cave.

Devi knelt next to Paxton and continued to transfer healing energy. "We could use the help of a healer. I don't know what is wrong with him or how to approach his healing. My specialty is defense, not healing. Although I do have some healing talents."

"It's a shame Paxton can't work on himself. He was an excellent healer." Tears formed in the corner of Samara's eye as she looked on. She wiped them away with her hand and lit a small flame on her palm to give Devi a break while she did her best for him. "I hope all that wasn't taken from him in the orb. It was a special gift."

Devi felt his forehead and shook her head. "He's burning up. I hope it's only because he's fighting whatever the orb did to him." She spent more time crouched over him, inserting healing magic until she slumped against the rock upon which she'd been sitting.

"You look exhausted," Samara said.

A weak smile crossed Devi's face. "Nothing a good sleep and a good meal won't fix."

Chilly morning air swept through the cave as the wind picked up outside.

Pushing down on her knees to help herself up, Devi

stood and headed to the entrance of the cave. "I'm going to make a proper fire in here. A magical fire would take too much needed energy to keep it kindled."

Samara joined her, quenching her small magical flame on her palm, and together they searched the immediate area outside for some twigs, leaves, and branches. Back within the depths of the cave, they built an A-frame with the smaller sticks over the leaves to use for kindling. Devi created a small flame to set the leaves on fire. When the fire was burning strongly, they added a couple thicker branches then logs to keep the flame fed. They stacked the extra wood a couple feet from the fire.

The orange glow filled the space, warmth flooded toward them, and the scent of the fire took away some of the dank, musty smell of the cave.

The familiars returned with a couple of small game, and after preparing them, they threaded the meat onto a thick straight stick and turned it over the fire at intervals. While the meat roasted, Samara added extra barriers outside the cave, and Devi injected more healing power into Paxton. Once the food was finally ready, they feasted on the cooked meat then slept some of the day away.

Samara's sleep was fitful, filled with images of orange tentacles reaching out to grab her, the orb wrapping itself around her. Trapped by its power, Samara struggled to escape. She was unable to break free as Paxton awoke, his eyes filled with evil and his power dark, no longer healing but life-sucking and destructive.

Samara jolted awake, drenched in sweat. She glanced quickly at Paxton, still lying on his back and unconscious, then glanced at Devi. The defense arts instructor sat with her elbows resting on her knees, the light of the fire illuminating her delicate face and pointed ears as she stared at Paxton's lifeless form. Zion lay by her side, facing the entrance of the cave as though on guard. Samara squashed down the pleasure of having her defense instructor by her side. As glad as she was that Devi was with her and could teach her more magic, she also knew that Devi had lost everything she'd lived for over the last several years.

Devi's eyes connected with Samara's. "Not a nice night's sleep."

Visible, Ulrieg sat in the shadow of a corner, his red eyes piercing through the darkness. They hadn't been here long, but the darkness was already getting to Samara. She wished they could move closer to the light at the entrance of the cave but knew it would be harder to remain hidden if the coterie members found the cave.

"You were tossing and turning. That's what my sleep's been like for the last several months." Devi rubbed a tired eye before picking up a stick and poking the fire, stirring and brightening the embers. A fresh wave of heat warmed the cave.

Samara pulled herself into a seated position and hugged her knees. "Do you mind me asking, when did you realize that the coterie was evil?"

"I've known for a very long time. Many years, in fact. I've done my best to teach apprentices and continue as though nothing is wrong. Hoping that one day there would be apprentices who see the truth, whose conscience wouldn't allow them to continue with the coterie and their treatment of the people of the kingdoms. Lo and behold, we happened to get a few honorable apprentices at one time. Maybe the winds are changing."

"What made you think that I was one of the good ones?" Samara fiddled with the edge of her dress.

"I had suspicions about the authenticity of your familiar, Gray, the owl." Devi half smiled. "I knew something was off with your connection. It's remarkable how you managed to train a wild owl to act like your familiar. Though, some of his actions were strange."

Samara huffed. "Those were probably the times Ulrieg forced the owl to do something."

"That would make sense." Devi rubbed an arm. "I watched you closely without you knowing, and I knew things were going missing from underneath the coterie building. I didn't go underneath very often, but I investigated after hearing rumors that things had been going wrong for the senior members of the coterie." She threw the stick onto the fire and looped her arms around her knees. "You're incredibly brave, doing what you've been doing. I didn't realize how disturbed the senior members of the coterie were until Callista asked for help one day. There was no denying it after that. I feel incredibly stupid for not having realized just how bad they were until then. Naturally, I was appalled and wanted to save all I could, but I was always outnumbered. Often, by the time I knew what was happening, the dragons were already deceased. I don't know how they could be so cruel, torturing the dragons like that. It's one thing to call someone your enemy—it's another to disfigure them for fun." Devi's face grew pale under the firelight. "I hid my feelings from Callista, and when I heard of the dragons disappearing, I investigated. With Zion's help, it didn't take long to work out who was behind the disappearances."

Devi threw her head back then continued. "Oh, when I

found out which senior coterie members were involved in the torture, I wasn't surprised. I knew there was something off with Zofia. I didn't like her from the start. She has always been cruel. The same with Kellam and Vexx." She shivered. "Callista's definitely managed to choose twisted border patrol sorcerers. But ever since I found out, I've been identifying certain students, talking to the quieter ones and training them to be stronger. Ones who seem to have good in their hearts and not evil." She scoffed. "The evil ones shine forward and take pride in it, like Kaine, Luna, and Mist. I hoped that by doing this, I was making up for time lost to my ignorance."

"Are any of the other coterie instructors good?" Samara rested her hands on her knees.

Devi shrugged. "I honestly don't know. It's not something we could just talk about. Although I wouldn't be surprised if Eliphas, the herbs instructor, has a good heart despite his eccentricity. I know he seems unusual, but he can use that to hide behind and blind Callista to his true heart."

They sat in silence for a while, Samara pondering over what Devi had said and what their next move should be. Her gaze turned to Paxton. He remained unmoving, although the sight of him breathing was a relief. He was alive, if nothing else. Although pale, he looked almost peaceful, as though in a deep sleep. She hoped they could heal him and get him back to normal. They could certainly use his healing power right now.

Ulrieg moved to sit by Samara's side, his red eyes passing over Paxton's still form. *Has anyone seen any sign of Jojo?*

Samara's heart dropped. "I completely forgot about him in our rush to leave the underground."

Although he was an important part of Paxton's life, the frog was tiny in comparison to other familiars.

Stones dug into Samara's knees as she knelt beside Paxton and patted his pockets. She double-checked the pocket on his tunic and felt something small within the material. Lifting it open, she apprehensively dug her hand in and pulled out a lax, unmoving JoJo.

CHAPTER TWENTY-FIVE

Samara's blood turned cold. It looked like JoJo was dead. After wetting her hands with water from her canteen, she placed the frog gently on her hand and stroked his back, hoping for some sign of life. She had heard that frogs will sometimes seem dead and come back to life once they're in a warmer climate. She hoped this was the case, but she couldn't be sure because no matter how much she prodded Jojo, he didn't move. She took him closer to the fire to warm his blood, protecting his amphibian skin from the fire's strong heat with her hands. The last thing she needed to do was cook him.

Wingless flight! That doesn't look good. Ulrieg snorted, careful to shoot his internal heat away from the small familiar's skin. *I'm talking to him, but he won't respond.*

Devi wet her hands and reached for JoJo. "Here. Let me have a go." Enclosing him within her palms, she closed her eyes and inserted Jojo with healing power.

Hand behind her back, Samara kept her fingers

crossed. She wanted him to survive. Then he might be able to give Paxton some more energy to recover.

After several tries, Devi let her hands drop to her lap, still cupping Jojo within them. "I'm not having any luck. He's not moving." Her face distraught, she shook her head. "There's no pulse. He may have given his last life to Paxton to keep him alive. Familiars can be rather giving like that."

Ulrieg nudged Jojo with his nose then pulled away, his glowing red eyes fixed on the small familiar. *I have heard of that happening before.* His eyes focused on Samara, and somehow, their red glow softened. *We'll do anything to protect our bonded.*

Samara returned the affection of his gaze yet couldn't pass up the chance to tease. "Are you getting all soft on me, Ulrieg?"

Ulrieg raised a scaly eyebrow.

"I'm just joking. I wouldn't want you to give your life for me. I couldn't stand being left behind without you." She ran the back of her hand gently along Ulrieg's jawline, avoiding the large horn under the tip of his chin.

The dragon tilted his head toward Paxton, his expression challenging. *Perhaps true love's kiss would wake him.*

Samara gazed down at her hands, and she could feel her cheeks flush. "I'd rather do that with him awake and reactive, but I'm willing to give it a go. I'll try anything if it might wake him up."

Go on, then. Ulrieg nudged her with his wing.

She shifted to her knees, pulling her skirt to the side and feeling the pain of the rocks digging into her skin as she leaned over Paxton's face. He had never been typically handsome, but his genuine smile and sensitivity had made him the most beautiful man she had ever known. How she longed to witness that again. She pressed her lips against his, and the heat of his fever warmed her lips even more than her cheeks before she pulled away and stroked the side of his face.

She willed him to wake. Several minutes passed, and still he didn't move. Her eyes met Ulrieg's. "It didn't work."

All teasing had left Ulrieg's eyes. *Wingless flight! I was half joking, but it would've been nice if it worked.*

Samara nodded in agreement as she slowly shifted back to the larger rock not far away.

The fire crackled, constantly fueling the dancing orange glow that filled their part of the cave. Although they had rested, they hadn't ventured out. The last thing they needed was for Callista, Zofia, or Kellam to catch them.

"Do you think Callista has given up the search by now?" Samara asked Devi.

Devi absentmindedly fiddled with the unmoving Jojo in her hands. "It's hard to tell. They can be rather persistent when they want to. Or they could've gone back to the building and sent some of their minions to do the work for them. I don't think Callista knows where you've been hanging out so far. So that could be an advantage."

Ulrieg climbed to his feet and stretched, pushing his backside into the air. *I'll go out and have a scout around. At least I can be invisible and fly close.*

Ulrieg turned invisible as he walked toward the daylight coming from the distant cave opening. Rocks clattered, and his talons clicked against the stones. When he launched into the sky, several more rocks clattered from the force of his jump.

Zion lay next to Devi, his head resting in her lap. Devi petted his head, her eyes wistful as she gazed into the fire. The senior sorceress had healed more of his wounds, leaving the sores in his fur less obvious. Eventually, the wolf familiar stretched out his legs then curled up next to his bonded, his back touching her side.

Samara stacked a couple more logs onto the fire, pausing as Paxton stirred slightly. It had been the first movement he had made on his own since they had pulled him from the orb. Excitement ran through her, but it quickly dissipated when the movement stopped and his eyes remained shut. If it wasn't for the steadily increasingly breaths, he could easily be mistaken for dead.

Noticing Samara's worry-filled gaze, Devi said, "That's a positive sign. But I think he has a long way to go." She yawned. "I'm going to get a little more sleep. I need to recoup before I can give him more healing energy."

"You do that, and I'll keep watching out for Ulrieg," Samara said.

Devi stroked Zion's head. "I'm sure Zion will be watching with you. He may appear asleep, but he's always on alert." Devi curled into a ball, making herself as comfortable as she could, her head on Samara's backpack. She had only meant to help Samara, so the instructor had left with nothing.

As the hours passed, Samara sat by the fire and kept an eye on Paxton, looking for any movement. Every so often, when she felt her magic strengthen, she gradually injected more healing power into Paxton. Her ability to heal others wasn't strong, but it would be better than nothing.

Her shoulder still twinged occasionally but had improved greatly after Devi injected some healing power into it. She hoped Paxton would have some ability to heal himself once he got to a certain point in his recovery. She had never asked him if he could heal himself, something sorcerers and magic wielders often couldn't do.

Paxton gradually began to stir, giving Samara more hope and encouraging her to inject more healing power into him when she had enough energy to do so.

Rocks scattered near the entrance, and she spun in time to see Ulrieg turn visible, his silhouette framed by the light from the distant mouth of the cave.

Relief flooded Samara when she saw he remained unharmed after going so close to members of the coterie. *How did it go?*

If anything, those senior coterie members are persistent. Ulrieg huffed, snorting a small flash of fire. *They never seem to give up. They're always keen to cause harm. It's sickening.*

I gather that means they're still following us and are close. Samara couldn't help smiling over Ulrieg's disgust, despite the situation.

Of course it means they're still following us. They're psychopaths!

Your life would be a lot less hectic if you hadn't bonded with me, wouldn't it?

Yes. Ulrieg grumbled. *But I'm glad I bonded with you. We wouldn't be able to help the kingdoms otherwise. There is no way we could do it alone.* He wandered to stand next to Paxton's unmoving form. *How's Sleeping Beauty?*

Do you mean Paxton or Devi? Samara smiled as Devi snuggled with Zion not far from Paxton.

Paxton, of course. Looking worried, he nodded toward the instructor. *Unless Devi's also lost too much energy from trying to heal him.* His gaze traveled to Jojo, sadness in his glowing red eyes.

Deep love for her familiar washed over Samara. *Paxton has moved a slight bit, which is giving me more hope. Plus, his breaths are stronger and more regular. But other than that, there has been no change.*

Looks like we're going to be here for quite a while longer. You might want to reinforce your boundaries around the cave to make sure the coterie members can't find us here. Either that, or we're going to have to leave, and that doesn't look possible with Paxton like this.

Good thinking! Samara rose to her feet. *I'll go do that now before they get any closer.*

CHAPTER TWENTY-SIX

For days, the large dragons spent as much time as possible with their bonded. The sight of a large dragon following closely behind a human had become common, and the bonds seemed to give the villagers something else to be proud of. The smaller dragons intermingled and talked with the humans, helping out when they could. Now that the stone wall had been finished, the homes destroyed by the coterie were being rebuilt at a rapid pace. The dragons' help with heavy objects sped up all processes.

After some convincing, Emelyne had even allowed work to start on the palace. The dragons knocked down the walls of the palace that weren't very stable, and the people—under instruction of the stonemason—rebuilt them, the dragons helping to lift the heavy stones. Once the dragons had placed the stones on top of the walls, flat side out, the villagers used mortar to hold the rocks together. Now not only were the buildings being rebuilt quickly, stone and wooden alike, but progress on the palace was also leaping forward, supplying Emelyne and her parents with a few dry and wind-resistant rooms—a welcome gift, considering the weather was growing colder.

The outside walls were wrapped with decorative steel bars that doubled as a strengthening agent blessed with dragon fire. These additions put the palace's past security measures to shame.

As the outside of the palace walls were rebuilt, other villagers set to decorating the inside. Supplies were sparse, but Emelyne didn't want extravagance and was happy with basic furniture. The outside was looking extravagant enough with the addition of the dragon-blessed metal and decorative emblems. The only people staying in the castle for now were Emelyne and her adoptive parents, Lozzeak and Gibobo. Some of the new families had been staying in the tunnels and caves below. They, too, could stay in proper rooms once they were built.

The work was demanding. Emelyne's every muscle ached during the night. She no longer needed to go flying every night to scout the surrounding areas, as the dragons did it for her. Still, she tried to make time to fly with Monut, as the fresh, cool air cleared her mind.

A week after the large dragons had bonded with their humans, Emelyne called them together in the afternoon. Monut walked next to her, dwarfing her figure as she led the large dragons and their riders from the back of the village. She'd dressed in a special leather riding suit—tailored by Paxton's parents—over tight tan pants and a long-sleeve tunic buttoned up the front. She felt the sleeve of the riding suit as she walked to a large clearing in the small forest to the back of Paddosha Palace village. They had tanned the leather perfectly, making it very pliable and comfortable.

Someone coughed, and she turned to see the other bonded humans and their dragons following, weaving through the trees. All the larger dragons were of a similar gray color.

Monut, are all large dragons gray? The smaller dragons seem to be different colors, but all of the ones who have bonded with humans are gray.

Ah, yes. That is because it is a dull color that blends with the sky in certain weather. We don't have the ability to turn ourselves invisible like Ulrieg, so it's our kind of camouflage, if you will. That is what I have been told. Although there could be special cases where the carrier dragon is a different color. Just like it's strange for Ulrieg to be bonded to a being, albeit a half human, half elf.

Emelyne slapped her thigh. *That makes perfect sense. Perfect for bein' the dragons of fightin' dragon riders. It's like that's the way it was intended.*

Several footfalls sounded to the side, and Emelyne turned to find Cyrra leading the smaller dragons to join them in the clearing.

"What are ya doin', Cyrra?" Emelyne asked.

The brown-and-beige-striped dragon almost looked surprised to be asked. *Oh, we're coming to watch. We might be able to help and give pointers.*

Emelyne frowned. "But ya aren't a dragon who gets ridden."

Technically no, but I did have Samara on my back for a little while.

"Really?" Emelyne asked.

Yes, she did. Monut nodded. *Samara was going to ride her initially because I wasn't going with the dragons to Dragoria. But it was too painful to watch. The flying consistency was all over the place because Cyrra was too small to carry even a thin woman. So I offered to take her instead. It won't hurt for them to watch. They could even act as obstacles.*

Emelyne shrugged. "Then they might as well come."

They reached the clearing by late afternoon, and the cool breeze picked up as the sun moved to the west. The dragons and their respective riders gathered in a large circle, the riders' faces expressing both excitement and apprehension. The smaller dragons watched from the edge of the clearing, under the trees. All eyes turned to Emelyne and Monut.

Emelyne took a long look at the dragons' choices. The ten villagers before her were a mixture of men and women all around Emelyne's age—in their late teens or early adulthood—and their bodies were lean and sturdy.

"Congratulations on bondin' together." Emelyne placed a hand on Monut's cheek, relishing the feel of his tough scales. "I'm sure by now, ya realize how special the bond is—to constantly have that companion with ya, either physically or in spirit."

She studied the bonded humans and saw the deep love and connection as they looked at their dragons. "That's great! I can see it in ya eyes." She smiled. "Now, which of ya have ridden ya dragon?" No one answered. Her eyes passed over each of them until they landed on a young man wearing long emerald pants and a long-sleeved tunic. She pointed at him. "You. Ya look adventurous. What's ya name?"

The man stood straight, pulled back his broad shoulders, and raised his chiseled jaw. "Kobi."

Dragging her tail across the ground, his dragon wrapped her long, pointy tail around the front of Kobi. Leaves and twigs jumped in its wake.

"Have ya tried to get on her back?" Emelyne asked.

He ran a hand through the chocolate strands of his cropped, wavy hair. "Ioldra has encouraged me to hop on a couple of times. We have walked around a bit, but nothing else."

"Ya haven't flown on her?"

He shook his head. "There's nothing to hang on to."

Emelyne frowned. "Show us where ya sit."

Ioldra lowered her torso to the ground and stretched out her wing. Kobi awkwardly climbed up and sat on her back in the space between her wings, one leg on each side. The dragon walked a few paces, and he tried to hang on to her scales.

Emelyne shook her head and held back a smile as she glanced at Monut. *I thought it would jus' be a natural position, but I guess not everyone has practical knowledge.* "That's a good way to fall off, especially if ya flyin'." She turned to the group. "This is how ya do it." She removed the saddle from Monut's back, and he lowered to the ground like Ioldra had. Emelyne climbed up, sat just in front of Monut's wings— her legs hooked over his arms—and hugged Monut's neck. "I have someone workin' on saddles for us all, but for now, ya need to learn without them. After all, ya dragons won't always have saddles on them."

The others followed her example. Soon they were flying low in the clearing, climbing higher as their confidence grew. Several cries of exhilaration rang out from the riders as Kobi and Ioldra led the others to greater heights. The dragons swirled and swerved, and the smaller ones flew between them just for fun, Cyrra leading the way. It was a shame Cyrra couldn't have a rider. It was evident she would like one.

After a while, Monut pulled back and hovered at the edge of the clearing as they watched the new dragon riders and their dragons get better acquainted.

Princess. Monut's deep voice rumbled through her mind. *This is the start of your dragon army. Big changes are in the wind. You should be proud.*

CHAPTER TWENTY-SEVEN

Several days passed, but Paxton remained unconscious, making it almost impossible to leave the cave. His movement had progressed to tossing and turning, yet his eyes wouldn't open. At least Callista and her gang had stopped searching for them. Each day, the familiars caught food and brought it back for them to eat. Once her arm was completely healed, Samara would also hunt, glad to escape the dankness of the cave.

Devi continued to teach Samara different spells while they were stuck within the shelter of the cave. Every day, they injected more healing energy into Paxton, hoping he would wake, although no visible improvements were evident. Perhaps time alone could help Paxton recover from the orb's twisted embrace. In the meantime, Samara would keep him hydrated by pouring small amounts of water into his mouth. She wished she could feed him as well, as he had lost so much weight while in the orb. His skin clung to his bones. If he didn't wake soon, he could starve to death. She didn't know how he had lasted this long without food. The only explanation she could think of was that the orb had magically sustained him.

The days passed painfully slowly as they waited for him to wake. If they had some spare energy, on the fine days, they would venture outside within the barrier to get some fresh air, sunlight, and water from the stream Ulrieg had found nearby. They also used the time to assess their situation. Each day, Ulrieg confirmed that the coterie hadn't resumed their search.

Devi taught Samara to levitate stones and shoot them into the distance. Samara practiced every day, improving her aim and embracing the satisfaction that came with hitting her mark.

"I'm really glad I have you to teach me more magic." Samara levitated another stone and held it in place. "I know I have a long way to go to have anything close to the power of the coterie members, and to add to it, I don't seem to have a special gift that is significant, one that makes me stand out from the others."

"Surely you must have some kind of magic that is different from everyone else." Devi watched Samara's technique closely then gave an approving nod. "And it's okay to not have the same magic as everyone else. Everyone is different, and each special gift is different, even if only slightly. If you're not as strong in the unseen magic, then you might be stronger in the physical magic." She indicated to Samara's bow and quiver lying on the bank of the river. "Like your talent for shooting spelled arrows and how those arrows affect your target. That *is* a special kind of magic. Perhaps all your special magic is connected to your arrows."

Samara lifted one side of her mouth. "It is a different

type of magic than I've seen others use, but it didn't seem to get stronger when I bonded with Ulrieg. And it would be nice to have a special magic that doesn't require a weapon to work."

"I understand. But haven't you used your arrows in other ways? I know Callista had you creating holes in walls. That's pretty special, and it wasn't something you could do before you bonded with Ulrieg."

Ulrieg bounced on a branch above them. *Ha! And didn't that shoot her in the foot, so to speak?*

Devi glanced curiously at Ulrieg. "What do you mean?"

The dragon chuckled. *That one thing Callista taught her, Samara has used to break down barriers between the realms.*

Devi's jaw dropped. "What?"

Samara felt her cheeks warm under the instructor's gaze. "I've discovered that with Ulrieg pressed against me, I can use his power with my own to create holes in the kingdoms' wards with my spelled arrows. I learned this on my trip with Callista. Henriette and I went for a wander in the middle of the night, and I created a hole into Slosiaran. I kept it there so our families could use it to escape Wraeyanor when we left the coterie."

"You mean you don't have to go through the border control manned by Vexx and Kellam?" Devi asked. "I was wondering how you got through the border to Slosiaran without being spotted by Kellam. That's a fantastic gift. Very useful and very special. Knowing this, how can you ever think that you don't have a special gift? I've not known anybody able to break those borders—not even I can put a hole in them."

"Like Ulrieg said, the thought started after Callista taught me to put holes in walls and doors, then I just played around at the border and was pleasantly surprised."

You should see the other realms she's broken into. Ulrieg landed next to Devi and puffed out his chest, widening his shoulders.

"What do you mean?"

Well, we believe we've cut through a ward and found Dragoria.

Devi's arms dropped to her sides, and her jaw slackened. "What? Are you serious? What makes you think this?"

Samara halted her stone-shooting practice. "It took a lot more effort to make a hole in that ward, and it was different. We couldn't see through to the other side. It was a full moon, when Ulrieg's senses were on high alert, and he had a strange sensation. We followed his gut instinct until it led us to a spot along a wall with an arched opening overgrown by vines. When we pushed through the foliage, we couldn't get through the barrier, and we couldn't see what was on the other side. I tried to open it like I'd opened the border to Slosiaran, with Ulrieg pressed against my skin, but it didn't work. Then I had Ulrieg breathe fire on the tip of the spelled arrow, and he pressed against me again as I fired it into the barrier."

"And what did you see?" Devi asked.

Samara sat on a flat stone near Ulrieg. "We saw a realm that looked rather tatty and a broken building in the distance that Ulrieg swore was one of the guard towers from when Dragoria was open and fighting for the other kingdoms. There weren't any paths, and the roads were covered in grass and overgrown with foliage."

"You didn't go into the realm?" Devi asked.

"No." Samara shook her head. "We had to go back to be with Forgrac and his traveling acting crew. And we knew we had a lot of work to do before telling the dragons inside Dragoria, if there are any left, about the hole. I don't think the realms are ready to know that Dragoria has been opened. But since then, we have sent some dragon friends into that area. They haven't come back yet, as far as we know, but they are discovering the realm. I'm sure they'll let us know if it's not Dragoria or if they don't find any other dragons. Let's hope the guardian dragons and all the other breeds are still alive in there."

Devi sat next to Samara and wrapped her arms around her knees. "Samara, you cannot say that you don't have a special magic. You have just accentuated how special it is. No one else can do what you've done. What you have done is about to change our whole world. We are on the crux of it."

"We figured that, but we also knew we needed to build up our side and gather people who are against the coterie. Did you know we have found the lost princess? She's not what we expected, but she is leading well and cares for her people—even though she didn't grow up with them. That's why we've been staying in Paddosha Palace village."

"I can't wait to go there. It's so comforting to know we have a way to get through the border without going through Kellam's watch, because he will certainly recognize us—unless you have the magic of disguise."

"No, I don't. I didn't know it existed," Samara said.

They headed back to the cave, arms full of firewood,

then stepped into the darkness and followed the light of the fire. They dropped the wood and sat by the fire, stacking a few logs on top. Paxton groaned and his breaths became ragged, drawing Samara's attention. Her eyes landed on his in time to see them fly wide open. His brown eyes had turned black.

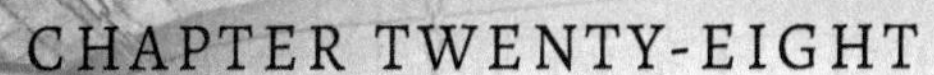

CHAPTER TWENTY-EIGHT

S amara flinched, pulling away from Paxton. Even the whites of his eyes were black. They shouldn't have been black. The change had made them look pure evil. That couldn't be a good sign. She glanced toward Devi, unable to hide her panic.

The instructor dropped the log she was holding and as it clacked to a still on the floor readied herself to defend. Samara wanted to grab for her bow and reach for an arrow from her back, but she halted. This was Paxton. She shouldn't have to hold arrows up against Paxton. She toyed with the idea of doing it just in case he wasn't the kindhearted man he used to be. Still, this was her sweet, caring Paxton—the man she had fallen in love with.

Ulrieg, are you seeing this? Samara couldn't see if he had returned to the cave when they did.

Am I seeing this? Are you kidding me? He looks pure evil. Has he devoured the orbs magic and kept it inside himself?

Paxton sat with his eyes wide. The light of the fire emphasized every crevice of his thin frame, making him look distorted. He observed his surroundings, his panicked breath slowly subsiding.

Eventually, his sight landed on Samara and widened farther with disbelief. "Samara?" He blinked rapidly.

Samara closed her mouth that she hadn't realized had dropped open. Stooping down to his level, she held out a hand to him, trying to act as though everything were normal yet also remaining on guard at the same time. "How are you feeling?"

A frown creased his forehead. "Strange. What happened?" He studied the surroundings another time, his eyes wide. "Where are we? Did we escape?" His eyes landed on Devi, and the frown on his forehead deepened.

She squeezed his hand. "We have escaped. It's the second time for me and the first time for you."

"What do you mean?"

"You were captured, and they threw you into the orb."

The tiny amount of color that filled Paxton's face vanished as his expression became one of disbelief.

It was uncanny looking into his black, evil-looking eyes when his reactions seemed so pure and innocent. Samara couldn't help but cast concerned glances at Devi. Clearly still on guard, the instructor's expression mirrored hers.

"Oh." Releasing his hand from Samara's, Paxton felt around his pockets. "Where's Jojo? I can't feel him." A deep sadness crossed his face, reflecting what Samara was feeling inside.

Slowly, she reached down to where they had placed Jojo, scooped him up carefully, and handed him to Paxton. "I'm afraid Jojo didn't make it. No matter how hard we tried, we couldn't get him to respond."

"Oh no!" Paxton shook his head, his eyes watering. "No. Not Jojo." Pain etched his voice, breaking Samara's heart. His shoulders caved as he cupped Jojo sweetly and stroked his back. "Not Jojo."

"I'm so sorry, Paxton. We tried everything we could." Samara said. "It was hard enough trying to wake you up and heal you. But JoJo didn't seem to have a heartbeat at all." To busy herself, she placed a hand on Paxton's shoulder, trying to comfort him, but there was nothing she could do. She had to let him grieve. It broke her heart as he tried to inject healing magic into his deceased frog familiar.

"I can feel it." Paxton sniffed.

"You can feel what?" Samara asked.

"I can feel that my magic has weakened. It's not as strong as it used to be. Right when I need it to be strong to heal Jojo."

Devi clasped her hands. "I'm afraid Jojo is past healing. And as for your power, that happens if our familiar has passed away."

Desperation in his eyes, Paxton turned to Devi. "Do we get to bond again?"

The instructor shook her head. "I'm not sure. It's rare that you hear of a familiar dying and then another bond happening for a sorcerer. Although I will never say never. There may be a possibility."

Samara loaded a couple more logs onto the fire and sat by Paxton, watching his every move in her peripheral vision, trying not to make it obvious that he was under investigation. He seemed normal, other than being fatigued and sad that he had lost Jojo, but with the blackness in his eyes, Samara remained wary. There was no telling what the orb had done to him during all that time.

Ulrieg nudged Samara in the side. *You should offer the poor guy some food. Remember he hasn't eaten in months. Don't you think he's starving by now?*

Shame washed over Samara. She had been concentrating so much on the change in Paxton's eyes that she hadn't thought about anything else. They even had some leftover meat from earlier that day. She reached over and grabbed some, placed it on a flat rock, and set it near Paxton. "Here, you must be starving. It's still warm from our lunch."

His eyes widened as he placed Jojo gently on his lap and picked up the rock.

Seeing the keenness in his eyes, Devi placed more meat on the rock. "You need to regain your energy because we can't stay here. We have escaped from the coterie, but they are still pursuing us, and we need to get to Paddosha Palace village to help protect it if we can."

Samara nodded, crossing her legs and resting her hands on her knees. "I have not been there for a little while, so hopefully all is good. Mist attacked it just before I left."

Concern filled Paxton's eyes before he took a bite of his rabbit and groaned with pleasure at the taste.

"At least I will be bringing two more magic wielders to help the human village," Samara said, watching him eagerly taking another bite. "Oh, and you'll be happy to know that your family is at Paddosha Palace village. They came a while ago. They sought refuge there with my family." Samara could feel the pride and warmth welling within her when she saw the relief on Paxton's face. The knowledge seemed to restore a bit more of his energy.

"That's good to know." He took another small bite of the rabbit. "I'm happy to help you as much as I can. Although I don't know how good I'll be anymore without Jojo as my familiar. My magic won't be as strong."

"It's too early for you to tell." Devi placed a hand on his shoulder. "Give yourself some time and some rest. I would hate for you to overexert yourself when you've just come out of such a horrific time, even if you don't remember it. Besides, we honestly believe it's possible that Jojo gave his life to protect you and help you survive by giving you as much magic as he could."

"I do feel weak," Paxton said. "But I guess that's to be expected—if that's what happened to me." He took another bite of the rabbit and groaned loudly. "It's been so long since I've tasted real food. I have missed it."

Ha. Can you believe this guy? He looks like something from the underground, and he's questioning if he really did spend time in that evil thing.

Samara hoped Ulrieg's snarky comment was only for her ears. She cast him an evil eye. *He's going through enough. Don't you dare say anything like that to him... even if we're all thinking it.*

Yep. There you go. You know the truth.

Yes, but I hope for the best. He seems to be acting like Paxton. His eyes are the only worrying thing so far, beside the death of Jojo. I was hoping to bring Paddosha Palace village more magic help. She gnawed her bottom lip.

# CHAPTER TWENTY-NINE

Each late afternoon, the dragon riders and dragons would gather in the clearing in the woods. Training the dragons and their riders was necessary, and even though all were tired from a hard day's work, they all found the dragon riding exhilarating. A week after their first gathering, Marcel and Jastira had finished the saddles for the ten extra dragons. Emelyne piled them on Monut's back, and he carried them to the meeting spot. When they arrived, the relief on the dragon riders' faces was palatable. Each rider had their own sense of adventure, but some security on the dragon's back would make for a safer and more pleasant ride.

In addition, Emelyne had asked Cyrra and a few other smaller dragons to bring along war darts, bows and arrows, and other weapons they could use.

I wish people and their weapons didn't weigh so much. Cyrra's back was loaded with bags full of weapons. *Just carrying Samara for a little while around the clearing was more than enough. It was very hard to stay in the sky.*

Monut chuckled, his deep voice rumbling. *You are not built for riding, little one. That is why you are so small.*

Huh? Cyrra huffed. *I'm much bigger than a lot of other dragons!*

Yes, you are. But you are still only half our size. That is why we carry the humans and their weapons.

The brown-and-beige-striped dragon tripped slightly and lost her footing. Slowly, she pried each leg from the ground and continued walking. *I just don't see why you large dragons get to have all the fun. It was fun giving Samara a ride, but she was just way too heavy—and she's thin.*

A *crack* sounded behind them. Grabbing the hilt of her sword, Emelyne turned to see what had caused the noise.

Cyrra continued. *And because of that, you large dragons get all the glory and praise, and we little dragons are merely ornaments.*

"Cyrra, shush!" Emelyne held a finger to her lips, her eyes peeled in the direction of the noise. Though the dragon wasn't speaking out loud, Emelyne needed silence in her mind as she listened. She didn't think anyone could get through the fence and into Paddosha Palace village confines, but she wanted to be sure. It could even be a bear or large predatory animal, not that she was particularly worried with so many dragons around.

The smaller dragon moved close to Emelyne, her eyes scanning the forest behind them. *What is it?*

Emelyne shook her head. "Shh!"

The *crack* of another twig breaking sounded to the right, and all eyes turned to investigate. The sound was soon followed by that of dried leaves crunching to the rhythm of light footfalls.

"Show ya-self!" Emelyne called, her hand still resting on her sword hilt.

A few moments passed before a small face peered past a large tree trunk. The sweet, serious blue eyes focused on Emelyne. "It's only me. I'm sorry. I really want to see the dragons and the riders train." Maisie shifted from behind the tree. The young girl's long beige pinafore was tucked in around her waist and flowed to the ground.

The princess's hand relaxed by her side. "That's all right. Ya jus' had us on edge with ya sneakin' 'bout behind us. Come on. But ya'll have to stay out of the way, as we're trainin' with weapons today."

I'll watch over her. Cyrra's whole body lit with enthusiasm.

A broad smile spread across Maisie's face, and she skipped toward Emelyne and the two dragons. "This is going to be fun!"

Cyrra walked alongside her to the side of the clearing. *Hello. I'm Cyrra. What's your name?*

"Maisie. It's really nice to meet you. I've seen you around the village with all the other dragons." Wide-eyed, the girl gazed at the dragons, waiting for them to start. "There are so many of you now. I like it."

The large dragons and their respective riders stood in a wide circle, chatting with each other. The love and commitment between the riders and their dragons shone through and seemed to grow every time Emelyne met up with them.

Cyrra plonked her backside down behind Monut and Emelyne. *Phew! I'll be glad to finally get rid of this load.*

Maisie placed a hand on Cyrra's leg. "You are carrying a lot of weapons. It must be very heavy."

Humph! Tell me about it. Cyrra moaned and collapsed, her stomach to the ground.

Emelyne addressed the group, indicating the large pile of saddles on Monut's back. "Good news! As ya can see, ya all have saddles."

All the riders cheered, and each approached Monut as Emelyne stood on his back and passed the saddles down, one by one. "When ya done puttin' them on ya dragons, grab ya weapons from Cyrra's back. After ya chosen ya weapons, ya'll be responsible for bringin' them along for other practices." Emelyne inspected each saddle briefly before she handed them down. Each was a work of art. The sturdy leather had tanned well, remaining thick and strong. For a couple who weren't warriors, they had thought of almost everything the dragon riders would need. There were many slots and pockets to hold different weapons, as well as small sacks to add essential supplies like food and water for long trips. On top of all of that work, they had embroidered decorative edges with swords, bows and arrows, and dragons.

The riders set to work, their combined effort making light work of the task. The saddles were soon on the dragons, weapons slotted in place.

After placing the final saddle on Monut, Emelyne mounted, tucked her weapons into place, and addressed the group. "I know ya have been trainin' with certain weapons on the ground. Now ya goin' to have to practice with these weapons in the air, on ya dragon. Anyone can attack anyone, but please remember, this is jus' a practice. We are usin' real weapons. I don't want anyone hurt badly." She held her sword high. "Prepare ya-selves. This is gonna be a wild ride."

The chilly late afternoon air brushed against Emelyne's face as Monut leaped into the sky, followed by the ten large dragons with their riders. She held her sword steadfast in her hand. As soon as Monut had flown above the treetops, he dived at one of the rising dragons. The female rider saw them coming and drew her sword, ready to strike back. The clang of steel as the swords clashed was deafening. Quickly, they pulled their swords apart and rallied for another attack. Emelyne swung high as Anayah swung low, the princess's force stronger than the slightly older woman's. Emelyne wasn't surprised.

"Looks like I need to get ya workin' in the blacksmith shop to build up ya muscles." Emelyne swung again, but the move was quickly blocked by Anayah. "At least ya have some quick reflexes." She swung a few more times, and Anayah blocked a few more before Emelyne eventually slapped her on the shoulder with the blunt edge of her sword.

An arrow whizzed past Emelyne's head, just missing Anayah. Emelyne yelled, "Oi! Watch where ya aimin' that thing!" She spun to see Kobi flying on Ioldra, a sheepish grin on his face.

"Sorry! I was bumped from the side," he yelled.

"All the more reason to be careful," Emelyne called back. "Ya don't wanna to kill ya own team."

They continued their practice for a while longer, the smaller dragons joining in and attacking from the sides, until the sun had lowered behind the horizon. The group descended to the sound of giggles.

Emelyne smiled. Below her in the clearing, Cyrra was running in circles, sometimes flying a couple of feet off the ground. Maisie was clinging tightly to her back, arms wrapped around her neck. The dragons landed in the clearing, and Cyrra halted, Maisie barely clinging on as she was flung forward.

"Well, look at ya. Ya look like ya havin' fun." Emelyne laughed at Cyrra's excited face. She almost seemed more excited than Maisie.

Maisie straightened and contained herself, her eyes bright in the twilight. "Oh, yes. Lots of fun!" She pressed her hands together as though in prayer. "Can I come do this every day? Please?"

Emelyne chuckled. "I don't see why not." She gave her a stern look. "As long as ya parents approve."

Maisie gigged again as Cyrra rejoiced, dancing from foot to foot.

I've got my own little rider!

The magnificent hues of orange, pink, purple, and blue were soon eaten by the darkness. Monut nudged Cyrra gently. *I think it's time you took the little one back to her parents. They will start to worry if she isn't home in time for supper.*

That I can do. Cyrra wandered off toward the village with an ecstatic Maisie on her back.

Once they were gone, Emelyne called for the riders' attention. "I realize that ya all are probably tired after the long day at work, then dragon-rider trainin', but I need to ask one more thing of ya. Now that there are so many of us, I think we can take turns patrollin' over the village and watchin' out for any unwanted visitors at night. This will give ya more ridin' practice under the cover of darkness, all while helpin' protect the village."

"I'll go first." Kobi stepped forward into the circle, his

hand resting on Ioldra's snout. "I'm keen to get some more practice. Just save me some supper."

Emelyne nodded. "Will do. But I'm sure there'll be enough."

"We'll scout after supper," Anayah chimed as her dragon, Jyzom, clawed at the ground and snorted his enthusiasm.

"Fantastic! As for the rest of ya, I'm starvin'. How 'bout you?" Emelyne asked.

She was met with a roar of approval, and the humans followed her back to the village while the dragons went to hunt in the darkness.

CHAPTER THIRTY

"Is there a river nearby?" Face slackened with sadness, Paxton focused his black eyes on Jojo as he cupped him in his palm—the frog slightly stiffened with rigor mortis.

Samara turned her eyes from the gesture, finding it hard to deal with. "Yes. There is one not too far away where we get our water."

"Can you take me there? I would like to bury Jojo near water. Somewhere nice." He looked up, and Samara still found it hard to meet his gaze. Those black eyes gave her the shivers.

"It's beautiful there." Devi answered for her, seeming to have picked up on how Samara was feeling. "We can both take you there. I don't think you're strong enough to walk on your own yet." She looked at Samara. "It's best to go now, before the sun sets."

Together, they helped Paxton to his feet, hoisting him up by his arms.

Paxton gently placed Jojo in his pocket, and the

women led him out of the cave. He squinted, the sun's bright rays too strong for eyes that had seen nothing but darkness for so long. "So, this is what the outside looks like." He smiled at Samara as though trying to ease some of the tension.

Samara squeezed his arm, focusing straight ahead. "I hope you have a lot more time in it. I know how much you loved the outdoors and nature."

Wingless flight! Just pile it on, why don't you?

Ulrieg, I'm trying to be nice. He could still be the nice Paxton that we love. Samara spoke through their bond as though with gritted teeth.

I know. But things are so tense. You're both acting as though he's about to smother you in evil magic.

I'm really trying not to, but it's hard with his eyes like that.

"Yes, I did and still do." Paxton's voice pulled her out of the conversation with Ulrieg.

"Huh?" Samara looked directly at Paxton, accidentally meeting his eyes.

Paxton smiled, the same smile Samara had fallen in love with. "You were saying how much I loved the outdoors and nature." He searched the trees. "Were you talking to Ulrieg? I haven't seen him yet. He is all right, isn't he?" Aided by the two women, he continued to walk along the slightly rocky river path, water gurgling in the distance.

"He certainly is and just as snarky as ever." Samara gazed around her. "Why don't you show yourself, Ulrieg?"

Dragon moon! It's almost like you planned that. He turned visible, perched in a tree a few feet in front of them. *I'm here, Paxton. It's been a while.*

Paxton smiled at him. "It has. It's nice to see you again."

I wish I could say the same. It's just you look like you've devoured something evil and haven't digested it properly. I'm not quite sure how to take it yet.

Ulrieg! Samara tutted.

Paxton frowned. "What do you mean?" He turned to Samara then Devi.

Samara sighed and frowned up at Ulrieg.

Devi squeezed his arm. "We didn't want to alarm you. You look like yourself… except for your eyes."

"What's wrong with my eyes?" Paxton asked.

Devi took a deep breath. "They're black."

"What?" Paxton yanked his arms free and felt his face, which was paler than the clouds in the sky.

"Honestly, everything else seems the same with you. It's just your eyes." Samara felt bad seeing him so shaken over his eyes being black. "It's only been a little while since you were pulled out of the orb. They may change back to the way they were—beautiful brown, with glowing rings of green when you use your magic. She reached to touch his face, hesitating before pulling back and shifting her touch to his arm."

"What if I've turned evil? Maybe the orb has turned me and the eyes are just the first sign." Paxton looked panicked. "You should probably leave me and go back to your village."

"We're not going to give up on you. Maybe Jojo died to save you and your goodness." Devi rested a hand on his shoulder. "Be patient."

Zion walked close by her side, his eyes wary.

Devi tried to reassure him. "We will continue to insert you with healing power, and hopefully, it'll be enough."

He breathed deeply, his panic settling. "I hope you're right. I don't want to put you or your village in danger." He started forward again. "Let's go bury Jojo. I can at least do that for him, after all he went through."

The women took him to the riverbed a few yards from where they had stopped. He knelt on the stoney bank and dug deep into the rocks lining the river's edge until he found some soil. Gently, he took his familiar out of his tunic pocket, placed him in the ground, held a hand over the burial spot, and closed his eyes. Using his magic, he wrapped the frog in a little coffin made of leaves and twigs. He then covered the coffin with soil and rocks, his face again drained of color from the exertion of using his power.

"Thank you, sweet friend, for being there for me and committing to being my familiar. You were the best. Your friendship meant a lot to me. You will be sorely missed." He sniffed. "This is worse than losing a friend." He looked weak.

Devi rubbed his back. "That is to be expected. Our familiars are bonded to a part of our soul."

Samara hooked her arm in his. "Come, let's get you back to the cave so you can rest. Devi and I will gather any berries, roots, and nuts we can find while the familiars go hunting for meat."

"I could stay by the river while you gather," Paxton said.

Devi shook her head. "I'd rather keep you hidden in case any of the coterie members come looking."

Reluctantly, Paxton nodded.

As they started toward the cave, Devi said, "We need to get you fully rested and nourished so you can walk on your own."

CHAPTER THIRTY-ONE

After almost a week of waiting in the dank cave, Paxton had finally recovered enough to leave. He was still very weak and slow at walking. The trip back to the village was going to be slower than it had been for Samara and Ulrieg. To conserve energy, they didn't erect any more barriers when they left the cave. They did, however, continue to look behind them to make sure they weren't being followed. The road was long and hard, and avoiding the border patrol, centaurs, and ogres required a lot of stops and detours.

They finally reached the kingdom of Slosiaran, putting Wraeyanor behind them. Paxton's eyes remained black, still no sign of the brown ones that had once gazed at Samara affectionately. Samara missed the way he used to look at her. The situation was made worse because they were stuck between villages, with no access to a library or materials for Paxton to do his own research.

"This will do for the night." Samara dropped her bag between some bushes in a small clearing. Her feet and body ached from all the walking, and she was certain the others were hurting too. The mountain blocking the Merciless Sanctuary towered in the distance, and thought of the place brought Samara fond memories of the time Monut and several other dragons were in hiding there.

Ulrieg spoke through their bond. *I guess we're going hunting.*

Yes, please, sweet bonded. Samara fluttered her eyelashes at him.

Ulrieg pushed off the branch where he'd been sitting, and Zion padded in the other direction.

Devi gathered leaves and twigs for kindling as Samara and Paxton collected a few logs and branches. They pooled the resources in a slight valley, hoping to keep the fire partially hidden.

After piling the leaves then the twigs, Samara ignited the pile with a small flame from her palm. Her father had taught her this trick when they'd been poor and were living in a barn. The uncontrolled and almost explosive nature of her magic was now a distant memory from before her time as an apprentice of the coterie. She piled thicker branches on top of the fire, eventually adding a couple of logs. Once satisfied the fire would burn successfully, she pulled away from it to find Paxton gone. "Did you see where Paxton went?"

Devi stirred a small traveling pot Samara had brought with her from the village then threw in a few tea leaves and placed it over the fire. "I think he's just gone for some fresh air." She sniffed the tea, seemingly satisfied with the strength of the smell. "I think he might need some alone time to process everything he's been through."

Samara sat on a log beside her, watching her work. "Does he seem the same to you?"

Devi paused from stirring and gazed at her. "Yes, I think so. I haven't noticed any difference in his mannerisms."

Samara watched the embers dance when she poked the fire. "True, but I'm still worried that the black eyes mean something."

"As I said to Paxton, it's too early to tell. They may change back. And it may just be a side effect." Devi tapped the stick on the side of the pot, the resulting *clang* loud in the quiet of the early evening. She poured some tea into two cups.

Samara took the cup by the edges, careful not to burn her hands. "I hope you're right. I don't want to lose him and his power to the dark side."

"We'll deal with that if it comes. Just do what you're doing and keep a good eye on him." Devi blew on her tea.

A soft thud sounded next to Samara, and she jumped, spilling some of her tea. Ulrieg's black form appeared in the firelight as he dropped an opossum at her feet.

Dinner is served. Ulrieg bowed mockingly, one wing folded over his abdomen, the other spread to the side.

"That was quick." Samara blinked.

I have a slight advantage. You know. It's called turning invisible. They never see me coming. He showed off his white and very pointy teeth.

"Ha." Samara nudged him playfully before taking the animal and preparing it to roast.

Not long after, Zion crept up quietly, his pawfalls softer than a mouse, and laid a rabbit at Devi's feet.

"Wonderful catch, Zion," Devi said before he took off with Ulrieg to catch their own meal.

A wolf howled in the distance, the sound easily heard over the crackling of the fire. Samara placed her opossum on a long stick and set it over the fire to roast before pulling her cloak over her shoulders to combat the cool autumn air. Soon Devi had finished preparing the rabbit and placed it next to the opossum.

Samara sucked in a deep breath. She quite liked sitting around a campfire and often found it relaxing. She would enjoy it even more if she didn't have to look over her shoulder all the time.

A movement caught her eye several yards away. She looked, expecting to see Paxton. Instead, she saw an owl perched on a low branch. She searched the nearby area for Paxton, but he was nowhere to be seen. She hoped he hadn't collapsed somewhere. Shaking her head, she reprimanded herself. He hadn't shown any signs of weakness lately. He hadn't completely recovered, but he looked far from the point of passing out. She should leave him be. Everyone needed their space.

She turned the opossum and rabbit to cook them evenly. Thanks to the familiars, they had plenty to eat this night. She could've caught her own food with her arrows, but Ulrieg knew she hated being the one to kill animals.

A strange laugh echoed in the distance. It sounded inhuman. She shivered. For some reason, it reminded her of how Mystique used to make her feel when she stared at her with those slitted yellow cat eyes. Something had always seemed off and often made her feel uneasy. She didn't know why until she found out the cat had been suspicious of her. Samara had been so naive to think she could get away with pretending the owl was her familiar and that Callista would believe it. As if she could fool a powerful sorceress who'd had five hundred summers to grow wise and who'd likely witnessed nearly every trick under the sun. Samara was glad to no longer be in the sights of the black jaguar and her bonded.

The night darkened further, and an owl hooted in the distance. Samara pulled her cloak tighter around her shoulders. She sniffed, the cool night air causing her nose to run. She felt a strange tension in the air and shifted her attention to the noises of the night, realizing everything had grown quiet. The darkness had become eerie. The only noise was the crackling of the fire. She scanned the trees surrounding them, searching for anything amiss.

Suddenly, Paxton emerged from the trees, his gait confident and strong, his footfalls almost silent. He looked revitalized. The change was disconcerting. His eyes focused on Samara, and in the firelight, his irises were vaguely visible—like the whites of his eyes were reclaiming their space. Yet his irises remained black. He smiled at her, and Samara could almost see the old Paxton, the one who had been there for her before his terrible stint in the orb.

Her heart softened. Perhaps he was completely the Paxton from before. As to where he got the additional strength, she did not know.

As he strode into the clearing, Devi watched him, her expression wary. She stood. "You look different." Unlike Samara, who had been disarmed by his smile, she seemed on edge.

Confused, Samara observed him more closely. "Did something happen to you while you were gone?"

The smile on his face broadened as he stepped closer to the fire. "You won't believe what has happened."

A shadow lurked behind him, then out of the darkness of the trees emerged a hyena. Lit by the firelight, it was clearly the size of Ulrieg, almost reaching Paxton's waist.

Samara quickly reached for her bow lying next to her, nocked an arrow, and pointed it at the creature.

Paxton moved in front of her. "This is Mynete, my new familiar."

Stunned, Samara froze, arrow still in place.

Paxton approached and pushed the tip down. "It's all right. She's with me."

Mynete cackled, and Samara realized that was the noise she'd heard in the distance earlier.

Still looking on edge, Devi moved closer. "Wow! You move fast. We didn't even know it was possible, yet you've achieved it quickly."

Paxton's smile broadened even more. "She approached me out of nowhere. Isn't she a sweetie?"

Samara looked at the humpbacked creature with small hips and a wicked smile. "It's an interesting match." She exchanged glances with Devi, finding her thoughts confirmed in the instructor's face. Hyenas were known to be nasty, deceptive creatures.

Scratching Mynete behind the ears, Paxton seemed radiant. "I didn't expect to find a familiar this quickly. Our bond has already given me extra strength, physically and mentally." He stretched out his hand, fingers spread, to the nearest tree. Roots slowly grew from the earth, intertwining as they rose from the soil.

The surrounding darkness and Paxton's spell pulled Samara's mind back to her recent nightmares of rapidly-growing roots wrapping around to secure and pin her, exposing her to danger.

As if feeling her distress, Paxton stopped, allowing the roots to return into the ground.

Still, the look in his eyes made her uneasy.

CHAPTER THIRTY-TWO

"Princess Emelyne!" Sweat beaded on Kobi's forehead as he ran up to her in the middle of an evening supper in the noisy tavern. "There's a small group of people heading this way. They should be at the dragon gate in a short while."

Emelyne frowned, balancing her bowl on her lap. "Who's crazy enough to visit a village at night?" Shaking her head, she put her empty bowl on the bar bench, swallowed the remaining bite of freshly baked bread, and chased it down with the last of her ale. She clapped her hands. "All right. I'll get Monut an' have a look to see who it is."

"Ya should have someone else doin' this for ya." Her ma dipped a chunk of bread into her stew and swirled it around, casting Emelyne a concerned glance.

Emelyne sighed. "I will, but at the moment, I'd rather check out things like this me-self, until the villagers are more competent."

"All right, then." Gibobo sighed and reached up to place a caring hand on her shoulder. "Be safe."

She rubbed her mother's shoulder. "I will. Besides, I have Monut."

The village was well lit. Sconces on every wall illuminated the village square and buildings lining the path, giving her a clear walkway to the front gates.

She called Monut through their bond. *Monut! Can ya give me a lift to see this small group comin'?*

I'll meet you at the front of the village.

I'm almost there. She passed the last of the houses and headed into the darkness, where Monut joined her moments later.

He snorted and shook his head. *Should I put on my vicious face?*

I don't know. They could be friendlies. She climbed onto his bare back, as she had removed his saddle earlier, after the dragon-riding practice. Although Emelyne felt more secure with the saddle, she didn't mind flying bareback. She had complete faith that if she fell, Monut would catch her.

Before long, Monut spotted the group. *There are only three beings. That's not many.*

That depends on whether they are magic wielders. If they are from the coterie, three is still many. Emelyne squinted, trying to make out the figures. They weren't much bigger than dots and were difficult for her to see in the darkness, especially since Monut was flying through cloud cover.

Oh, that's not good.

What's not? She tightened her grip under his scales as she peered farther over his side.

They have two animals with them, skirting the outside. They could be familiars.

Emelyne groaned. *I can't see that far. Is there any way we can get closer?*

Something dark appeared in front of Monut, and he swerved at the last second, narrowly missing it. *What are you doing, you weirdo? You nearly ran into me.*

Peering behind them, Emelyne spotted the black dragon. "Ulrieg!"

Nah. I'm some other black creature that looks just like a dragon. He snorted a small plume of fire. *What're you two doing all the way up here? Can't you see it's Samara in the middle?*

Monut slowed down, allowing the smaller dragon to keep up.

"We were keepin' our distance in case ya were coterie members," Emelyne explained.

The black dragon's wings flapped twice as quickly as Monut's. *Well, you got that right. That's three coterie members down there. The only difference is that they are now ex-coterie members.*

When I saw two animals traveling with them, I worried that they were familiars. Monut began a slow descent.

"Who are the other two people?" Emelyne asked.

One is an instructor from the coterie, and the other is Paxton. Ulrieg descended with them.

"Isn't Paxton Samara's beloved?" Emelyne gazed over the side of Monut, trying to get a better look.

Yes, he certainly was. There was a strange tone in the black dragon's voice.

"What do ya mean 'was'?" Emelyne knew how much Samara had missed him.

Well, I guess he still kind of is. It's just that his time in the orb changed him. He could be the same person, but you'll see what I mean when you meet him.

They circled down, catching the attention of the three on the ground. The two animals on either side narrowed in. Emelyne was shocked to see a copper-colored wolf beside a tall, thin elven woman. She moved with grace and carried herself with confidence, her hair short and spiky with a salmon-colored tinge. On the other side of Samara was a young man with semipointed ears similar to Samara's and a low dark ponytail. Even through his expression of surprise, his face was plain and kind looking. But when she looked into his eyes, she was taken aback. They were unnatural. She didn't know whether the moonlight was landing strangely on his face or his eyes really were black.

Quickly, Emelyne slid off Monut's back, approached Samara, and lightly backhanded her upper arm. "Hello, stranger!" She grinned. "Nice to have ya back. Did ya knock off a few coterie members while ya were there?"

Samara shook her head. The pink coloring was completely gone from her hair, and it had grown a little longer during her time away. "I'm afraid not. Devi came to help me get Paxton out, but she ended up needing to flee as well. I thought you wouldn't mind an extra set of magical hands. Not only that, but she's also my defense arts instructor."

"In that case, ya more than welcome." Emelyne smiled.

Samara indicated the man beside her. "And, Princess, this is Paxton."

Emelyne waved a quelling hand. "Please, call me Emelyne. I'm lovin' pullin' these people together an' seein' the changes for the better, but I ain't need all this royalty stuff." Though she half joked, she couldn't get over the blackness of his eyes. She thought at times she caught a glimpse of the whites of his eyes, but the moon wasn't bright enough. Ulrieg had been right. She hoped Samara knew what she was doing and that her beloved hadn't been tainted by an evil force.

"Thank you." Paxton inclined his head. "I hope I can help. It's wonderful to finally see a true dragon rider. I researched as much as I could at the Sacred Flame's library. They had redacted a lot of information about the dragons, although some things, I could just barely make out."

When Emelyne noticed the animal standing next to him, she struggled not to flinch. "Is that a hyena?"

"Yes." Paxton straightened his shoulders. "Mynete is my new familiar."

"Jojo, his original familiar, died in the orb," Samara interjected. "We think to protect Paxton. It's unusual for a sorcerer from the Sacred Flame coterie to bond with a second familiar."

"Oh. All right. It's strange to think of a hyena as friendly." Emelyne frowned, feeling unsure. Hopefully Samara was seeing things clearly when it came to her beloved. Emelyne glanced at the teacher. The elven lady seemed sensible and caring. Perhaps she would say something to Samara if she thought something was wrong with Paxton.

Monut turned and started to walk toward the village, Ulrieg beside him. The group followed while Samara told the story of Paxton's rescue and their narrow escape. Emelyne updated Samara on the centaur attack and their progress rebuilding the village. Soon they reached the metal dragon gate, and the guard opened the doors wide.

Emelyne splayed her arms as they stepped through. "Welcome to our village."

CHAPTER THIRTY-THREE

Samara couldn't believe the difference. "Wow! The village looks spectacular!" Eyes wide, her head swung from side to side as she studied all the work that had been completed while she was away.

Emelyne looked bashful. "We started from the main street an' are workin' our way back through the village to the edges. Since the weather has cooled off, the villagers have insisted on startin' on the palace. That's probably a good thing. Now visitors have somewhere to sleep. The inn is full of villagers still waitin' on their homes to be made livable. We have managed to pick up the pace since the dragons came back from Dragoria—with extra dragons."

"They have?" Samara spun to look at Emelyne. "And there are more dragons?"

"There sure are. An' we have more dragon riders." Emelyne smiled and eyed Monut affectionately as he walked close behind her.

"Wait, you found Dragoria?" Paxton asked Emelyne.

"Actually, Samara an' Ulrieg found Dragoria. The dragons who were hiding with Monut in the Merciless Sanctuary went to visit the realm recently an' brought back a few more dragons."

He turned to Samara. "You didn't tell me that."

"Sorry. I was distracted, worried about whether you were going to heal properly and be your normal self," Samara explained.

He pushed his lips to one side. "Fair enough. I'd love to hear about it later." He addressed Emelyne. "Did they bring any guardian dragons?"

Emelyne shook her head. "The guardian dragons decided to stay in Dragoria for now."

"That makes sense." Samara rubbed her chin. "They have more to do with the elven side, as that's where the dragon elves should live. Because of their size, I imagine they would be safer in Dragoria until they find their dragon elf."

"Have you opened a portal into the elven side?" Devi asked Samara.

Samara shook her head. "I have a lot of work to do yet. I'll have to look into that as soon as Paddosha Palace village is fully established and their defenses are strong enough." She glanced sideways at Paxton, her mind awash with worry for his wellbeing.

"Can we see the dragons?" Devi asked.

"They're out huntin'. They could be gone a while." Emelyne led them along the main road, which was illuminated by sconces.

People passed by, eyeing the strangers with their familiars.

Ulrieg snorted. *Jeesh! Anyone would think we'd brought*

the enemy into the village by the way they're looking at the newcomers.

I can't blame them after all the trouble they have had with the coterie. It's safer for them to be apprehensive. Samara watched a couple walk partially backward after they had passed, making sure to get a good look at the ex-coterie members and their familiars.

Paxton breathed in deeply. "What's that smell? It smells so good."

"I'll show ya." Emelyne led them to the village square, where the food stalls were set up for supper and the tavern was almost bursting at the seams with joyous villagers getting their fill of food and ale. "Ya must be hungry." She motioned to the stalls. "We've pooled our resources while the village is bein' rebuilt. Even the food is prepared in bulk. Help ya-self. I'm goin' to grab me-self an ale. Ya can either grab some of this for ya familiars, or ya can send them outside the village to hunt their own. As long as they don't eat our livestock." Her expression seemed apprehensive when she looked at Mynete, but the princess quickly wiped it away.

The hyena seemed to mock her with her mouth open, showing off her teeth.

"Once ya have had ya fill, I'll show ya where ya sleepin'."

Samara, Paxton, and Devi huddled together after sending their familiars to hunt in the wild.

Samara studied the different stalls manned by villagers serving up food, and her eyes landed on a very familiar face. "Look who it is." She hurried over to the stall, and Devi and Paxton followed. "Forgrac!" She opened her arms, and the dwarf ducked out from behind the stall to give her a hug. "I missed you."

"Aye! I missed ya more." The dwarf hugged her tightly. He nodded to Devi. "Nice to see ya, instructor. Thanks for keepin' an eye out for me favorite apprentice."

"It's the least I could do," Devi said. "She did most of the work herself."

"Rubbish," Samara objected. "She did much more than that."

"An' ya saved Paxton." The smile faltered when his eyes connected with Paxton's, but he quickly changed his expression to be more upbeat. "It's nice to see ya." He tapped Paxton lightly on the arm with his palm. "Let me get ya some food." He dashed to his stall, grabbed some plates, and served up some freshly roasted vegetables and mutton topped with gravy. "They have me runnin' the cookin' side of things." He handed them each a plate, which they accepted gratefully.

"An' he's been doin' a brilliant job too." Emelyne joined them, slurping down a large gulp of ale from her tankard.

"Of course he has," Devi interjected, lifting a spoonful of roasted potato to her mouth. "The food quality at the coterie increased greatly after Forgrac became our cook." She groaned as she savored the potato.

Although they had been getting their fill of meat and berries, the properly cooked and seasoned food tasted so much better. Even eating off a plate was a luxury. Samara had packed lightly for her journey, and Devi and Paxton had nothing to carry since they'd exited the coterie with no notice.

"Forgrac, you've outdone yourself again." Paxton

complemented him as he forked roasted meat into his mouth.

The dwarf waved his hand dismissively. "Aye, ya too kind. It's jus' ya haven't eaten a proper meal for so long, bein' stuck in that orb an' all."

"Don't dismiss it. You're a wonderful cook, as always," Samara said. "The village is lucky to have you."

Forgrac looked bashful. "Ya such a sweet girl. No wonder I was drawn to ya at the coterie." He turned to Emelyne. "She was the first apprentice to actually pay attention to me after eighteen summers of servin' at the coterie. She acted like I was jus' like her. All the others, includin' the instructors, acted like I didn't exist. Like all their maintenance an' cookin' jus' did itself." He shook his head.

Emelyne nudged Samara playfully and snorted. "I knew I liked ya for a reason—once I got past the distrust from ya coterie hair." She chuckled then halted quickly as she eyed Devi's short salmon-colored hair. She slapped a hand over her mouth.

Devi kindly dismissed her comment. "It is weird how they want our hair to be so bright. Paxton's wasn't so bad when he was in the coterie, as it was a deep green. But yes, brilliant pink or salmon aren't blending colors. Makes me think they force the colors so they can find us easily if we try to escape."

Ahh! Samara! Samara! It's so good to see you. I've got something for you.

Recognizing the voice, Samara turned to find the overly energetic dragon. "Cyrra!" She placed her plate on a bench nearby.

The dragon jogged from the far side of the courtyard,

from the direction of Paddosha Palace village's woods, a bag slung over her neck. Her eyes were lit with enthusiasm, and she was followed by a trail of dragons of different sizes.

"Wow!" Paxton muttered beside her as he and Devi observed them in awe.

Cyrra stopped short a couple of yards from Samara, spotting her companions. *Oh, hello, new people.* She spotted Devi's salmon hair and leaned in close to Samara, her voice changing to a whisper. *Did you know that lady's from the coterie?*

Samara placed a hand gently on her jaw. "Yes, that is Devi. She was my defense arts instructor, but she's on our side."

Cyrra pulled up straight. *Oh, good. You had me worried there for a second.* She turned to Paxton and pulled back. *What's wrong with your eyes?*

Samara could feel the tension radiating off Paxton, but still he faced the dragon. "I'm sorry if they scare you. It seems to be a side effect from being trapped in the orb for so long. We're hoping they'll return to normal soon."

Yeah, they are kind of scary. Cyrra giggled. She turned back to Samara. *Anyway, before I forget, this bag is for you.* She lowered her head so Samara could lift the bag from her neck. *It's from the guardian dragons. They wanted you to have it.*

"Really?" Samara retrieved the leather bag, placed it on the bench, and pulled it open. Inside was a large leather-bound book that looked worn and very old. Carefully, she retrieved it and opened the cover to find the title page. "Ancient Magical Spells." Her eyes widened with wonder, and she began to turn the pages, glancing through the different spells.

"What a fantastic book." Paxton peered over her shoulder.

Samara glanced up at Devi. "Do you know these spells?"

Devi took a look as Samara flicked through a couple more pages. "No. Many of these are new to me. We should pore through this book together." She looked at Cyrra. "Did you say the guardian dragons sent this?"

Cyrra jigged from talon to talon, her eyes expectant. "Yes. Did I do good?"

"You did very well, Cyrra. This book is going to be cherished. It may give us more ammunition against the coterie," Samara said.

"Spells that they may not be able to combat," Devi added, eyeing a particular spell.

CHAPTER THIRTY-FOUR

Exhausted from their long travel, Emelyne had organized for four canisters to be filled with ale and led the newcomers to the palace to show them their rooms.

Samara was grateful for somewhere to rest and looked forward to a relaxing bath, keen to clean off the smell and dirt from their long travels. The princess also organized new clothes for them. Once they were clean and well rested, they would look around the village some more and take Paxton to see his parents. The rooms were sparse, decorated with limited basic furniture, yet they looked clean and comfortable—stone walls on all sides, with a window and a thick wooden door.

She was amazed by how much the villagers had accomplished with the dragons' help while she was away.

She left the window open for Ulrieg, glad she didn't have to go to the front door to let him in. Feeling groggy after finishing the ale and taking a nice warm bath, she pulled back the blankets on her bed and slipped between the sheets, resting her back on the firm yet soft surface. Her muscles thanked her for it, and she had almost fallen asleep when Ulrieg called to her through the bond.

Samara, where are you?

I'm in the palace, on the second floor. I'll stand near the window so you can see me. She flung back the blankets, the cool night air wrapping around her. Shivering in her thin white nightdress and keen to return to the bed's warmth, she peered out the window at the flickering flames of the sconces lining the main street and village square. The firelight gave the newly renovated part of the village a certain charm.

A push of wind blew back her hair, and she stood to the side, giving Ulrieg room to land. His talons clacked on the windowsill, and he turned visible. His glowing red eyes surveyed the room. *Paxton's not in here?*

Samara felt her cheeks warm. She hadn't invited Paxton in. She probably should have, as he might need some reassurance and comfort, but her emotions were unsteady around him. "No. I kind of need some time alone to process everything. Maybe being alone and getting a good night's sleep will help him heal quicker."

Ulrieg tossed his head. *I don't blame you. I was mainly asking so I could speak freely.*

"I don't think that has stopped you before."

You're right. But I thought I shouldn't say this in front of him at the moment, not until we know what is going on with him.

Samara tiptoed back to her bed and drew the blankets up, longing for the warmth to embrace her again. "What is it you want to say?"

His familiar is a nasty eater. It's very disturbing.

"What do you mean?"

The way she kills her prey and tears it apart. I mean, it's just nasty.

"Don't you and Zion kill your prey and tear them apart?"

Ulrieg snorted. *Yes, but Mynete tears from the stomach, before the creature is dead. It's unsettling!*

Samara pressed her lips together. "I don't know. She is a hyena. They aren't known to be nice."

That's an understatement, from what I saw. I hope it's just that. Otherwise, I'd be getting worried about Paxton's state of mind.

She wrapped a strand of hair around her finger and tugged. "I admit, I'm worried. But I'm trying to be open-minded and hoping for the best for Paxton."

As long as you're aware. You're often naïve, and that worries me at times, especially when it comes to matters of your heart.

"I've definitely been guilty of that in the past, but I think I'm getting better. I'd be lying if I said I didn't long for the Paxton prior to the time in the orb. I miss him greatly in many ways."

Ulrieg paced the floor, his talons clacking on the stones. *Well, I've told Monut to get one of the smaller dragons who can fit inside the corridor to guard Emelyne's room.*

"Really?"

He stopped and faced her, his red eyes glowing with determination. *I'd rather be safe than sorry. And that's what I told him. We can't lose the princess, especially to someone we brought with us. I think the whole plan to squash the coterie would die with her. It would be much harder to rally the people if their leader was gone.*

"You're right, of course." Samara lay down and stared at the ceiling. "I hope it's just a side effect, like he said. We could really use his help."

~

A TAP SOUNDED at the door, stirring Samara from her slumber. She lay still with her eyes closed, her body half asleep. The tapping sounded again. Her body was rocked roughly.

Samara, get up. Ulrieg's talons dug into her arm as he shook her again. *There's someone at the door.*

She groaned, stretching under the covers, and cracked open an eye. "But it's not even light yet."

I think it's close to dawn. I can feel it in the air, and there are birds chirping in the distance. He shook her again.

"All right. All right. I'm getting up." Throwing back her blankets, she sat up and kicked her legs over the side of the bed before shuffling sleepily to the door.

The person banged again when she was a yard away, startling her. She placed a hand over her heart to calm it before turning the handle and pulling the door open. Paxton stood on the other side, his face cast in eerie shadows from the sconce burning in the corridor. Mynete sat open-mouthed behind him. Samara pulled her eyes away from the strange creature and focused on Paxton.

Stifling a yawn, she said, "Morning, Paxton. Is something wrong?"

His gaze traveled over her thin nightgown, and he grinned. "No, I thought maybe you would like to go for an early-morning walk."

She used to love the way he looked at her and felt

some of that old bashfulness come over her again. This was the guy who had seen through to her heart, who had helped her rescue dragons and research the coterie's history. The person who had seen through the facade of insincere people like Kaine. He deserved her time. He probably needed help to heal his heart after what he had been through. She nodded.

"Just give me a couple of minutes to get dressed." She closed the door.

You know I'll be following you, right? And watching his every move. Ulrieg's talons clacked on the floor before he pounced onto the foot of her bed.

"I wouldn't expect anything else." She changed into a clean beige tunic with a pale-blue pinafore then tied a belt around her waist, brushed her hair quickly, and pulled on her boots.

Just before she opened the door, Ulrieg turned invisible.

Paxton, still waiting on the other side, peered past her. "Where's Ulrieg?"

"I'm sure he'll follow." She closed the door behind her.

Their boots stomped softly on the stone floor as they left the corridor and descended the stairs to the front door.

"How are things going with your new familiar?" Samara peered over her shoulder to see Mynete watching her with deep-brown eyes. When her mouth was closed, the hyena looked almost cute.

He opened the door and led her outside, a faint light rising in the east. "We are getting to know each other. I miss Jojo and didn't get much time to mourn him, but

Mynete is helping me get past that. That is why I came to get you."

Samara frowned. "I don't understand."

Paxton grabbed her hand, and she let him. Warmth flooded through her arm as memories of how special he used to make her feel came flooding back.

He squeezed her hand. "I don't know how my power has been affected by what I've been through and the change of familiar, so I'd like to practice, but I wanted your company." He faced her, the sconces along the street lightly illuminating his face. "I have complete trust in you. I also can see how my eyes are affecting you. I think they are clearing, but if I was in your shoes, I would find them scary too."

With a few words, he had not only acknowledged how uncomfortable he was making her but had also exonerated her of any guilt. That was the Paxton she knew and loved.

He continued, "I would also like to sort out some of this and hopefully lose the blackness in my eyes before I see my family again. It would be hard for them to accept."

She squeezed his hand in return. "Then let's go and work this out."

CHAPTER THIRTY-FIVE

When Monut told Emelyne he had organized a dragon guard, she almost laughed. But when he said whom he wanted to protect her from, she understood. She was excellent in physical fights, but Paxton was a sorcerer. Not only that, but he had also been trapped in the dark magic of the orb for so long they didn't know for sure which side he was on. Monut waited the whole night outside her window just in case the dragon on guard saw him approaching Emelyne's room. If that happened, she would climb onto his back through the window, and they would fly to safety. She had to give it to him. It was a clever escape plan considering they could have brought an enemy directly into her palace. Still, she hoped that wasn't the case.

When morning split the darkness and pushed it from the sky, Emelyne woke and got ready for another day.

Morning, my bonded. Monut's snout stuck through her window. *I hope you slept well.*

"I did. Thanks. I felt very safe knowin' ya were at me

window an' a decent-sized dragon was guardin' me door." She dressed in her riding leathers, strapped her sword to her hip, and exited the room.

Standing outside her door was one of the new dragons. He had a thin build and was beige with black dots. Smaller than Cyrra yet larger than Ulrieg, he filled most of the narrow corridor.

She addressed him. "And who do we have here?"

I am Chorug, from the land of Dragoria. The dragon sounded formal, much like Monut.

"Nice to meet ya. Thanks for ya protection last night. I hope ya didn't have any trouble."

No trouble at all. Not even a mouse.

Emelyne slapped her thigh as she laughed. "Fantastic! I guess the palace is too new. Plus, we're too far from the kitchen to attract mice." She turned to leave but halted. "I'm goin' out for the day, so you're free to go. Thanks again."

I'm happy to do it again if the princess needs my service.

"I may need ya tonight. Come. Follow me out an' go do as ya wish." She trailed down the corridor and descended the stairs, Chorug following closely behind. Emelyne stopped in front of Samara's door and knocked.

The young sorceress and her dragon aren't in there. They went for a walk with the black-eyed man and his hyena just before light.

When Emelyne gave him a questioning look, he explained, *Ulrieg kept me informed after he found out I was guarding your door.*

She looked up at him. "So ya could've finished ya duty much earlier."

I wouldn't leave you alone. I didn't know if they would come back while you were still asleep.

"Ya take ya job very seriously." Emelyne smiled at him and continued down the stairs to the bottom level, out the large palace doors, and into the bustling courtyard. People filled the village square, grabbing their breakfasts of freshly baked pastries or bread.

Chorug headed out of the village toward the woods as Emelyne joined the villagers for breakfast. She spotted Devi, who was hard to miss with her spiky salmon-colored hair. The defensive arts instructor breezed through the crowd, her long brown gown sweeping across the pebbled street as she sauntered through the stalls. The light-copper-hued wolf sullied with flecks of gray padded by her side, his eyes alert as he studied the surroundings. There was a gracefulness in both of them as the elf and wolf moved among the villagers.

After grabbing a couple pastries, Emelyne jogged to catch up with the sorceress. "Good mornin', Sorceress!"

The elegant elf turned to face her. Her brown eyes shone with warmth. She looked to be in her thirties, but Emelyne wouldn't be surprised if she was a lot older. Elves rarely showed their age. "Good morning, Princess. Thank you for your hospitality last night. It was very nice to sleep in a bed after all this time. And please, call me Devi."

She threw back her head. "Ha. Then ya gotta call me Emelyne. And if ya a friend of Samara's and help the village, ya welcome in me palace anytime."

"Thank you, again. It's been a long time since we left the coterie. It is nice to find some hospitable people." Her familiar shifted closer and listened to their conversation, his eyes assessing Emelyne.

The princess chuckled. "Don't worry, I'll find some way for ya to pay me back. No one stays in the village for free."

After a quick scan of the bustling villagers around her, Devi shook her head. "No. I can see you have everyone busy. But again, everyone is also fed and provided for, by the looks of things. That is a sign of a true leader." She picked up a large chunk of bread, broke some off, and popped it into her mouth. "When you think of some way I can contribute, let me know."

Emelyne snorted as though the sorceress had made a joke. She slapped her lightly on the upper arm. "I'm sure I'll put ya to good use if the coterie come knockin'. We need more magical power to go against them. Someone with ya skills."

The elven sorceress only inclined her head graciously and accompanied Emelyne as she passed through the village, wishing others a good morning as they passed through the streets peacefully on their way to work. The villagers seemed to be in good spirits. Though they eyed the sorceress apprehensively, they clearly trusted Emelyne's choice of companions. Emelyne grabbed some extra pastries and led the sorceress to her father's blacksmith shop. The autumn breeze was cool, but it couldn't have been a clearer day.

Emelyne. Something is wrong. In three words, Monut had shattered her peaceful morning.

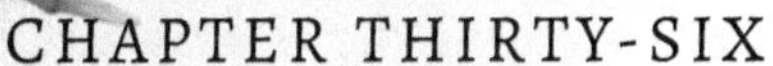

CHAPTER THIRTY-SIX

Samara and Paxton walked to the woods behind Paddosha Palace village, Mynete several yards behind them and Ulrieg visible in the trees, leaping from branch to branch. Unable to help it, Samara glanced repeatedly over her shoulder at the hyena. She didn't know why she found her so disconcerting. The familiar wasn't doing anything wrong, although the cackling she made every now and then was definitely off-putting. The branches above rustled, bringing Samara comfort at the knowledge Ulrieg was close by.

The morning wind seemed extremely cool. She pulled her long brown cloak tighter around her shoulders, feeling the weight of her bow and quiver on her back. They walked in silence for quite some time, observing their surroundings until the sun had crested over the tops of the tall trees.

Keeping Samara's hand in his, Paxton led her past the clearing where the dragons often gathered. They continued to the far edge, just inside the stone wall surrounded by the steel-bar fence. He paused, glancing toward the forest then back, where Samara noticed a gap in the stone wall exposing the several-yard space to the metal-bar fence. It appeared Emelyne had left a few gaps in the stone wall so the villagers didn't feel trapped but still had enough wall to hide behind if attacked.

She didn't want to admit it, but she was still on edge. Until she knew for sure Paxton was the same person and hadn't been influenced by the orb's power, she didn't want to let her guard down. "Is there anything in particular you are looking for?"

His black eyes connected with hers, and he shook his head. "No. I'm looking for privacy and nature. As you know, my magical specialty was related to healing and nature." He released her hand and removed his bag from his back. "Besides, I picked us up some breakfast before I came to get you."

Mynete stopped several feet away at the edge of the woods, staring at the stone wall and the gap to the steel fence. Ulrieg perched in the trees and caught a bird to munch on.

Sitting with his back against a tree, Paxton pulled out a package and unwrapped the rough fabric to reveal a large chunk of bread, a few pastries, and two fresh apples.

Samara sat near him, a smile on her lips. "What a sweet gesture! And I thought we were out here for just business." She selected a pastry with strawberry filling and took a bite. She groaned. The pastries were still a little warm. It had been so long since she had eaten proper meals and fresh-baked goods.

Paxton offered her wine from a canteen, and she took a large swig.

"You certainly know your way to a women's heart." She savored another bite of the pastry.

He grinned. "I know you've had a rough trip to rescue me. I would've invited Devi, but you know what they say—three's a crowd. Besides, you should always have a good breakfast before you get to work."

Her guard softened, opening her heart a little to him again. As she looked at his face and expression, she still had hope he was the old Paxton, not influenced by the orb's power.

Birds sang joyously in the trees as the sun's rays grew stronger, illuminating the sky and chasing away the night's coolness. There was something magical about the early morning. Everything seemed fresh and ready for the new day.

He shifted closer to her so their sides were touching. She leaned into him, resting her head on his shoulder, and he wrapped an arm around her. In that moment, happiness was an understatement. They ate without too much talk. Samara filled him in on things that had happened from the time she had left the coterie until she had rescued him from the orb. Paxton had little to say because he couldn't remember anything from inside the orb.

When they had eaten their fill, the day had already reached midmorning. They rose to their feet and dusted themselves off.

After giving her half a smile, he looked for Mynete. "I think it's time to see what my change of familiar and the time in the orb has done to my powers."

The hyena trotted up to him, looking slightly

disjointed with her high shoulders, low hips, and beige, brown-striped coat. She sat by his feet and pressed up against his long brown pants.

Samara prepared herself, not knowing what Paxton's next move would be.

This is the area where I buried the crystal. Ulrieg's voice cut through her edginess.

She paled and looked around. *Are you sure?*

Yes, it's not far from the palace's underground tunnel exit.

Let's leave it for now. Maybe we should only retrieve it to give it back to the princess. She couldn't see any disturbed dirt. The foliage had grown over the ground, as though nothing had been buried there.

"Here goes." Paxton stood next to a tree on the outskirts of the woods, his voice pulling her away from the conversation with Ulrieg. He closed his eyes, tilted his face to the sky, rubbed his hands together, squatted, then slammed his palm against the earth near his feet.

The ground rumbled, and Samara splayed her arms, feeling uneasy. She hadn't known Paxton could make the ground shake. She spread her feet hip-width apart and braced herself, using her arms for balance. Leaves fell from the branches above, showering around them. A large flock of birds took flight from the trees around them, then the woods became eerily quiet.

Ulrieg grumbled. *What is he doing?*

I don't know. Samara glanced at Paxton, trying to read his expression, but his eyes were still shut. *He doesn't seem to be healing anything.*

It feels more like damage. Almost like he's trying to shake me out of this tree. Argh! I'm taking flight.

Looking up, Samara saw her familiar push off the

branches of the tree and hover several feet above before making his way to the stone wall. The mortar was holding fast and keeping the rocks in place despite the shaking.

Something wrapped around Samara's ankles, tight and uncomfortable. Glancing down, she saw roots reaching up from the earth and grabbing hold of her legs. She gasped, trying to kick them away, but her feet couldn't move. They were already too tight in the roots' embrace.

"Paxton!" she called. She saw that his eyes had opened, his face blank as he stared into the sky.

The darkness in his eyes had deepened. Worry clawed at her heart. Surely her Paxton hadn't turned to the dark side. He'd seemed genuine when he took her hand and led her here.

The roots grew, wrapping farther around her legs. "Paxton!" She called louder. The young sorcerer was too engrossed in his magic, both palms planted on the ground, Mynete cackling as she maintained contact with her bonded.

Samara tried blocking spells, but this wasn't something being thrown at her. The roots were touching her, wrapping closely around her skin. She tried a barrier spell, one she had learned recently from Devi. It did nothing. She grabbed for her quiver, feeling for the hand knife she kept strapped to it. At the same time, she searched for Ulrieg. She couldn't see him. Knowing him, he had probably turned invisible. *Ulrieg! Help!*

A large gash suddenly appeared on Paxton's pale face, crimson dripping down his cheek. He recoiled to the side.

Samara watched for Ulrieg's next attack while clasping the knife firmly and slashing at the roots winding around her legs. The wood was too thick. These weren't vines of fresh green sprigs but roots of old wooden trees, tough and hard to hack through, growing too fast for her surface cuts to have any effect.

Another deep gash sliced up Paxton's shoulder. He didn't even cry out in pain as his tunic was split open and blood oozed down the material. Suddenly, several more roots shot out of the ground around Paxton and Mynete, growing taller than he. The roots swatted from side to side, making it impossible for Ulrieg to get past their defenses.

A thud sounded on the ground near her as though something heavy had been walloped to the ground. *Wingless flight! I'm sorry, Samara. I can't get past those swinging roots.*

I know you'll think of something, Ulrieg. Please do it quickly. I'm running out of time. The roots reached Samara's hips, wrapping around her, quickly ascending her waist. Her lip quivering, Samara called out to the man she loved, her voice desperate. "Paxton!"

He didn't respond, his hand still flat against the earth. The cackling of Mynete made the situation even scarier. It was like something was controlling Paxton, as though he was a mindless creature being used as a pawn to abuse his power.

"Paxton. I know you're in there. You must fight this. This isn't you." She sucked on her bottom lip.

He didn't even glance her way.

"Paxton, please. Fight this." She squeezed her fists. At least the roots weren't squeezing her to death. "Paxton. I know you. You want peace... and for the dragons and the kingdoms on their side to win against the coterie's oppression. Please." She pleaded again. "Fight this." The roots squeezed tighter—but still not too tight—as they reached her shoulders.

Suddenly, the ground started churning as thick, strong roots crawled under the surface. The concentration of roots moved as the roots around Samara reached her neck. The roots under the earth's surface shifted roughly until something hard was ejected from the soil.

She blinked, unable to believe her eyes. The crystal. A little dirty yet still a large semipillar with cut edges and magnificent color. Once the crystal was completely out of the soil, the roots beneath it stopped churning. They seemed to have settled... until more shot through the gap in the stone fence, wrapped around the crystal, then pulled it toward the outward steel fence. The same roots then created ladders over the steel-bar fence and down the other side. Several more roots joined in to create more of the same. Samara couldn't see the full extent of the damage, but she saw parts of ladders spreading past the stone walls, leading her to think he had created even more where she couldn't see.

Paxton stood, the roots around him retreating into the earth. Shoulders broad, ignoring his injuries, he headed to the steel fence. His expression was blank—almost as though no one occupied his body. He grabbed the crystal, hoisted it onto his shoulder with inhuman strength, climbed the ladder, and descended the other side. His hyena familiar squeezed through the steel fence after him.

Samara, barely able to see him through the gap in the stone wall yet still secured by the tree roots, tried again to connect to the sweet man she knew was inside his body somewhere. "Paxton. Wait! This isn't you."

He didn't even look her way as he turned and walked away with the crystal.

The roots wrapped loosely around her face and covered her eyes.

CHAPTER THIRTY-SEVEN

What is it? Emelyne asked through their bond, her hand instinctively grabbing the hilt of her sword.

Monut's large gray form seemed to drop out of the sky before he descended onto the courtyard. *Ulrieg said something has happened to Samara at the back of the woods. She needs help. And bring anything that can cut.* He looked down by her side and spotted her hand still on the hilt of her weapon. *Good. I see you have your sword.*

"I never leave home without it." She smirked.

A gentle but firm hand grabbed her upper arm. "What's going on?"

Turning, Emelyne faced Devi. "Samara is in trouble. I ain't sure exactly how, but I'm guessin' she's bound." The princess climbed up Monut, who had already been saddled.

"Can he carry more than one? I'd like to help." The sorceress's brown eyes were filled with genuine concern.

Emelyne wasn't sure what she was getting herself into. *Monut?*

I believe I can carry two adult beings a short distance. Climb on, Sorceress.

Without hesitation, Devi awkwardly climbed up Monut's side, her skirt wrapping around her legs at inopportune times. Emelyne grasped her hand to help her with the final steps. Devi hitched up her skirt, showing off her slim legs, sat behind the princess, and grabbed her around the waist.

Monut pushed off, and Emelyne felt the sorceress's fingers digging into her as they rose.

"Are ya all right?" Emelyne asked.

"Yes. I'm not the fondest of heights, and I've definitely never done this before." She chuckled.

"This height is nothin'. Monut's only gonna rise jus' over the trees. His favorite place is among the clouds." Emelyne pointed toward the light-gray clouds in the overcast sky.

Devi glanced up. "I think I'll leave that flying for you."

On dragonback, they traveled quickly to the back edge of the woods. In the distance, over the steel fence, Emelyne spotted two figures heading away from the village—one a being and one an animal. She tapped Monut on the shoulder. *Can you see who that is over there?*

The dragon's large gray head turned in the direction Emelyne had indicated, the two horns on his crown framing the figures in the distance. A deep growl reverberated in his throat. *That is the new young wizard. The one that is supposed to be Samara's beloved. He seems to be carrying something big. What has he done?* Monut started to descend as two large figures flew overhead.

Emelyne looked up in time to see two of the large gray dragons flying in the direction of the fleeing sorcerer and his familiar, Ulrieg leading the way.

Monut landed beside the gap in the stone wall. *Samara is around here somewhere.*

They spotted a strange root formation not far from the woods. Emelyne dismounted, followed closely by Devi.

The sorceress motioned toward the root formation. "That looks like the work of Paxton. We need to see if anything is inside."

A muffled sound reached their ears, urging Emelyne into a run. She reached the tower of roots, which were about her height and as thick as her arm. She peered between the cracks. "Samara!" She pulled at the roots, trying to pry them away. They were set, unbudging. She called over her shoulder to Devi as the sorceress approached. "We're gonna need a saw or some very sharp tools to cut through this." She pulled at a different root. "They won't budge."

"I've already had a go at them with my hand knife." Samara's voice echoed out to them. "It did nothing, and it's pretty sharp too."

What about me? Monut stood beside them. *I'll see if my talons will rip through them.*

"Jus' be careful not to scratch or pierce Samara. The roots ain't far from her flesh," Emelyne warned.

I promise I'll be very careful. Monut moved closer. Using his front talons, he grabbed parts of the roots on the outside of the cocoon-like entrapment. The mound shifted slightly with each pull, likely yanking Samara around a little inside, but they wouldn't break. *I think they have been reinforced with magic.*

Samara groaned. "I thought he was getting better too. I guess he had me fooled. I'm so sorry I brought him here."

"Don't beat ya-self up." Emelyne met her gaze through a gap in the roots. "I've been guilty of trustin' people I shouldn't too."

"I'm just as much to blame for this one, Samara. We remained on edge, but as time went on, it felt like he was improving, getting back to the Paxton we used to know." Devi placed a hand on the roots and muttered a spell. Nothing happened. "These must be reinforced in magic. That spell didn't do anything."

"I should have known better, though. I knew him better than anyone at the coterie. I guess he blinded me by impersonating his past self. Especially this morning. He even packed us breakfast before this trip." Samara's sigh echoed through the root cocoon.

"And what would you have done differently? Probably nothing," Devi reassured her.

"I wouldn't have brought him out here, for a start. And I certainly would've kept a better eye on my feet and moved quicker once I saw the roots coming out of the ground." Samara's bottom lip protruded slightly. "I tried to stop them from growing around me, but none of my spells worked."

"So there ain't much ya coulda done," Emelyne summarized. "Stop ya worryin', an' let's get ya outta here." The princess started swinging her sword, the blade creating small nicks in the hard roots. Instead of deterring her, the minute progress seemed to spur her on. She swung and swung until a root finally broke. "It worked for that one, but it's not goin' to be as safe when I get closer to ya skin." She chipped away at more roots. "I might have to go back to the village to get a saw when I get closer to ya flesh."

"I trust you to do your best. The bad news is he also created several ladders over your steel fence. They will have to be removed as well," Samara warned.

"At least they can be cut down with axes." Emelyne paused to catch her breath then set back to work.

"I'll have a look to see how many there are." Devi wandered through the gap in the stone fence and halted before calling over her shoulder, "There are a lot of ladders. You're going to need more help to get them removed."

Two large shadows blocked the sun for an instant, and Emelyne looked up to see the two large gray dragons who had flown over the fences toward Paxton. They landed inside the stone wall. In their talons, one carried Paxton and the other his hyena familiar. By some of the markings on the large dragons' faces, she recognized them as Ioldra, Kobi's dragon, and Jyzom, Anayah's dragon.

Ioldra kept the sorcerer pinned to the ground. *Princess, what would you like us to do with these two?*

Ulrieg landed next to them. *Monut, we couldn't recover the crystal. Can you fly out to get it?*

Emelyne paused and looked at him. "What crystal is this?"

Your crystal, Princess. Ulrieg explained, *Well, one of the ones that belong to Slosiaran, your kingdom. We were waiting for you to have your palace rebuilt before we brought it up. Samara and I saved it from Callista when we visited here the first time.* He stood tall and squeezed his front talons as if to make a point. *I could drag it through the underground, but I'm not big or strong enough to fly it all that distance.*

Hearing this, Monut pushed off to search in the direction Paxton had headed.

Emelyne watched him go then eyed Paxton and Mynete. "Devi, can ya stay with Samara for a short time to make sure she's safe? I'm goin' to lead these dragons to the dungeons an' have our first prisoners locked up. Then I'm goin' to bring back a saw and hopefully some more strong people to cut down these ladders."

"Of course," the sorceress said as Monut returned with the large crystal in his talons.

CHAPTER THIRTY-EIGHT

Sconces lit the wall, and a dank, earthy smell smothered them as they made their way through the wide and tall corridors of the palace underground. Emelyne led the three large gray dragons and their prisoners to the dungeons. No trees or greenery decorated this part of the palace. The lack of sunlight made it almost impossible for any fauna to grow, and the dungeons were far from the underground pool where Princess Bianca had survived the attack on the palace a hundred years ago. Instead, the gray stone walls looked almost orange under the glow of the flames.

She peered over her shoulder, eyeing Paxton and his hyena as they were urged along by the dragons, Monut bringing up the rear as he carried the crystal under one wing.

The sorcerer wasn't what she'd expected from the coterie. He didn't have the evil intent written over his face. Instead, he looked torn—almost disappointed in himself. Samara had held so much faith in him and how he used to be, yet given what he just did, he had clearly turned.

She hoped Samara's judgement and faith in people could be trusted, as she would likely bring more people into the village. Perhaps she got this one wrong because of her love for him. Samara had described Paxton as an intelligent, caring, and affectionate person who showed empathy for the underdogs. Emelyne saw a shadow of this etched in his confused face, contradicted by the black eyes.

They reached the dungeons, and she unlocked two with the key hanging on a wall nearby. Without a struggle, Paxton entered one, and Mynete entered the other. The cells were bare, made of stone—not a chair or bed to be seen and no flora other than a couple of small mossy mounds in the corridor. After locking the barred doors behind them, Emelyne hung the keys back on the hook, out of the prisoners' reach.

I will stand guard for now. Jyzom, Anayah's dragon, stood by the cells.

"Thank you, Jyzom. I will have to organize permanent dungeon guards. I will send some later. But first I must deal with these ladders Paxton has created and finish freeing Samara." Emelyne looked at Paxton briefly, puzzled by his haunted face. If it meant anything, she would deal with it later. She turned to leave.

"I'm sorry, Princess!" Paxton's voice echoed slightly in the empty dungeon. "I didn't mean to do it."

Emelyne faced him. His face looked more distraught than before. She didn't know if it was an act, didn't know if she could trust what he said.

His hands shaking, Paxton's gaze fell to his fingers

with an expression of shock and disgust. "It wasn't my intention to trap Samara like that or to build ladders over your fence. I don't know what came over me."

She approached the cell.

Careful, Princess! Monut dropped the crystal and stormed to the cell bars, towering over the prisoners. *It could be a ruse.*

She touched Monut gently on his large scaly leg and looked into his golden eyes. *I know. I promise I'll be careful.* Turning to Paxton, she studied his face. There was so much remorse there. Still, as Monut had said, it could be an act. She couldn't let her guard down. "Then I'm sure ya understand that we need to leave ya in here. If you truly mean what ya say, ya won't try to escape or cause any trouble."

"Of course, Princess. I understand completely." He looked down to the floor, brunet strands of hair from his ponytail falling over his shoulder. "Can you please tell Samara I'm sorry?"

She hardened her face. "I'll see what I decide. I don't want to cause her any more grief than she is already dealin' with."

Monut gathered the crystal under his wing again, and Monut's and Ioldra's talons clacked against the floor as the three of them headed out of the underground. Emelyne's ancestors had created an impressive network of tunnels under the palace—solid and steadfast, even after all these years, with a vast array of rooms and enough space for dragons.

When they exited the underground into the harsh light of the midmorning sun, Emelyne asked Monut to place the crystal in a safe place for now then headed to the blacksmith's to grab a saw, leaving Ioldra in the village square. The early-morning breakfast rush had disintegrated, leaving only a few people wandering the streets as they went about their daily tasks. The sun warmed her skin, yet her heart was cased in ice over what had happened that morning. The dangers of the coterie were never far away, even though they had almost built a fortress.

"Mornin', Pa! Mornin', Silut!" Emelyne called over the din of the blacksmith shop. The two blacksmiths were hard at work forming the steel needed to reinforce the palace and the weapons the villagers required.

"Mornin', love," her adoptive father called. Lozzeak placed his hammer and current project on the bench. The heated end of the steel turned dark as the metal cooled. "What can I do for ya?"

"I'm needin' several axes an' a saw. An' do ya know of any tree loppers?" she asked.

Lozzeak shook his head. "I have the equipment you need"—he indicated the back wall filled with newly made weapons, axes, and an arrangement of saws—"but I ain't know of any loppers."

Silut placed his equipment down and wiped the sweat from his brow with his long sleeve. "I know of a couple of burley men who could help with that."

A loud horn sounded, and Emelyne froze, her panicked eyes connecting with her father's. "Shattered anvil! That was the alarm. That's not good. We have ladders constructed over the steel fence, an' Samara is trapped in a cocoon of roots."

Her dwarven father looked puzzled. "What?"

"I ain't got time to explain." Emelyne grabbed a saw off

the wall and turned to Silut. "Can ya organize those tree loppers with axes an' saws an' send them to the back of the village, beyond the woods? There are several ladders there that need cuttin' down."

"On it," Silut called, heading out instantly.

"Pa, can ya round up the weapons an' get Finlay to organize an' gather the fighters at the front of the village?"

Lozzeak inclined his head. "Of course."

She ran out of the blacksmith shop and through the village, dodging panicked villagers as they rushed through the streets. She reached the village square, where the two dragons waited. "Ioldra, call Kobi to round up the dragon riders to get their dragons saddled an' meet at the front of the village inside the walls. Monut, take me to Samara, quickly."

The female dragon flew off, and Emelyne strapped weapons onto Monut's saddle before he lowered for her to climb on. Once he was in the air and skimming the tops of the village buildings and trees, Emelyne gazed out as far as she could see. Clouds of dust swirled in the distance to the front of the village as a swarm of beings rose over the horizon. She swallowed the lump in her throat. That was more than a few attackers. It looked to be ogres, centaurs, and trolls, with what looked like members of the coterie leading the way. Turning back to face Monut's front, she saw similar clouds of dust in the rear of the village, heading right toward Paxton's ladders.

Emelyne clenched her fists. "I hope Silut rounds up those loppers quickly. This looks like it's gonna be an intense battle, an' the last thing we need is for our enemies to have easy access."

I have every bit of faith that Silut will pull through. He is determined to make up for his earlier betrayal. Monut flew a few wing beats in silence. *It may be the same with Paxton. We don't know what the coterie may have over people, or in Paxton's case, how they have managed to dig their claws in because of his extended exposure to the powerful evil orb. It took a long time for my ancestors to banish the orb to its current confinement. At least, that's what I've been told by the dragons who have come from Dragoria. They have much knowledge of how our worlds used to be. The guardian dragons have passed on much information.*

Emelyne bit her bottom lip. *I don't know, Monut. I hope ya right 'bout Paxton—for our sakes an' for Samara's.*

Monut landed near the root cocoon, Devi still standing guard. The sorceress seemed agitated.

Emelyne grabbed the saw from its restraint and dismounted. "Are ya all right?"

Devi flayed her hands. "I'm annoyed that I didn't act sooner with Paxton. All of this could have been avoided if I'd acted in a more cautious manner."

"I don't think that's all on ya, Devi. I don't know much 'bout magic an' its hold, but I think Paxton may be conflicted. Either he's a very good actor, or he's battlin' with the dark magic that the orb has instilled in him." Emelyne bent, lining the saw up with the roots.

"What do you mean?" Devi looked shocked.

Emelyne started sawing slowly. "He's apologized for what he has done, an' he actually looks horrified."

"Really?" Samara asked, her voice still muffled by the roots.

"Seems like it," Emelyne answered.

The senior sorceress thrust her hands by her side. "I long to look through the book that Cyrra brought back from Dragoria for Samara. I would like to see if there are any spells in there that would bind the parts of the orb residing in Paxton."

"You're welcome to it. It's in my room at the palace."

Hope ignited on Devi's face from Samara's words.

The root gave way, and Emelyne started on another. "I think Paxton's gonna be a problem for another day. Right now, we have invaders rollin' in from the horizon, an' we're gonna need all the help we can get to defeat them."

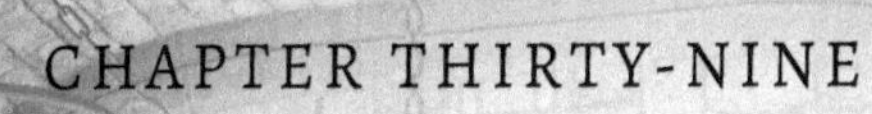

CHAPTER THIRTY-NINE

Thick limb-like roots wrapped around Samara, constricting and strong. There was no way she was getting out of this by herself. She peered out of the small space between the roots cocooned around her.

I told you his eyes were a worry. A sign that the orb had instilled some of its evil power into him. Ulrieg paced around Devi and the root cocoon as they waited for Emelyne to finish sawing through the enclosure. *But no, you always have to give someone the benefit of the doubt.*

She narrowed her eyes when she spotted him. *You don't need to lecture me, Ulrieg. I'm already punishing myself enough. Besides, you liked Paxton, and I'm sure underneath, you were hoping he'd stayed the same even after being exposed for an extended period to the orb's evil influence.*

Ulrieg snorted, causing Devi to jump.

"It's all right. He's just annoyed because he knows I'm right," Samara reassured her, knowing the defense arts instructor hadn't had much contact with dragons.

Devi placed a hand over her heart. "I think I'm just

jumpy. I feel like I should be doing something to protect the village."

Emelyne paused from sawing to glance at her. "Monut can take ya wherever you need to go, if ya don't mind ridin' him alone."

The senior sorceress eyed him skeptically. "Can you keep close to the ground and fly steadily?"

I can restrain myself. Just for you. Monut lowered to the ground, and Devi climbed unsteadily onto his back. She wrapped the leather strap around her waist right before Monut leaped into the sky.

After a few more cuts, Samara managed to squeeze out of her entrapment. "What a relief. Thank you."

The *thud* of a heavy landing sounded behind them, and Samara turned to see Monut had already returned.

The enemy is closing in quickly and is much closer at the back. We need to get those ladders down. Monut bounded over to the ladders and set one alight with his dragon fire.

Emelyne, Samara, and Ulrieg followed, the extent of the ladders far greater than they had expected. The ladders lined the wall far beyond where they could see.

"How did Paxton create so many ladders is such a short time?" Samara was flabbergasted. So little time had passed since Paxton had placed his hand on the ground and entrapped her, and now he'd already finished building the ladders. "He must be far more powerful than before, but now his magic is tainted." Samara grabbed a few arrows and began spelling and firing them into the bases of the ladders on all sides. Each arrow exploded, creating holes in the roots and causing them to break away. "It's such a shame. We could use his power to help protect the village."

Emelyne admired Samara's handiwork. "Ya have a spectacular gift as well. It's a shame ya couldn't use it when ya were trapped."

The princess helped as Monut lifted the ladders that had been freed and pulled them over the barred fence to the inside, the ladder he'd set alight still burning. The enemy in the distance was closing in rapidly.

"Everyone's gift has its limits, advantages, and disadvantages," Samara said. "I didn't think mine was much of a gift until I could open holes in the magic wards between the kingdoms." She shot four more arrows into the base of the next ladder, causing it to shatter, then Monut flew over and hoisted it to the village side of the fence.

Emelyne glanced down the barrier, seeming to assess how many more ladders they had to get rid of. The line still stretched as far as the eye could see. "We need to work faster." She grabbed the saw and started on the next one.

Several men carrying axes and saws filed through the opening in the stone wall and started cutting down the ladders in the other direction.

Her face pale, the princess turned to Samara. "It looks like the intruders at the front of the village are closer. I should go an' assess the situation an' make sure they're ready."

Would it be better if I go? Ulrieg landed beside her. *I can report back to you. Samara doesn't need me for these spells, and I'm not doing much here at the moment anyway. I'll be quick.*

"Thank you." Emelyne went right back to cutting the ladders. The task seemed endless as they made their way down the fence. "I can't believe after all this effort to create a dragon-blessed fence that it was compromised within moments by plant-made ladders."

Samara shot off another arrow and was rewarded with the sound of wood shattering. "I'm sorry. Going against magic wielders is like that. It's not going to be an easy battle to push back the coterie."

"Well, it's a battle I ain't gonna back down from." Emelyne sawed faster, sweat pooling on her forehead and the back of her neck.

Monut roared and blew fire onto the next ladder, setting it alight. *Hear, hear, Princess. I know the dragons will agree. We are over being oppressed and scattered. Together we shall rise and fight.*

Emelyne smiled. "We're gonna need an alliance between the dragons, the humans, an' any magic wielders we can muster." The princess wiped the perspiration from her brow.

The sun had risen to the midday point, its rays sweltering them as they labored over the ladders.

A soft *thud* sounded beside them. Samara turned to find Ulrieg had returned, ready to report to Emelyne.

The dragon riders are gathered with the trained villagers at the front of the village. Devi is also with them. They are on edge, as expected with the invaders nearby. He fluffed his wings, standing tall and proud. *I've had a quick look at the crowd rounding the horizon. I can't see Callista or Vexx, but Kellam and Kaine are definitely at the forefront.*

Emelyne looked at Samara. "What does that mean?"

"It's good news that Callista isn't with them—but bad because Kellam is just as evil and very powerful. It's a strange combination, as Kellam hates humans and half bloods and Kaine is a human. Kellam oversees the border between Slosiaran and Wraeyanor, and Kaine—"

"Yeah, I know who he is. He killed me best friend jus' for delayin' him a bit." Emelyne scowled. "He's a narcissistic psychopath."

You've got that right! Ulrieg showed off his expanse of teeth in what was likely supposed to be a smile.

"Whatever you do, don't let him touch you. He has the ability to charm you into telling him whatever he wants." Samara shot another arrow into a ladder and was loading another when a piece of splintered wood hit her boot from the explosion.

"Ha. If I get close enough for him to touch me, I'll be stickin' me sword into him. A little repayment for what he did to Thiznabo," Emelyne promised. "An' I won't be givin' him any warnin'. Jus' like he did to me best friend."

"Be careful, though. Just because Ulrieg didn't see more of the coterie members doesn't mean they aren't here. Maybe some of the less-senior ones but still strong contenders," Samara warned.

"Don't worry. Jus' because I'm hungry for Kaine's blood doesn't mean I ain't gonna keep an eye on others." Emelyne walked to the next ladder as Monut lifted the one she had felled over to their side of the fence.

Samara groaned. "This is taking too long. I think I have to climb over and start creating wards so they can't reach the ladders."

Careful you don't wear yourself out quickly. You're going to need your power when they arrive. Ulrieg flew over the fence to stand by her side, ready to lend her any familiar magic she might need.

As Emelyne and Monut continued to help as they

could, Samara alternated between setting a ward to barricade four ladders and spelling more arrows to explode the legs of the next four. She tried not to show how much of her energy was depleted each time she created a ward. She couldn't stop now. The village was counting on her.

Although Samara's wards helped them progress more quickly, they still had many more ladders to abolish. The grounds of Paddosha Palace village were vast with all the farmlands included.

A loud commotion came from the direction the men had gone to cut down ladders. Samara turned to find the men running toward them.

A stocky man with bulging muscles led the group. "Princess! They're getting over the fence. We need fighters on this side of the village, now!"

Not far behind them, trolls approached, their intimidating forms towering over the top of the stone wall. Samara froze as bad memories of her first real battle flooded her mind. Even back when she'd thought the coterie was good, they'd made her battle trolls without using magic. She had been captured that day, and if it hadn't been for Ulrieg, she would probably be dead. The trolls grew closer, and she shook her head to clear the distraction and prepare for the biggest battle of her life.

CHAPTER FORTY

A chill ran down Emelyne's spine. Paddosha Palace village was under attack again—this time from an even stronger force. It seemed enemies were approaching on all sides. She dropped her saw, made sure her sword was secure in its scabbard, climbed onto Monut's back, and strapped herself to the saddle as he took to the sky.

Samara quickly climbed back over the fence, exhaustion evident on her face. She had expended so much power putting up the wards along the outside. Emelyne cringed. She didn't need anyone to be worn out at this stage, especially the ones with magic.

The young sorceress pulled back her shoulders and marched to the area the men had just run through between the steel and stone fences. Right before the gap in the stone wall, Samara clapped her hands, spread them wide, and planted a hand to the ground, creating a ward. She'd stepped back, her chest heaving as she tried to regain some energy, when four trolls ran straight into the invisible barrier.

Flying at twice their height, Emelyne gaped at the trolls. The beings were huge—in height and in size—with large, bulky muscles. Their flesh was partially covered with animal hides. Some of the trolls had one eye, while others had two or three. Their feet were bare and calloused. They stopped, their height allowing them to see over the stone fence and gape down at the humans. The troll in front thumped his chest and let out a guttural roar at Samara, who was standing on the other side of the wall, surrounded by the men who had run her way.

Monut rose higher into the air, hovering for a moment before diving over the top of the trolls, raining dragon fire upon them. Some of the trolls' hair was burning, and they flailed their arms over their heads, trying to block the fire's heat. The dragon paused for a moment, banked in the opposite direction, then did it again. The trolls thumped against the stone wall, causing stones to dislodge from their mortar. Quickly, Samara grabbed her arrows and charmed one before firing it at a troll. The troll fell to the ground, petrified.

An arrow whistled past Emelyne. She scanned the ground below, spotting rapid movement. Centaurs galloped back and forth on the outside of the steel fence, their long, loose hair flowing behind them.

Another arrow lodged into the stone wall below, not far from Samara. The sorceress turned and fired an arrow through the gap in the stones in return, followed quickly by a second. The sorceress darted behind the wall, taking cover as she shot several more arrows at the centaurs while also spelling and firing more arrows at the trolls. The men waited near her with their cutting tools in hand, ready to use them on the trolls if they broke through.

A flame billowed after a couple of centaurs, narrowly missing them as Ulrieg followed them in his invisible form. The sky filled with fluttering wings as the smaller dragons joined them in the battle. Several dragons dived at the trolls, dousing them with fire and scratching them when they could get their talons close enough. Yet the trolls kept coming, their massive arms and bodies breaking through parts of the village's stone wall, eliminating some of their protection.

The loppers hurled their axes at the trolls, some nicking the skin and drawing blood. Others ran to get more help after having exhausted their weapons. Emelyne sheathed her sword and pulled out one of her war darts. Only one troll had been felled so far, and they were only petrified until the spelled arrow was removed. This needed to change, especially since the trolls were on the village's side of the fence. Monut steadied, and she hurled the dart at the troll who'd traveled farthest onto the village land. The dart pierced the troll's heart, and he fell to his knees before slumping to the ground, unmoving.

That troll's death only seemed to spur the others on. Six more trolls climbed over the distant ladders and joined the three who remained. The dragons attacked with fury, lighting them up with dragon fire and ripping at their skin with their talons. The trolls were either too stupid or too determined, for they kept coming.

Samara raced in front of the area where the trolls had broken through then repeated the gesture for her warding spell. Ulrieg stayed pressed to her leg as she worked on another barrier. She finished just in time to stop the trolls from entering the hole that had been created in that part of the stone wall. The giant beasts worked on felling another section, and the sorceress headed in that direction, her limbs slack and her pace slow. Before long, and she would surely collapse from exhaustion. She managed to hold up her spelled arrow and shoot a troll, sending him to the ground in a petrified heap. The sorceress spelled and shot a few more arrows. With the exhaustion Samara was clearly battling, her aim wasn't true, and the arrows skimmed over the distant wildflowers.

Something had to change soon, or their odds weren't looking good. Emelyne pulled another war dart from Monut's saddle and threw it at a troll who had just created another hole in their stone wall. The troll fell and blocked the gap, only to be yanked aside by the troll behind him, exposing the hole again for the other trolls to enter.

Look out! Monut shifted rapidly, jerking Emelyne in the saddle.

An arrow whistled past her ear, slicing through her hair. *That was close! Thanks for moving in time.* She pressed a hand against his scales.

Monut's affection radiated down their bond. *I'll do my best to dodge them, but you also need to watch the centaurs. They have their eye on you and will fire if they think the arrow will reach.*

At least their hooves will stop them from climbin' the ladders. Emelyne gripped the saddle as Monut swerved away from another arrow. She slipped out a dagger and threw it in the centaur's direction. The centaur swerved just in time.

Monut circled father from the centaurs' reach. Emelyne reassessed the trolls. The next troll in line attempted to push through the hole in the stone wall, only to find that Samara had erected a barrier right before he'd tried to enter. When he was unable to get through, the troll hit and punched the barrier and swatted at the attacking dragons.

Seeing that her barrier was a success, Samara backed away from that hole and headed to a spot where another troll was thumping his way through. The sorceress was almost there when she buckled to her knees, falling face-first into the wildflowers. The black dragon, half her height, pulled her against the part of the wall that was protected by Samara's barrier and protectively spread his wings over the sorceress's body before turning invisible, hiding Samara with him.

Emelyne blinked. *I didn't know Ulrieg could do that. I thought he could only turn himself invisible.*

Monut's throat rumbled. *I believe that is how he hid the crystal from the coterie and smuggled it out of the palace grounds. I don't think it's something he does very often.*

Her heart warmed at the thought of the snarky black dragon's love for his bonded, but the feeling was rapidly pushed away by another arrow whizzing past her. *I'm glad he can keep his bonded safe this time, but we need a break-through if we're going to defeat these trolls.*

Another of the giant beasts slammed against a section of stone wall, several stones crumbling to the ground. Out of war darts, Emelyne aimed a dagger at the troll's single eye. Narrowly missing the mark, the weapon pierced the troll's forehead then fell to the ground, causing a trail of crimson to trickle into his eye. The troll yelled his disapproval and swung at some dragons that had attacked at the same time. He slammed harder into the wall, and more rocks tumbled to the ground.

Shattered anvil! These trolls are not only destroyin' all our hard work—they are also breakin' through into our village. Emelyne clenched her fist as she searched for another weapon to throw.

The troll shouldered the wall another time, loosening enough stones to clear a path.

Hang on! Monut dived at the one temporarily blinded by blood, jolted up as he reached the troll's front, and dragged his claws up the troll's abdomen.

The troll screamed in rage and pain, lifting a leg to walk through the gap he had just created.

Emelyne's heart sank. This was it. The trolls were getting through. She was out of darts, and Samara was out of commission, probably not to recover while this battle raged.

CHAPTER FORTY-ONE

Samara held her breath. The troll was breaking through. Soon the others would follow, and she could see Emelyne was out of large throwing weapons. Samara had almost completely blacked out after creating her last barrier. She knew Ulrieg had dragged her to a safe place and cloaked her with invisibility to keep her hidden from harm. She wanted to get up and fight for the villagers. She had more than herself to think about—especially with the friendships she had formed with Emelyne and the dragons. Her good friends were residing here, seeking Paddosha Palace village's protection, as was her family. Her friends' families had also traveled here to escape the coterie's evil wrath. Samara had a lot to lose.

I must help. She spoke to Ulrieg through their bond, her words muffled even though she didn't physically speak them.

Nonsense! You're not in any position to do anything at the moment, other than get yourself killed. That's not going to help them in the slightest. You're staying put.

I can't do that. They need my help. She tried to move, but Ulrieg pushed her weakened body back easily with his wings. She slumped back to the ground. He was right. Still, she wanted to try. Staying put didn't sit right. Plus, a troll had almost broken the wall and was about to create a hole to step through. The others would soon follow.

Despite Emelyne's and Monut's best efforts, the troll succeeded. Though something seemed to knock him back. Samara frowned, straining her eyes to get a better look. Her vision had become fuzzy in her weakness, yet she could easily see the size of the troll stumbling backward. He readjusted and tried to push through the gap again, only to stagger back into the trolls behind him.

Can you see what's going on?

Ulrieg's breath warmed her against the cool air. *No. The troll is behaving oddly, and the trolls behind are getting agitated with him for not passing through the gap.* The dragon's body stiffened as he studied the scene. *Wait. I saw a slight glimmer.* There was confusion in his voice.

What do you mean? Samara squinted harder, trying to see what Ulrieg saw. Stones crumbled to the ground from the force of the trolls shoving against the one in the gap, but every time the troll tried to move forward, he seemed to be pushed back.

Yep, there it is. I think someone is invisible on our side of the barrier.

What? I don't know anyone on our side who can turn invisible other than you. Do you? She concentrated hard on the area in front of the gap, but her sight was never going to be anywhere near as good as Ulrieg's, especially with this exhaustion.

Suddenly, a couple of trolls fell backward, yet nothing

had been thrown their way. They seemed to have been struck by an invisible force.

All right! I definitely don't know anyone who can turn invisible and blast defensive blocks. Samara shook her head. *I don't believe Devi has learned to turn invisible. Although I'm pretty sure she can shoot defensive blasts.*

Confused, the trolls went to another section of the wall and started knocking it down. Yet the result was the same. They created a gap but couldn't get through. Samara was just as puzzled as the trolls. The trolls walked to the next gap in the stone wall and tried to pass through, only to be met with the same resistance.

Monut said Emelyne doesn't know what is going on either. I just asked. Ulrieg shifted slightly, giving Samara a better view of the battle.

Something flickered behind the stone wall, out of the trolls' line of sight, then it turned solid, completely visible from the village's side.

Samara gasped. Standing by the wall was a tall young man about her age wearing a large cloak, the hood pulled over his head.

Huh! Would you look at that. It's Peadar. His invisibility spell must have worn off. Ulrieg turned visible and showed off his vast array of teeth as he furled his wings, exposing Samara as well.

Seeing Ulrieg, the young sorcerer smiled and pulled back his hood, exposing his short bright-yellow hair and his semipointed ears. Ziggy, his racoon familiar, clambered out from the protection of his cloak, nearly tripping him.

Monut started to fly at him, but Ulrieg tried to call him off.

Wait, Monut. We know him. He's with us and the reason the trolls couldn't get through,

The large dragon pulled up at the last second and hovered near Samara and Ulrieg.

Checking over his shoulder, Peadar made sure the trolls weren't getting through. He then walked over to Samara and Ulrieg, stumbling over a clump of wildflowers. His lanky form looked slightly weary, but nothing like Samara felt at the moment.

When he neared, Samara called out to him, "Can you turn invisible?"

He stopped before them and shook his head. "Henriette is here also. She made my cloak invisible."

His kind light-brown eyes were a welcome sight after the morning Samara had experienced. The trolls grew impatient with the spot they couldn't get through and moved farther away to find another entrance.

Monut and Emelyne flew to follow them, and Peadar watched them go. "Wow! I can't believe it—a real dragon rider and a huge dragon. Is he friendly?"

Samara nodded. "If you treat his bonded well."

When she noticed Peadar wasn't worried about the trolls looking for another entrance, Samara motioned in that direction. "Is Henriette down there?"

Peadar nodded. "It's good to see you. I hear you broke Paxton out. Is he around?" He searched this side of the woods.

Samara shook her head. "He is here, but I'm afraid the orb got to him. Plus, he has a new familiar, as Jojo died. It's a hyena."

"Such an unusual choice for Paxton." He frowned. "Is

there anything that can be done to free him from the orb's grasp?"

"We haven't had a chance to investigate yet. I only found out this morning, then the village was attacked." Samara slowly climbed to her feet.

"You look worn out." His eyes were muddied with concern.

"I run out of energy quickly when I create barriers." She tilted her head. "You hardly look worn out at all."

"I was blasting the trolls as they tried to step through, not creating barriers. Plus, I always had Ziggy pressing against my flesh. That keeps me stronger for longer. You should have Ulrieg constantly press against your skin until you feel more revitalized." Peadar eyed Ulrieg and all the horns covering most of his upper body. "I guess it's a little hard to snuggle up with something so prickly. A racoon is a little cuddlier."

And that's the way I like it. I'm not some cuddle toy. Ulrieg pressed his side to Samara's legs.

She reached down, cupped him under the chin—avoiding the long horn sticking out from under his jawline—and looked into his red eyes. "You're like a prickly pear cactus. Hard and thorny on the outside yet sweet in the middle. I know you care." She released his jaw.

Ulrieg looked almost bashful as he turned his eyes away. *Argh! You're so mushy.*

Samara smiled, already feeling her energy increase. "I know you like it." With her energy returning, her mind started to function better. She turned to Peadar. "Why are you and Henriette here?"

"We've been sent by Callista to attack Paddosha Palace village with Kellam and Kaine. Naturally, as soon as we could, we broke off from them and said we'd control the trolls at the back. Our real plan was to stop them if they got through. We weren't sure how strong your protection was. We knew that Devi had escaped with you." He looked around the area. "I guess she is somewhere else?"

"I believe she is at the front, where Kellam and Kaine are."

"Where is Paxton?" Peadar scratched Ziggy on the head when his racoon familiar brushed up against him.

"He's currently secured in the palace's dungeon. He lost control of his power. It's like the orb's magic took over."

"Is he going to be released?" Peadar looked concerned.

Samara shrugged. "Paxton is all right physically, but his magic and mind have been tainted. He created all the ladders made out of roots and is the reason the trolls got in. We'll find out more after this battle is over." Slowly, Samara started to walk in the direction Henriette and Emelyne had gone, Ulrieg by her side. "We should check on the other two to see how they are doing against the trolls."

Peadar and Ziggy fell in step. They followed the stone wall and fence line, finding many of the ladders burned or chopped down but no sign of the trolls. The area was deserted other than the occasional centaur galloping past, looking for a villager to shoot with an arrow through the steel-barred fence.

Their path led them past more farms until they finally reached the front section of the village. The enemies in the back seemed peaceful in comparison to what surrounded the front and sides of the main road, waiting to attack and bring down the village. Emelyne and Henriette had joined Devi in front of the dragon riders, and the extended group—including the villagers and dragons—looked ready to defend.

CHAPTER FORTY-TWO

Emelyne was startled when a lanky half blood about her age with brilliant-yellow hair suddenly appeared on their side of the fence. Monut seemed just as startled and dived to attack the second the man became visible. She didn't know people could turn invisible, but she also didn't understand why he didn't remain invisible and continued to concentrate on stopping the trolls—if it was he who was stopping them. Samara seemed to think so, and again, it was another of her friends. After their encounter with Paxton, she hoped the rest of the people Samara recommended were true helpers and not more miscalculations. They didn't need any more enemies on their side of the fence. Paxton was enough.

Emelyne followed the trolls as they tried to get into the village area, but again, the trolls were stopped by some-thing. She kept an eye on them for a while longer before a female human with pale skin and long turquoise hair down to her waist appeared out of nowhere. A panda ferret ran out from her long cloak and sniffed around before running back into the material's protection. Unlike the man who stopped to talk to Samara, the woman continued to block the trolls from coming inside the village area.

Emelyne watched her for a while longer before joining the smaller dragons in destroying the ladders that had been left behind. "I hate to admit it, but there's something about that human sorceress that I like."

Monut watched the sorceress at work, and amusement crossed his face. *It's not because she is calling to the trolls to tell them to go a certain way then purposefully blocking that way with a ward and laughing at the trolls when they run face-first into it? That actually sounds like something you would do if you could.*

Emelyne slapped him playfully and chuckled. "You know, that could be it. She has a sense of humor and knows the trolls aren't very smart."

Following the sorceress, the smaller dragons had set several of the ladders on fire. Emelyne set to cutting down the ones they hadn't gotten to, and Monut lifted them to the village side of the fence.

The ferret remained in almost constant contact with the woman, either on her shoulder or hiding within her clothes, chattering away. The young sorceress answered as though she understood the ferret, which meant the animal was her familiar.

Annoyed with their lack of success in breaching the stone wall, the trolls left the Paddosha Palace village grounds, exiting over a ladder and stomping their way around the outside of the bared fence toward the front of the village. Seeing that the immediate threat had left, the sorceress approached Emelyne, giving the princess a better look at her plain yet friendly face. She was close to Emelyne's height, making her slightly taller than Samara. Her charcoal-colored dress hugged her average-width waist and swished through the wildflowers as she walked. Once she was close, Emelyne was held captive for a moment by the palest-blue eyes she had ever seen.

The human sorceress smiled. "Hello. I'm Henriette, a friend of Samara's."

Suddenly, it all clicked for Emelyne. She smiled broadly. "Ya the sorceress Samara said saved our village from the lightnin' sorceress. Thanks so much."

Henriette's smile broadened, almost looking mischievous. "I got rid of the pest at least, but I believe she caused a fair bit of damage before I stopped her."

The princess slapped her thigh. "Ha. I like that. *The pest.* I'm Emelyne."

"The princess?" Henriette looked surprised. "Of course. That makes sense. And this is your dragon." She looked at Monut, who was tossing another ladder away from the fence. "He's impressive."

"Yes, he is." Emelyne looked at Monut with affection.

Henriette glanced over the princess's shoulder. "Did we leave the others behind?"

"They haven't caught up yet. I think Samara lost a lot of energy. I'm sure they'll catch up when they can. I must head to the front of the village to see how things are goin' there. What is ya plan?"

Henriette's smile faded slightly. "I can't go back to their side now. The trolls have seen me go against them and will probably report it. That's it for my life with the coterie."

Emelyne threw an arm over Henriette's shoulders. "Well, ya can stay here. We could use ya help."

The ferret ran from Henriette's shoulder up Emelyne's arm and stopped on her shoulder to study her face. The ferret had a white head and chest, black legs, and white paws, with long black fur on her body.

"And this is my familiar, Pixie." Pride filled the sorceress's voice.

"She's adorable." Emelyne said, squealing with delight when Pixie gently nudged her with her nose before running back along Emelyne's arm to Henriette.

"She likes you too." Henriette smiled.

As they approached the front of the village, they saw several centaurs with their arrows aimed at the village. Several ogres, looking ready to knock things down, waited impatiently next to the trolls. In the center of the crowd, Kellam and Kaine faced the village gate. Kellam's face was set with disapproval, his eyes narrowed, seeming aware yet also ignoring the snub-nosed monkey sitting by his side. The man's orange hair was alight with the sun.

Emelyne remembered this sorcerer. He and his monkey had chased her and her adoptive mother out of the dwarven village, Mirwohr, at the Perpetual Vale. They had nearly been captured then. And the handsome sorcerer standing near him—she certainly knew him. Kaine. He killed her friend, Thiznabo. Her gaze hardened. She longed to see him punished.

Henriette looked worried, her pale forehead creased and her mouth in a deep frown. "I hope they are standing there because my wards are blocking them. But I don't know. I made the ward specifically for Mist. Maybe those two can still get through."

Looking on her own side, Emelyne spotted the ten dragons and their riders sitting ready on their saddles. The dragons stood behind all the swordsmen and archers instructed by Finlay, who was perched near an arrow hole on the watchtower. In front of the large gray dragons, Devi stood with her legs shoulder-width apart and hands lifted to waist height, ready to defend. The smaller dragons landed behind the dragon riders, recouping the energy spent fighting off the trolls. The dragons, large and small, stirred restlessly, ready to take flight.

Emelyne could feel the tension in the air. She walked over to Devi, Henriette following closely behind. "What has been happenin' so far?"

Devi faced her and nodded at Henriette. "Kellam has been demanding that the villagers open the gates." Her eyes circled the people behind the walls. "As you can see, they haven't listened. I had heard that these villagers had been persecuted into doing Callista's will. I wish to congratulate you on turning them around in such a short time. I'm sure they are scared after what they have faced in the past, but they look to be steadfast."

The princess gave her a half smile. "It's amazin' what a bit of kindness an' support can do. Along with positive steps toward rebuildin' their beloved village."

"Good points. Not to mention that the return of the lost royal would also give them hope," Devi said.

Surprised over the lack of fighting, Emelyne said, "I must admit, I thought the battle would've commenced by now. It certainly did at the back of the village grounds. Thanks to Samara, the half-blooded sorcerer, the smaller dragons, and Henriette, we managed to kick the trolls back out."

Devi focused her brown eyes on Emelyne. "I don't think it'll be long. Kellam and Kaine don't like to be disobeyed. Although, they will probably split to attack the village because Kellam never works with humans."

"So I've heard." Emelyne rolled her eyes. "It makes no difference to me."

A male voice carried over the fence, the volume accentuated by magic. "How dare you defy me. Not only that, but you go against the Sacred Flame coterie by displaying dragons, of all creatures, on the front of your gates."

The princess had heard that voice before, had even run from it.

Kellam continued, "I give you ten seconds to open these offensive gates, and if you don't, then expect to be bathing your land in your blood. You are fools to think a couple of fences will keep us out."

Emelyne clenched her fists. She hoped the dragon-blessed fence would keep them out, but she knew it wouldn't stop their magic from entering. Looking at the people around her, the ones who had rallied behind her, she hoped they would all survive. She didn't want one to die. Yet she knew the chance of that was slim.

"All right." Kellam's voice boomed. "You've had your chance. By the end of this day, your crumpled village will be painted red with your blood."

CHAPTER FORTY-THREE

Thunder and lightning gathered in the sky. It had been clear earlier, the ominous clouds forming out of nowhere. Emelyne gazed up. The dark clouds swirled, an unnatural formation for a storm, reminding her of when the sorceress Mist had attacked their village. She hadn't known the sorceress was here, but this was a tell-tale sign. She scanned the enemies before her, trying to spot the sorceress.

Henriette moved next to her, the young sorceress's face even paler than before. Her long turquoise hair whipped around in the wind, and she flicked it over her shoulder. "I think Mist must be far back, behind the group. The wards should stop her from passing, but the barriers won't stop her attacks by lightning."

Emelyne nodded. She didn't know of anything that could stop a storm, even a magically created one. She glanced at Devi. "Do ya know how to disperse storm clouds created by a magic wielder?"

With a grave face, Devi shook her head. "Mist has an

unusual talent, one that I haven't seen in my hundred summers."

The clouds swelled, circling wider, and the wind picked up. Thunder roared, and lightning cracked through the darkness. The sounds were terrifying, let alone the ominous display before them.

Someone retched, and Emelyne didn't blame them. The tension passing through their group could be cut by a knife. Thudding footsteps galloped around the entrance of the village as centaurs paced back and forth, their bows ready and nocked. After more retching off to the left by the same person, a couple of villagers moved closer to comfort him.

The clouds swelled larger and lightning split the sky as the storm continued. The pressure continued to build. The ogres and trolls stood ready, bouncing from foot to foot with their eyes glued to the front dragon gates.

The wind whipped into a frenzy, chased by more thunder that almost canceled Kellam's voice as he yelled, "Charge!" Ogres and trolls bounded toward the front gate, shoulders tilted as through ready to ram into it. At the same time, a thunderous sound was followed by lightning, which hit the gate and bounced back. The front line of charging trolls and ogres was hit by its force and knocked to the ground, unmoving.

Emelyne cheered inside. The dragon-blessed gate had held. *Good job, Monut!*

We have had one small win. Monut sounded pleased with himself. *I'm glad I could help with that, at least.*

Thunder cracked again, and lightning shot down, hitting a group of people on the inside of the village boundary. The smell of burnt flesh disgusted Emelyne as screams of terror reined.

More retching sounded in the corner. Even Emelyne's stomach was stirring. Instead of being sick, she clenched her jaw and pulled back her shoulders. She had to be strong for the people. She sucked in a deep breath and pulled on Monut's strength, reinforcing her own.

Devi and Henriette worked together, their hands and arms weaving about as they built a ward over the top of the people. More lightning struck down on them, some crackling off the surface and some finding its way around the edges of the sorceresses' defense to hit within the stone walls.

Finlay caught Emelyne's eyes, and she nodded at him. He raised his hand and called out, "Attack!" The archers fired. Their arrows curved upward and gravitated down toward the attacking crowd, many hitting the enemy. A second lot was fired from on top of the walls and in between the arrow slits. Many more arrows lodged into ogres, trolls, and even some of the centaurs, but the magic wielders managed to knock them away.

The centaurs fired back through the steel fences, aiming for anybody they could see.

The dragon riders climbed onto their dragons and headed into the sky. The dragons dived low and shot fire over the groups around the palace walls. Cries of pain reverberated from the targets.

Emelyne and Monut took to the sky. Devi and Henriette protected them with different spells, which enabled them to rise high into the sky, out of the arrows' reach. Emelyne was in shock over the number of enemies outside of the village, ready to attack. The beings continued way beyond the first hill and wrapped around the majority of the village.

A weird pulse knocked Monut sideways, and Emelyne grabbed on tightly to the saddle as he flopped about. He managed to straighten before circling farther away from the group below. The dragon riders attacked, focusing on the outskirts of the enemy and avoiding the sorcerers. The dragons stooped low and breathed fire over them, the smaller dragons doing what they could by tearing up backs and shredding skin, knocking the attackers about, and breathing fire over them. Again, the smell of burnt flesh was sickening.

The main sorcerer continued to throw powerful blasts of magic at the people he could see through the steel fence. He shot several bursts of power at the stone wall, blasting away pieces of it then aiming for the villagers made visible by the breach. Several villagers fell, their bodies thrashing in pain on the ground. The gap also left them susceptible to arrow attacks from the centaurs scouting around the fence.

Emelyne threw a dagger, narrowly missing the main sorcerer, Kellam, as he dodged slightly to the side. *Shattered anvil! That sorcerer is as slippery as a snake.*

Monut encouraged her. *But he can still be brought down, so keep trying.*

The cries of war were deafening and disturbing. The screams of someone losing their life and in deep pain were not something Emelyne enjoyed. Yet each time someone from the village cried out in pain, she swore a disgusting, pleasured look crossed the faces of the two male sorcerers.

Monut dived, fast and strong, heading straight for

Kellam's back. Emelyne clung to Monut tightly, her hair whipping back in the wind and her cheeks stinging with the coolness of the breeze. During their descent, Emelyne grabbed her spare sword and threw it at one of the ogres heading toward the front gate. It hit him in the shoulder, leaving him madder, more determined, and seeking revenge.

Several ogres pounded at the front gate, but thankfully, between the dragon-blessed bars and the hard work of the dwarves, the gate was holding.

Devi and Henriette moved as quickly as possible, not only to create wards to stop Mist's lightening attacks but also to put up barriers at the places Kellam had destroyed the stone wall. Mist's attacks continued. The lightning bolts aimed mostly for the fighting villagers, occasionally shooting more closely to the center of the village and destroying farms.

Flickering orange lights caught Emelyne's attention, and she turned to find several burning homes, farmhouses, and crops. She cursed. The houses and farms they had just fixed were burning to the ground.

Some centaurs continued to gallop around the outside of the fence, shooting at any person unlucky enough to be exposed, while others ignited their arrows and shot them into the produce fields and woods, setting them on fire.

With a wave of his hand, the young half-blooded sorcerer with the yellow hair quelled some of the fires, stopping them from consuming the village's supplies as he rounded the corner with Samara. The young man caught Emelyne's attention with the way he waved his hands, stumbling over minuscule objects before blasting out magic to protect the village. He seemed so clumsy for a sorcerer of the Sacred Flame coterie.

Samara shot a few arrows at the circling centaurs and felled some instantly, leaving them either petrified or thrashing in terror.

After helping Devi with another protection spell, Henriette pulled the hood of her cloak over her head and disappeared. Only the felling of an enemy by an unexplained blast gave away the young sorceress's whereabouts.

Monut circled. *That's not good.*

Emelyne squinted to work out what Monut was referring to, only to see Kellam blasting his magic at the dragon gate over and over, the hinges rattling and shaking so much that the pegs started to wriggle out of place. The handsome yet devious sorcerer joined Kellam in his quest. If they weren't stopped soon, they might get through the gates after all.

Emelyne wrapped the saddle strap around one hand, clasping tightly as Monut ascended before plunging straight for Kellam.

CHAPTER FORTY-FOUR

T he storm had started. An almighty boom had cracked the sky, and lightning had shot down at them.

All Samara could think was *not again*—not Mist attacking the village again with lightning. It had taken them this long to recoup and rebuild just part of what had been lost. They were so close to finishing. Having to rebuild again would be a devastating blow.

Right as these thoughts were whirring through her head, another huge bolt of lightning hit the ground near her, narrowly missing several of the villagers taking refuge behind the stone wall.

Arrows flew in all directions as the villagers defended their home and the centaurs attacked.

A thunderous pounding reverberated across the front of the village as trolls and ogres stormed the gate, shoulders angled down. The beings were halfway to the entrance when lightning struck the front of the dragon-blessed steel gate. The bolt hit the dragon emblem, bouncing off and redirecting straight toward the stampeding trolls and ogres. The large beasts fell in unison, their bodies sizzling from the inside and releasing that sickening smell of burnt flesh.

Ulrieg chuckled. *That was a pretty awesome trick by Mist. I wonder if she can do that again to help us out.*

Samara lifted one side of her mouth. *I wouldn't count on that. I don't think that was the result Mist wanted. I think she was trying to blast open the dragon-forged gates to let the stampeding beings in.*

Oh, I know. That's why it's funny.

The ominous storm clouds continued to swirl above, large bolts of lightning announcing their sinister intensions and growling thunder emphasizing its point. The strikes were getting too close for comfort.

Trolls and ogres gathered on the road, apparently getting ready to run the gates again. Certainly, Mist had learned from the first attempt that bolts striking the gate would backfire.

Hopefully, the dragon-forged gates would be strong enough to keep the large beings at bay for quite some time. She searched for something she could use to help. So much was going on, but she had to be careful. Her energy had recouped enough to walk to the front of the village but not enough to create any more wards. She spelled some arrows and fired them at any centaurs who came near her. Years of practice had made her aim truer than most. Each arrow she fired had the centaur writhing in pain, living in nightmares, or petrified. Any way she went about it left them useless to the other side.

A large dragon with a rider scooped down and grabbed a centaur by the back, picked him up, and threw him to the side, breaking one of his equine legs. The centaur tried but was unable to get up.

Samara shot an arrow at the centaur, petrifying it in the hopes of putting him out of his misery until someone decided to finish him off. Not long afterward, one of the dragon riders flew past and threw a sword into the heart of the centaur, taking away any chance of a recovery.

A loud bang pulled Samara's attention to the front gates. The steel doors rattled wildly as many of the ogres and trolls rammed against them. When the doors didn't budge, they circled back. Mist's lightning was no longer a threat to the large beings, as the sorceress had directed her powers toward the rest of the village. They repeatedly circled back and rammed the gates. Each time, the gates shook. The actual gate did not give in, but the pins in the hinges were slowly rising.

After firing a few more arrows at the centaurs, Samara looked back to check on the hinges. The pins were a quarter of the way out and seemed to be wriggling farther.

We must do something! Ulrieg's voice was strained with panic.

Samara raced to the gate and climbed up the stone steps to a platform behind the safety of the wall but from which she could see over the top, enabling a better view of the rammers below. She charmed an arrow and stood, bowstring taut, as she watched the trolls run toward the gate again. Releasing, she fired the arrow into the nearest troll. It lodged into the flesh of his bare stomach and knocked the troll to the ground, petrified. She aimed at the ogre next in line then watched as he dropped to the ground as well, writhing in pain.

The rest of the large beings kept ramming the gate, the hinge pins working their way up farther. She fired more arrows, felling the beings one by one and causing them to suffer a specific spell. The problem was that each of the felled trolls and ogres were quickly replaced with another waiting to join.

The pins are still working their way out. This isn't good. Ulrieg sounded as panicked as Samara felt.

She glanced at the pins, seeing what Ulrieg said to be true, and Samara worked quicker, spelling more arrows and firing them at the large ramming creatures.

She watched as more ogres and trolls joined the stampede, always another to take the place of her target. All her work wasn't taking the pressure off the hinges.

She grunted. *This is ridiculous! They seemed to have an endless supply of replacements. I've never seen so many large beings.*

Still, she refused to give up. The rammers didn't even stop when the unconscious bodies piled up in front of the gate—so high they could hardly get around them. She just couldn't stop them from shifting the pins.

A dragon dived from the sky, its rider hanging on tight as the dragon aimed for the ogres in front. Suddenly, a bolt of lightning shot down, hitting the dragon rider. The dragon was knocked off-balance and careened to the ground on the side of the enemy, hitting with a sickening *thud*. The noise counteracted the pounding footsteps of the large beings trying to break down the gate. From a fall like that, the dragon would have many broken bones. The dragon thrashed, seemingly injured and unable to get up. The rider remained still.

Samara cringed as Ulrieg growled. *That has gotta hurt.*

Samara wondered if he meant they would have lived through that.

The enemies piled on top of the dragon and rider, towering over them with arrows and swords. Ogres and trolls thudded their fists against them, blocking all view of the dragon and its rider.

Samara fired arrows at the beings attacking the dragon, their bodies falling away only to be replaced by others. Many of the villagers fired with her, trying to get them away from their fallen comrades, but the effects of their arrows were not as potent as those of Samara's spelled ones. Thankfully, Samara couldn't see what physical effect the attacks were having on the victims, but she knew it wasn't good. She would not have been able to save that rider or dragon even if they had survived the fall.

Lightning struck again, but still the archers from the village continued their rapid fire at the attackers. An invisible blast hit the mob of beings, pushing them away. Peadar hovered in the background, his hands raised, ready to send another blast. The centaurs, trolls, and ogres were shoved aside, exposing the dragon and the rider.

Samara's heart broke. There was so much blood—a terrible amount of blood. The dragon writhed weakly but couldn't get up. That was not good. The effect on the villagers would be devastating. They were down a dragon and a rider. The enemy crowded around the dragon and rider again, resuming the attack.

Another blast pushed them away, but this time, they did not go back because the dragon lay still along with its rider. A combined roar echoed among the dragons as the loose dragons and those with riders dived at the many trolls, ogres, and centaurs who had brought the dragon and rider to their deaths.

Kaine cut through the back of the crowd. The handsome sorcerer edged his way forward, his palm up, blocking all attacks on the beings who had felled the dragon and rider. A cocky self-assuredness was evident on his face as he advanced behind his magical barrier. A chill crept up Samara's spine. He was pure evil.

He might have been human and Kallem elven with a hatred for humans, but they were very similar in personality. Maybe they were sent on this mission together for that reason.

An arrow shot past Samara, narrowly missing her head. Following its trajectory, she saw the flaming tip enter a pile of dried bushes, igniting them instantly. The fire spread toward the village.

I'll put that out. Ulrieg's launch sent a breeze around her, then he quickly stifled the fire, patting it down with his invisible wings.

A loud thudding distracted her, sounding repeatedly over a short time. Samara faced the front of the village to see that, once again, the trolls and ogres had started ramming against the gate. They must have known they were getting somewhere. Otherwise, they would have given up by now. But even though they still hadn't broken down the gates, they didn't give up. They continued to walk back and charge, shoulders first, and each time, the gates wobbled a little more.

Samara set to work charming more arrows, noticing her supply was running low. She would have to grab some from the reserve shortly, as she was unable to collect any of the ones she had fired. She felled more trolls and ogres, but they did not stop coming.

Another bolt of lightning shot down from the sky, hitting the village farther in, closer to the parts that had been rebuilt. The smell of burning wood reached her nose, but she couldn't stop now. She had to keep trying to stop these trolls and ogres from breaking through. The villagers were being kept busy by the centaurs, who were still galloping around the outside of the wall and shooting arrows through the bars at anyone they could see. The continuous attack made it impossible for anyone to hammer the pins back into the gate's hinges.

More centaurs shot ignited arrows into the village boundaries, hitting several people and many areas that would burn rapidly. On Samara's left, a farm had started to burn after a centaur set it alight, and a farm not far behind it had been struck by lightning. Several of the village women who were not fighting ran toward the farms with wet blankets to stifle the fire before it burned their crops. Other women carried shields to protect the women at work.

She was distracted from this as another hit shook the gate. The pop of a pin sent terror through Samara as the dragon gates folded in and slammed to the ground.

CHAPTER FORTY-FIVE

Violation and destruction. Emelyne saw it all from Monut's back. Her beloved village was under attack. The violence below was devastating. The centaurs were shooting flames, catching things on fire, and lightning, which nobody could do much about except for Devi and Henriette—was shooting from the sky. The sorceresses blocked some of the parts of the village, but the lightning still got through certain parts because the area was too vast for them to protect it all. Parts of the woods were set alight, along with a few wooden buildings. In such a short time, her precious village that they'd only just rebuilt was already being burned. They'd have to battle the fire later, though. For now, they needed to stop the invasion. One dragon rider and his dragon had already fallen, and while she was still mourning the loss, the trolls and ogres had barged through the gates. She had seen Samara felling many of them, creating a heap of petrified bodies, but more kept turning up to ram the gates, bypassing the mound of their own kind to follow the order of the sorcerer.

She was especially annoyed when she noticed the sorcerer Kaine blocking all attempts to fell any of the beings that had attacked the dragon and his rider. The handsome sorcerer continued to block all fire, and as soon as the gates burst open, he walked right through them, following a group of trolls, ogres, and centaurs.

The villagers retaliated, the swordsmen coming out from behind their protection to fight off the giant ogres and trolls. They aimed for the lower parts of the body with swords and shot arrows at their eyes in their attempt to stop the monstrosities from entering the village. The villagers' persistence in fighting an enemy far larger than themselves filled Emelyne with pride. They were going above and beyond what they had practiced. She knew they were scared, as they hadn't done anything like this before.

Her attention folded back onto Kaine, and wrath welled deep inside her, heating her up from the inside. The sorcerer who dared to kill her friend had walked into her village. She had to stop him. He was more unwelcome than any of the others.

Monut, get him!

Her dragon didn't ask whom she was intending. He seemed to know, and he dived, beelining from high in the sky. Emelyne leaned back in the saddle and gripped the reins, her knuckles white and her hair standing straight up as gravity pulled them down. She knew there was a battle at hand, and she knew she could trust the villagers to fight the best they could alongside the magic wielders who had joined them. As much as she wanted the battle to stop, she had her eyes set on Kaine.

The sorcerer reached out to touch someone, and Emelyne grabbed her dagger, threw it, and sliced the sorcerer's arm. He pulled it back quickly, assessing the cut that bled through his cloak before turning to the skies, looking for the owner of the dagger. His eyes connected with Emelyne's, and a sneering confidence washed over him as he pulled his shoulders back and focused solely on her. He ignored his surroundings, seeming to think he was impenetrable by all others around him as he waited for Monut's attack.

The wind brushed hair into Emelyne's eyes, causing them to water and making her vision blurry. She trusted Monut to know what to do. He kept plummeting, and Emelyne blinked, getting the tears out of her eyes just in time to see Kaine raise a palm when Monut was only a few feet away. Monut banked roughly to the right, flipping his legs. He avoided the block yet reached his talons around the barrier to tear at the sorcerer's arms. Somehow, her bonded dragon was accurate at diagnosing where the barrier had gone and where he needed to maneuver without even nicking it. Scratching his talons along the confident sorcerer's arms at the same time was an added bonus. Crimson trails ran long his sleeves, dripping to the ground.

That was fantastic, Monut! She reached for an arrow, nocked it, and fired it at the sorcerer once they'd flown around to his back. He twisted, rotated a palm to face them, then blocked the arrow, causing it to slam into the invisible barrier and drop to the ground.

Emmeline cursed. *Shattered anvil! He's too quick.*

Suddenly, Kaine whipped out two throwing knives from behind his back. She swerved, catching sight of one slicing off some of her hair. She quickly grabbed for another arrow and fired at him, hoping to get through his barriers, his protection. The blue-haired sorcerer knocked it aside with his second throwing knife then whipped it toward her.

Monut took them up higher, dodging the throw as Emeline kept her eyes fixed on the sorcerer. She released the arrow, and again the sorcerer blocked it with his spells. She growled in frustration. She wanted to wipe his condescending smile off his face, if only she could get to him.

Kaine's palm shot out, and Monut was suddenly knocked off course. The large dragon battled to straighten and maintain his flight.

That wasn't fun. Monut flipped to face the sorcerer. *He blasted me with some power to knock me off course.*

Kaine shoved another palm toward Monut, muttering the word *"Petra."* The large dragon dodged to the side before rising farther.

The arrogant sorcerer traveled farther into the village, and an older villager ran at him, sword drawn high, ready to swing. Kaine reached out a hand, dodging the sword, and touched the man, then he watched as he dropped to the ground, lifeless... exactly how her best friend had fallen.

Anger welled deep within Emelyne's heart. "No!" she cried out as she recognized the sweet man she had talked to only yesterday in the middle of the village. He had helped unconditionally with the rebuild of the village.

Monut flipped and dived again at the sorcerer, trying

to catch him unawares, but Kaine turned up his handsome face, searching the sky for him, just as the dragon drew near. Once again, he drew up a palm, blocking him.

This time, Monut landed feetfirst against the invisible barrier, pushed off, and flipped back into the sky.

As Monut rebounded, Emeline fired another arrow at the sorcerer. With a swipe of his hand, he cut the arrow in half, the bits dropping to the ground like two useless sticks. Monut swerved suddenly, knocking Emelyne to the side, and an arrow flew past her. She glanced down to see a female centaur had fired at her. She fired back at the centaur, hitting her in the heart, and the centaur fell to the ground, body thrashing.

She turned her attention back to Kaine to see him heading intentionally toward someone. When she studied his line of sight, he noticed the small form of Lozzeak not far away, swinging his sword to protect their village. She didn't even know her adoptive father had joined the battle. Yet the dwarf was attacking the trolls and ogres with an unmatched bravery, his sword swinging professionally as though he had been doing it for years. She hadn't seen him practice with the swords much because he had often left his testing of the swords to her friend Thiznabo. To her horror, she realized her father didn't see Kaine coming. Even though his skill was impressive, he was too focused on the troll in front of him. He sliced the troll's Achilles heel, impairing the troll instantly.

Emelyne fired at Kaine, but again he seemed to have a sense that she was there. He swiped his hand up, slicing the arrow in two. His footsteps were confident and assured as he headed straight for Lozzeak.

Hurry, Monut! We must get to him.

The large gray dragon flipped and dived at Kaine, his nose first.

Shoulders back and sight fixed, the sorcerer seemed to block out all other fighting except for her adoptive father. It was almost like he remembered him from the dwarven village.

As they plunged toward him, Emelyne held on to the hope that this time, Kaine was too distracted to notice them coming. But just as Monut was about to hit him again, he turned, hand already lifting to block or attack. Emelyne's heart dropped with disappointment, but suddenly, the sorcerer was knocked from the side by an invisible force. He was launched several feet to the left, Devi marching toward him.

Monut maneuvered quickly, preparing to land just near Kaine, and Emelyne disembarked before Kaine could rise to his feet. She stomped toward the sorcerer. The handsome man climbed to his feet only to be knocked down again by a blast from the side as Devi flung out her hands, muttering a spell as she walked. Emelyne took the opportunity. She whipped out her sword, the metal screeching as it scraped along the scabbard, ready for action.

CHAPTER FORTY-SIX

Emelyne marched quickly, her sword held high as she stomped toward the sorcerer she despised more than anyone in the world. He was not getting away with this, and he was not about to harm her father after he had already killed her friend.

Again, Kaine tried to rise, halting when he spotted her marching toward him. He quickly lifted a hand toward her as if to cast a spell, but said hand was shoved to the side by an invisible force.

Emelyne reached him before he could react and slammed the sword into his heart. The sorcerer writhed when shoved by the force of the blade, back pressed against the ground, the sword pinning him like an insect to a collector's board. Blood oozed from his mouth, and he coughed, flinching from the pain. All arrogance was gone.

Emelyne straddled him and leaned over the sword, pressing down. She stomped on the sorcerer's hands, palms down, so he couldn't cast any more spells. Bending over his face, she hissed, "That is for my friend. That is for Thiznabo. She didn't deserve to die, especially the way you killed her."

With two hands on the hilt of the sword, she twisted and yanked it out then wiped the blood off on his large cloak.

Heading toward Monut, she glimpsed Devi's face. The sorceress seemed strangely happy that she had removed one of their enemies. After Emelyne mounted Monut, she peered back to make sure Kaine hadn't moved, and she saw Devi standing over him as though making sure he'd died. Emelyne wished she had time to revel in her victory over Kaine. The sorcerer would no longer torment her. She had finally avenged Thiznabo, but there were too many threats to take time away from the battle.

Quickly, Monut climbed into the sky, and Emelyne fired some arrows into the centaurs breaking through the gate, followed by the trolls and the ogres. The dragon riders dive-bombed them, aiming for each large creature that had come through the fence as the civilians sliced with their swords and axes and shot arrows, trying to fell any creature that came through. But too many were coming at once—in large streams, their feet stomping on the dragon-blessed gates.

The scene before her was a mess of diving dragons. They seemed to be winning against some of the trolls and the invaders, but then lightning struck another of the dragons and its rider. The dragon instantly swerved from the force, which knocked it out of the sky. If they hadn't been killed by the lightning strike, then the fall would certainly end them. They hit the ground with an audible *crack*, the rider lying limp near the dragon the dragon's limbs lying in unnatural positions.

Again, the invaders swarmed the fallen dragon and rider. Monut and the other dragons dived, all pulling together to save their fellow dragon and rider. Alas, when they finally chased the enemy away, it was clear that they could not be saved. The bodies were a mess.

Lightning cracked above, and thunder roared through the clouds. Someone had to stop Mist, and they had to stop her now. Emelyne searched for the magic wielders now on their side, all split in all different directions. She couldn't find Henriette, probably because she was still invisible, but she could see the young man with yellow hair as he blocked several attacks, still stumbling his way around.

Each seemed to be doing their own thing. Although they were productive, the effort wasn't enough. Villagers swarmed around the giant trolls and ogres and slowly felled one at a time, the giants' cries of pain ringing throughout the air, the sound drowning out other cries of pain from the villagers as they were injured or slain.

Something changed in the way the magic wielders moved, and as if they were able to talk to one another, three of them congregated, seemingly working together. Devi was in the middle, clearly blocking any of the attacks from around them. Samara gathered on the right, along with the yellow-haired man Emelyne had not yet met on the left. They stood in the center of the road, farther into the village than the attackers. Henriette appeared next to Samara, bringing all four together. They joined hands, their familiars touching their sides. Devi called to each one of the magic wielders.

Emelyne couldn't hear what was happening, but the senior sorceress seemed to be instructing them to do something. Emelyne spotted Kellam heading toward the magic wielders, and she fired an arrow at him then followed it up with a dagger aimed straight for his heart.

The snub-nosed monkey screamed a warning to his bonded of the impending doom. The cloak fell from his head as he looked up, exposing his orange hair. A sinister smirk was on his face as he quickly pushed a palm her way.

Instantly, Monut rolled into a backward somersault, flipping out of control.

Emelyne didn't know whether Monut was going to be able to find his balance. Her heart tightened in her chest, and she braced for an extreme fall, picturing herself ending up like the other two dragons and their riders. When she gazed down to the ground, she saw herself careening toward where the four magic wielders stood. At least she was heading into the village and not away from it. If she survived the fall, they might have a chance, as long as the attackers didn't progress too quickly.

There were still so many fighting at the front gate, breaking their way into the village and past the villagers defending their home. Her knuckles were white as she braced against the saddle and the strap. She was glad to be strapped in, but the spinning was worrisome. She didn't fear heights, but this was not a pleasant feeling. If her adrenaline hadn't kicked in, then her hands would've been weak from exhaustion and shock.

It wasn't far now until she would land near the magic wielders below her, none of them aware of her as they pulled themselves together and joined hands.

Emelyne screamed at the top of her voice, "Look out!" She didn't want to take them out with her. She wanted her village to live and survive and rise against the coterie. Monut was lowering close to the tops of the trees. Before long, she would be smashing into them.

She called out again, "Look out!"

They didn't seem to hear her as she and Monut plummeted toward the ground. At the last second, the yellow-haired sorcerer looked up, his eyes wide. He shoved his palm up toward them.

Something slowed Monut, cushioning his fall as though he had been held with an invisible barrier. Monut stopped thrashing once he realized something had slowed his descent, and he steadied his fight. The yellow-haired sorcerer slowly shifted his hand, lowering them to the ground.

Emelyne connected eyes with the young half-blooded sorcerer's, and she was treated with a quick smile before he turned his concentration back to Devi and the other magic wielders.

CHAPTER FORTY-SEVEN

The battlefield was covered in devastation. On this day, red wasn't Samara's favorite color. It might never be. The invaders had stormed the gate and now pushed through to the stone wall, making their way to the front of the village.

The villagers were fighting courageously. As simple villagers and farmers, they were doing so well, but they were losing the battle. Something had to be done.

Samara heard her name and saw Devi beckoning her over. Peadar and Henriette soon joined, and Devi lined them in a street where the invaders had not yet reached.

Devi instructed, "We're going to join hands, close our eyes, and we're going to bond our power as one. It's the only way we have a chance. If you don't have your familiar with you, call them. They are needed."

Zion sat near her feet, pressed up against her. Peadar had Ziggy, Henriette had Pixie, and Ulrieg joined them as well, each of the familiars pressing up against their bonded's flesh, contributing to their strength. Together, the magic wielders—the ex-coterie members—joined their hands, tilted their heads back, and closed their eyes.

Samara had never worked together with other magic wielders and found the initial sensation strange. At first, she felt as though her strength was being pulled from her, but she surrendered to it, trusting the process and Devi. She felt connected. As the power leached from her, she sensed it pooling with the others'. She experienced a surge as Henriette's and Peadar's power joined hers and Devi's. Their power grew as they congregated around the senior sorceress.

Samara opened her eyes slightly. She was unable to see the power, but she felt it pull, twirl, and intertwine, a stronger weave of magic taking its time to build.

Samara had never felt such strength before. She hadn't known it existed. In awe, she allowed the power build and build until she felt the pressure was going to explode. Devi thrust her chest forward and arched her back, and the power burst out of her, attacking only the centaurs, the ogres, the trolls, and knocking Kellam at least a hundred feet back through the gate.

The villagers stood stunned, blinking, shocked. When Samara opened her eyes, the enemy had disappeared from inside the village. Somehow, Devi had managed to control the magic to affect only their enemies.

The magic wielders kept their hands joined as the villagers dusted themselves off and checked on their comrades. The four were about to separate to check on the fallen who needed aide when the enemy began to stir. Some had extra broken bones from being thrown so far, unable to rise to the occasion. Many of the centaurs with their horses' legs broken lay in agony on the ground.

Kellam dusted himself off and straightened his cloak, looking peeved and ready for blood as he stormed toward them, his familiar by his side. Lightning cracked in the sky, causing Devi to look up as though reminded of Mist's ominous threat.

Bolts shot down, hitting a few of the villagers who had just been saved. Their flesh sizzled, taking away the joyous feeling Samara had felt only seconds before. Another bolt hit the other side of the road.

Devi grabbed Samara's hand, stronger, tighter, and she closed her eyes as Kellam approached, commanding the trolls, ogres, and the centaurs to get up and fight. Devi pulled again from their strength. Samara could feel it building, rotating, weaving, intertwining. She tried hard to ignore the approaching sorcerer, the rumbling thunder, and lightning cracking in the sky from the dark, gray clouds. The magic wielders' power built and built, and she felt as though it was constantly nudging against a solid wall. Like a pot ready to boil and send the lid chattering. When the pressure was almost overbearing, Devi again pushed forward with her chest, releasing the power.

This time, it also aimed up, knocking the storm clouds away. It split them in half and stopped the whirling.

Kellam flew backward. His head hit a solid post of the steel fence, knocking him out. The trolls and the centaurs were sent flying backward as well, some with broken limbs and unable to move. Others who were able to move spotted the sorcerer out of commission. An uninjured ogre picked the sorcerer up and threw him over his bare shoulder before stomping off in the other direction. The enemy retreated, their number much smaller than when they'd arrived.

A strange sense of ease passed through the village. Devi released the magic wielders' hands, watching as the sorcerer was carried away. The clouds dissipated, letting the sun shine through.

It had been several hours, and the sun had sunk midway in the west. Soon it would be midafternoon. They had a lot of cleaning up to do and a lot of wounds to heal. Samara felt exhausted, but she knew her time wasn't up and her work not done.

Emelyne had unhooked herself from the saddle and climbed off Monut, studying herself for any wounds. She was surprised that after such a fall, there was not one scratch on either of them, thanks to the young sorcerer. By the time she'd turned her attention to the magic wielders, they were putting on a great display, twice knocking the enemies away and dispelling the storm clouds.

Emelyne approached the magic wielders. "That was impressive! I'm so glad ya on our side. I was worried after Paxton acted the way he did, but clearly Samara was right in trustin' ya lot."

Guilt covered Samara's face. "I am sorry that he did that and that I trusted him. I put your village in danger because of it. I shouldn't have let my heart do the speaking for me."

"Pfft! We've already been through this. Ya suffered enough. I was jus' makin' a point about anybody else ya brought here. It would be hard to know what he would do after bein' exposed to so much evil power for so long. Although, I do hope ya have better sense next time." Emelyne slipped her sword back into the scabbard, and her eyes turned to the yellow-haired sorcerer, admiring his lanky form as it towered over her. "Thanks for rescuin' us. It wasn't lookin' good for a moment."

The sorcerer's eyes softened. They were a beautiful light brown. "Of course I would rescue you. It was my pleasure." There was a goofy kindness about him, and it had her wondering what his natural hair color might be when it wasn't the coterie yellow. "I'm Peadar," he offered, pulling her out of her thoughts.

"Thanks for joinin' us. I'm Emelyne."

The princess! Monut stood protectively over her, his chest puffed out.

Emelyne nudged him with an elbow. "Ya don't have to emphasize that."

Monut gave her a stern eye. *Of course I do. He must know who's in charge.*

Peadar took her hand and lightly dipped his head. "It's nice to meet you, Princess. I have heard nothing but good things about you."

Emelyne felt her cheeks flush. Never in her life had she felt that before. His hands were so soft. He was definitely not a warrior, but with that power, he didn't have to be. She backhanded him lightly on the upper arm. "Oh, you're so sweet. Jus' call me Emelyne." She retracted her hand quickly. Trying to hide her embarrassment, her eyes traveled over the gate toward the retreating enemy. "Hopefully, they've learned their lesson and we've stopped them from comin' for a while."

"I'm afraid the coterie is very determined to be the

oppressor." A sadness crossed Devi's features. "They may be finished for today, but I would not class that as the end. I would say they only retreated because Kellam was knocked out and you had destroyed Kaine. I don't know where Mist is, but once I dispersed her clouds, she must have also retreated. Unfortunately, I do believe that they will be back."

Emelyne sighed. "Maybe one day we'll have peace. For now, we have another cleanup, an' looks like a lot of people need healin'. I'll have to set up an infirmary. We have lost many people today, an' a couple of dragons, but at least we have kept our village away from the coterie. This was only possible because of the alliance with ya four an' the dragons. If we didn't have ya help, we wouldn't be here."

AFTER THE VILLAGERS had cleaned up and the sorcerers, including Samara, had done the rounds to heal as many people as possible, the infirmary still housed plenty in recovery. Many were left with non-life-threatening injuries that the magic wielders didn't have enough energy to heal. They had used a tremendous amount of energy during the battle.

Samara's mind traveled to when Paxton would heal with little effort, and she wished she could see if Paxton would be able to help. But the memory of him sealing her in the root cocoon pushed away any hope of his help. It would be too risky, and she wasn't sure he could even heal anymore. His energy might only be good for destroying, the opposite to how it used to be.

The night sky was filled with stars, hardly a cloud in the sky. A perfect night for the party Emelyne had thrown. As the villagers were already eating together, she asked the preparers to add extras. That night, they mourned the losses of people and dragons. Yet at the same time, the village celebrated their victory, the free wine and ale spurring the party along further. The celebration was well deserved, and she felt as though she was the only one who wasn't feeling the cheerful vibe.

Samara heard loud cackling, and she turned around to find Emelyne slapping Peadar on the upper arm and snorting. The princess appeared to have connected well with Peadar, and her half-blooded friend seemed to lap up her attention.

Samara sat in the corner, eating her stew and feeling grateful for the time with her parents and siblings after being away for so long. Yet her emotions were mixed from what the day had brought. Her attention wavered over to Paxton's family. She hadn't yet told them that Paxton had returned. She didn't know how to tell them he appeared to have turned evil. Telling them would be difficult after they'd raised such a son who cared deeply for everybody.

The dragons had gone off to catch their food, mourning the loss of the couple that they had brought back with them from Dragoria. Ulrieg had gone with them. He now had some of his own kind to hang around, something he had not had for a very long time. On top of that, they were from Dragoria—a dragon's dream.

Not in the mood to celebrate, Samara finished her meal, kissed her parents on the cheek, and left them to enjoy their drinks. She wandered into the palace and down into the underground, heading toward the dungeons. She had to see Paxton. She had to find out what he was thinking. Emelyne had said he regretted what he did, but she had to see it for herself.

She traveled deep into the underground, through the tunnels and past the pond where Princess Bianca had been marked by the water dragon. The trickling of water echoed through the tunnels as water leaked through from the tiny little stream underground. The underground smelled dank. After picking up a sconce from the wall, she carried it with her through the tunnels, the stone walls glowing orange under the sconce's light. The air was still, and the distant sound of cheering villagers chased her along the corridors.

The cackling of a hyena echoed down the halls, sending a chill down Samara's spine. She probably should have warned Ulrieg that she was coming down here, but it was too late now. He would probably be most upset that she had gone without him, but surely Paxton couldn't do any damage to her down here. No plants would grow without the sunlight or the fresh air.

She pushed through to the next room and into the dungeons. Chorug stood purposefully on the side, guarding Paxton. "Hi, Chorug. What happened to Jyzom?"

The dragon stood tall. *I released him to go fight with his rider.*

At least the dragon had been safe while guarding Paxton. Paxton turned when he heard her, catching her attention. He had been sitting in the middle of the cell floor, his back to the door.

He moved to the bars, his hands grasping them, his

eyes pleading, his face apologetic. "I'm so sorry, Samara. I don't know what came over me."

Samara swallowed as she stepped farther into the room, eyeing the hyena in the other cell. She turned her attention back to him and caught his gaze. She was taken aback. The whites had returned, like some of the evilness had left him. The change sent her mind whirling. She didn't know what to think.

"Will you ever forgive me?" he asked.

She swallowed again, but the lump wouldn't budge. "I don't know if I can trust you, Paxton."

The words hurt to say, but she knew they were true. It was something she'd never thought she would have to say to him, but after what he did to her and to the village, she didn't know him.

His eyes dropped to the ground. "I understand. I just hope I can make it up to you and prove differently."

"I'm afraid it'll be up to Emelyne whether you can be released or not. I can no longer trust my emotions when it comes to you." She scuffed the toe of her boot on the ground. "I haven't had it in my heart to tell your parents that you're here. I don't know what to tell them. I don't want to break their hearts."

His shoulders sagged. "That's understandable. It's nothing more than I deserve."

Samara's heart broke seeing him like this. This was her Paxton. Her kind, caring, loving Paxton, who always liked to help people. Despite this, she could not trust him.

He studied her beseechingly. "I will make it up to you someday. I promise. The more I know what is inside of me, the more I can deal with it. The more I can fight it and push it away. Once I work out all of that, then perhaps I can use this terrible energy to help the cause of Dragoria, to save all the dragons and go against the coterie."

She stepped closer. Gently, Samara placed her hands on top of his on the bars. Her heart pulled toward him. She wanted to run into his arms and be embraced, to be told it would all be okay, and to believe every word he said. She ached. "For all our sakes, I hope you're right."

~~~~~

THANK you for reading Royal Alliance. If you have a few minutes, I'd love for you to leave a review or rating on Amazon. Your feedback helps to spread the word about my books.

YOU CAN FIND the next book here: Royal Resistance.
~~~~~

ACKNOWLEDGMENTS

I would like to thank all of my loyal readers for their support.

The last couple of years have been a big rollercoaster ride. My hereditary kidney disease has thrown me into the end stages. Thankfully, modern medicine has progressed over the last two generations, and kidney disease is no longer terminal. However, it is a lifetime of treatments, including dialysis and hopefully a transplant for a fuller life.

I'm currently undergoing regular dialysis treatments that suck the creative energy away, although they make me feel better than before I started them. I do my best to write when my head is clear and my days aren't filled with medical appointments and operations.

Because of this, my story production has been slower. But thankfully, the editors can help me produce quality stories when my brain lacks the alertness that comes with health.

Hopefully, I'll receive a transplant soon, along with the health benefits and energy that come with it.

As always, my husband and sons have been tremendous supporters. My husband has been a helpful first reader and, at times, been an excellent motivator.

A huge thank you to my editor, Meghan P., for her

editing and writing tips and my proofreader, Libybet R. G., for picking up the things we missed.

Thank you to all my readers who have loved my work and continue reading my stories. I'm looking forward to writing many more.

BOOKS BY KATRINA COPE

Pre-Teen Books

<u>The Sanctum Series</u>

JAYDEN'S CYBERMOUNTAIN

SCARLET'S ESCAPE

TAYLOR'S PLIGHT

ERIC & THE BLACK AXES

ADRIANNA'S SURGE

~~~~~

Young Adult Urban Fantasy

<u>Afterlife Series</u>

FLEDGLING

THE TAKING

ANGELIC RETRIBUTION

DIVIDED PATHS

TRUTH HUNTER

<u>Afterlife Novelette</u>

THE GATEKEEPER

~~~~~

Young Adult Urban Paranormal Fantasy

<u>Supernatural Evolvement Series</u>

(Associated with the Afterlife Series)

WITCH'S LEGACY (Prequel)

AALIYAH

<u>**Dragoria: the Lost Dragon Realm**</u>

DRAGON MOON

DRAGON HEART

DRAGON BREEZE

DRAGON'S ROYAL

ROYAL ALLIANCE

ROYAL RESISTANCE

ABOUT THE AUTHOR

Katrina is an author of several books in epic fantasy, young-adult fantasy, and a middle-grade sci-fi thriller series.

Her series include:

Dragoria: The Lost Dragon Realm - Coming of Age Epic fantasy

Valkyrie Academy Dragon Alliance - YA High fantasy

Thor's Dragon Rider - YA High fantasy (Spin-off of Valkyrie Academy Dragon Alliance but can be read separately)

The Afterlife - YA Contemporary fantasy

The Sanctum Series - Middle-grade Sci-fi thriller

She often talks to creatures of all kinds and has a passion for animals, nature, and travel. She lives in Queensland, Australia, with her husband and has survived teaching her three children how to drive.

Katrina's online home is at www.katrinacopebooks.com

You can connect with Katrina on:

tiktok.com/@katrinacopebooks
facebook.com/Author.Katrina.Cope
instagram.com/katrina_cope_author
bookbub.com/profile/katrina-cope
x.com/Katrina_R_Cope
pinterest.com/katrinacope56